John's Shadow

by

Rosemary Westwell

Acknowledgements

Grateful thanks to copy-editor Kate Jackson (roughseasinthemed@gmail.com) and to all the family and friends who have patiently assisted me with the making of this book.

# Prologue

The clock on Ely Cathedral chimed the hour. Mark King slowly uncurled his naked body, stretched out, and leaned back on the pillow. He clasped his hands behind his full head of hair and stared up at the ceiling. This was the best time, a time to pause, to savour the moment. Making love was one of the amazing mysteries of life when the whole body and soul for one moment were united. His eyes traced the shadows above him as they darkened in the dusk. The one leading from the ceiling light was plump and curvaceous – just like Vicky. He glanced down at her. She lay with her back to him, her rounded body curled into a foetal position. She was tranquil, well satisfied after their precious hour together. He slowly stroked the pale, smooth skin next to him. She murmured a few contented sounds, turned and rolled over to face him, her green eyes gazing into his, her long, dark hair framing an impish face.

'I must go,' he said. He leaned over and kissed her gently with a long, sensuous kiss. The bedroom clock ticked. He finally released her, turned and let his legs drop over the side of the bed, his bare feet revelling in the soft pile of the carpet. Mark sighed. Everything was as it should be: the perfect wife, a mistress by his side, a promising future.

A strong, dull pain niggled in his chest and he suddenly felt tired. He waited until the pain eased slightly. Warning signs, his doctor had said, but he was too young to have any heart problems, it was just indigestion. What did the doctor know? He slowly started dressing.

'Don't forget to collect the keys. They're in the box in the hall cupboard. The ones with the globe fob,' Vicky said, as he slipped out of the bedroom.

'I know, Anthea told me,' he called back, as he eased his way down the stairs. He smirked. Little did Anthea know. Fancy asking him to call into Vicky's! If she knew the truth, that'd be the last thing she'd do, wonderful, naive Anthea. For a moment the pain in his chest returned. He paused and forced himself to breathe deeply, until it had subsided. He swung open the cupboard door and scrabbled inside the box for the keys. Just as his fingers clasped the little globe, he felt a sudden severe pain in his finger, as if someone had stuck in a huge needle.

'Ouch!' he yelled. 'What do you keep in here?' His voice echoed in the hallway. Vicky gave no response. His hand throbbed, but he didn't have time to stop. He had to go. Anthea was expecting him to be outside the cathedral at the interval and he must get there on time. 'Can't let the wife know what I've been up to,' he muttered. With his other hand he flung open the front door.

'Bye!' he called, and pain shot up his arm and into his chest. It was so terrible that his yell sounded no more than a strangled croak. He couldn't stop, he must get out and go to the cathedral. As he stepped into the darkness, his hand useless by his side, his chest and head ached like the onset of flu. Anthea would be coming out of the cathedral now, waiting for him. With all his might he slammed the door shut but the world swirled in front of him. His whole body was wracked with pain and he was fighting for breath. Not now, please, not now. He stumbled out into the cool autumn air.

# Chapter 1

I was angry, boy was I angry. It was John as usual. I was revving up for a flaming row, although I knew it would be useless. John just couldn't help himself. He was – my hands stopped their work in the sink full of dirty pans as I thought about him – he was just John, an irritating, irascible, jokey man that I loved, not in an all-embracing lovey-dovey way, but the man who was my lifetime partner. The man I could never imagine ever being separated from in spite of his annoying ways. I lifted a wet hand up to my sweaty forehead and tried to brush away a thick curl that kept flopping down. I failed. The story of my life. I blew a sharp breath up towards the lock of hair, but the curl was  obstinate. Just like John. Time and time again I'd drummed into him that he had to come home by seven o'clock so that I could get the dinner done, have time to mark a few books, get to bed in time to sleep so that I could get up early in the morning to – I could go on, but I won't. Time is too short to be bogged down with the drudgery of life and the treadmill of work.

It wasn't as if he didn't work, it was just that he couldn't be trusted to keep his job. Last time he had such a row with the foreman that he could never show his face there again. Come to think of it, neither could I. I sighed, finished washing the saucepans and stacked them roughly on the draining board. I was just pulling the plug out of the sink when the phone rang. Who could that be? I smoothed my damp apron in a half-hearted effort to dry my hands and picked up the receiver hoping I wouldn't be electrocuted.

'Sally?'

'Yes.'

'It's Gale. Are you all right?'

'Sure, except for John who is late for dinner as usual. I don't know why he does it. He knows darn well that we have dinner at seven. Even when I serve it later, it doesn't make the slightest bit of difference. He never turns up! He's usually annoying some neighbour or other.' Perhaps … 'He's not there with you is he?'

'No. He's not.' Gale cleared her throat. After what seemed like ages, she finally spoke. 'I'll come round.' The phone clicked.

I stared at the dead receiver. What on earth was that about? Gale, my ever-patient best friend, was never abrupt like this. Something was up. John wasn't with her, so it wasn't him for a change. Maybe she was having trouble with her hubby.

The doorbell rang.

When I opened the door Gale's face was pale and grim. We stood looking at each other. Something *was* wrong. Gale took a tiny step forward.

'Are you going to let me in?'

'Oh, sorry.' I moved back and let her walk into the sitting room.

She looked so serious; I decided to let her speak first for once. I hadn't seen her like this since our cat had been run over. Gale touched my hand.

'I was at the doctor's surgery this afternoon.'

I stared at her blankly. Was Gale ill? Did she have cancer?

She continued, 'Your husband came in and started haranguing Mrs Wells – you know, the old lady opposite who has a heart complaint?'

'Not again! He's always going on at the poor woman.' My words tumbled out. 'He always likes the old folk and they are the ones who are least able to deal with him. It's like he's suddenly an old man himself.' I looked down at the pile of newspapers spilling onto the floor next to John's chair.

Gale spoke clearly and slowly enough to be understood but not slowly enough for me to interrupt again. 'Sally, the doctors have sectioned him. He's in Gravesall Hospital.'

John, sectioned? I knew he'd been getting worse, tending towards moments of insanity but who didn't have bad moments? OK, so he was getting impossible to control, no matter how I used my teacher's commanding voice, but *sectioning*, this was a bit drastic, a bit too soon. I sat down, stunned. John, incarcerated in hospital, with a lot of people out of their minds? At first a great feeling of relief overwhelmed me, but then came the guilt. I had been pushing for something to be done, there was no doubt we needed help, but this, this was so final. I smiled weakly. I could feel my eyes filling with tears. No, I was not going to cry. I looked at Gale. 'Well he was always joking about men in white coats coming to take him away, but I never thought—'

'We all knew your John was a bit of an eccentric and he was getting more difficult to handle. It was bound to happen sometime.'

'I know, I know.' I looked into Gale's large eyes.

'Look, I'll stay for a while eh?'

'Yes, thanks.'

It would help to have someone with me while I came to terms with the terrible news. My life was going to change radically. We talked and talked well into the night. An empty bottle of red wine stood on the mantelpiece with two drained glasses when we finally parted.

I slept fitfully that night, dreaming of John, his troubled face contorted with anger as he was being forced into a van, men in white coats either side of him, gripping his slim arms with iron fists, forcing him into the dark interior of the hospital van.

Chapter 2

A stream of sunlight stretched across the bedclothes. My pillow was damp and my head ached. I suddenly realized why I had cried all night. I put my hand on the bedclothes next to me. It was true, John had gone. The room was silent except for the alarm clock ticking beside me. It would jangle loudly soon, my head wasn't ready to take it. I leaned over, pushed down the alarm button and rolled back, my eyes gazing blankly above. The early morning sun lit up the room, making a pattern on the ceiling. I stared at it for a few moments.

I put my hand on the bed next to me again and stroked the empty space, willing John to return. For one moment I could believe that he had just gone to the toilet and would climb into bed next to me at any minute, but he didn't. John wasn't there and wouldn't be coming back. I sighed, rolled over, grabbed my towel and stumbled sleepily to the shower. Routine, keep to the same routine, I told myself. As the warm water soothed me I thought of school. Should I tell my colleagues? I remembered how cruel some of them were to Bill, and he was only slightly eccentric, he wasn't nearly as bad as John. No, no, I wouldn't tell anyone, not unless I was forced.

I finished dressing and put on my make-up. I could hear the neighbour's car revving as it was driven into the street. I had never really noticed it before, but now, now I was sensitive to every sound, I was hanging onto every sign of human life. I will never get used to this silence. I waited for John to ask where the paper was, or to insist on making some inane remark about what I was doing, not listening to my reply and following up with another irrelevant question. Troublesome as he was, I already missed him terribly. I sniffed. No, I wasn't going to cry. I didn't have time to redo my make-up. I would just have to buckle down, accept the situation and stand on my own two feet. After all, I'd had hard times before.

Over a decade before, the merciless Madge had made my life hell at boarding school. But I survived didn't I? What did I do? That was it; back then, I decided my only hope for some kind of bearable existence was to 'turn the disadvantage to an advantage'. None of the other girls would speak to me, Madge had bound them in some secret pact that I was untouchable, a vile creature that was to be sneered at, mentally tortured or simply shunned. I was alone, absolutely alone, even though I was surrounded by students. Thus I had all the time in the world to do what I wanted to do, alone. So what did I do? I practised the piano for hours, whenever I was free from duties. My horrible classmates could not interfere with the joy I felt when I revelled in the emotional turmoil of Beethoven or the scintillating beauty of Debussy. I could hear the strains of 'Au clair de la lune' as I sat at the piano in that dark, gloomy boarding school dining room that was my practice room. As a result of all those hours of practice, I became scholarship material. My career, if nothing else, was flourishing while the horrible child bullies were forced to stay in their little backward townships in the back of beyond Down Under. I had the final victory. But my job, my qualifications, even my love of music meant little to me now while I thought of John, struggling with his failing mind. I shook my head. I had to stop thinking like this. I had to win this battle too. I grabbed my school bag. Right, I needed to deal with my husband's sudden incarceration, and somehow find something positive out of this distressing negative situation. But how? How could I ever look at my husband's insanity in a positive way, or turn it into any sort of advantage for either of us?

I climbed into Bumble, my little red car, turned on the engine and drove out into the road. I was later than usual but I would still be able to dash into the assembly hall in time to tune up the orchestra. What would they play today? The 'Funeral March' – that would suit my mood admirably but it wasn't on their list, thank goodness. I would let the leader choose.

As I turned my car into my usual parking space I noticed tight groups of children and parents gathered at the front door. With their heads almost touching, they were obviously talking about something new and important. I snatched my bag from the back seat, slammed the door shut with my foot, locked the car and walked directly to the nearest huddle.

Little Helen Ballister broke free and ran to wards me. 'Miss! Miss! Mr King has been rushed to hospital!' Her wide eyes met mine.

'Hospital?'

'Yes late last night! Mummy says she saw the ambulance in front of the cathedral when she was giving our dog a short walk last night. She won't tell me any more.'

'Perhaps she doesn't know any more. I'm sure he will be all right. Now we should go inside, the bell will ring soon.'

As I spoke, Leonard Hall, the deputy headmaster, tall, lean and hungry-looking, stood at the school entrance.

'May I have your attention please!' his strident voice penetrated the whole car park. 'I am sorry everyone. You've probably heard the sad news about our headmaster. He died unexpectedly in the night. School will continue as usual. I shall take a special assembly for the children at quarter past nine.' The groups of parents and children rushed forward but stopped when Mr Hall held up his bony hand.

'There is no more information I can give you now. Please go home. Your child will be given a letter to take home tonight that will give all the information you need.'

I watched as the parents filed past talking to each other in hushed tones. Leonard Hall scanned the car park and his eyes finally came to rest on me.

'Mrs Wilks!' he called. 'There will be a staff meeting in ten minutes. Please tell any colleagues you see.'

I nodded, glancing around to see if anyone was approaching. Henry had just locked his car so I waited.

'What's up?' Henry Matthews, the fair-haired art teacher, came up to me, his right hand wedging a large file of artwork to his side.

'Mark King died suddenly last night,' I said, my voice sounding distant, as though unattached to the reality of the news and the consternation in the playground. We both stood still, trying to absorb the information.

But he was fine yesterday. What on earth happened?'

'I've no idea.' I sighed. I had enough on my plate without this happening as well. Then I just remembered in time. 'Oh, there's a staff meeting in a few minutes – pass the word.'

'Right.' Grim-faced, Henry walked towards the school entrance, saying a few words to other staff as they went towards the door. I followed.

The staffroom was stuffy. Leonard Hall sat in the head's chair, his face tilted upwards, as he launched into the usual platitudes. I found it very hard to concentrate. Flashes of Mark King interrupted my thoughts. Mark stood, tall, confident, undefeatable, soothing parents and staff with silken words. What could have happened? I shook my head and listened to Leonard's dry voice. Then John's face, contorted with anger and confusion flashed into mind. What would he be doing now? I could see him jabbing his finger into the chest of a nurse, haranguing the poor girl over some freaky idea he had. I ought to go and see him after school. Leonard Hall's voice droned on. I heard snippets of information – something about a visit to see Mark's wife, Anthea, and Leonard taking over the school.

His opportunity at last, I thought to myself. I glanced around; other staff members sat slumped in their chairs, equally despondent. Henry was next to me doodling on his pad. The caricature of Leonard was spot on. He'd caught his mean streak perfectly. I smiled briefly but images of John invaded my thoughts again. How was I going to cope without him? I suddenly felt cold inside. I remembered the stark silence of the house when I woke. What was I going to do? Routine, I reminded myself, I must just stick to the routine and then everything would work itself out.

'So the head's death is routine huh?' Henry grinned at me as we struggled out of the narrow staffroom door along with the rest of the staff.

I could feel my cheeks burning, 'No, I was just telling myself how to cope with all that's going on. I think the best way will be to stick to my routine and just get on with it.'

'It's a bit of a shock hearing about the headmaster, but we'll cope. No one's indispensable; Leonard's not really that bad, I'm sure everything will just tick over as usual. Besides, Mark was always a bit aloof, no one really knew him very well, not even his wife I believe. Come to think of it, you never really liked him anyway did you?'

Ignoring Henry's last comment, I said, 'It's not him or his death, there's something else I have to deal with.'

'Oh?' Henry looked at me, his pale blue eyes not missing a thing.

'Not now. I might tell you some time later.' I looked down.

'Now I really *am* intrigued.'

I turned away from him and walked quickly to my classroom, emptied my schoolbag of books onto the desk and got out the register. Henry stood in the entrance, his eyebrows raised. My cheeks burning, I focused on the list of names. Out of the corner of my eye I saw him shrug, turn and slowly walk away. Pity he was already married, not that it stopped Rita I thought, as I recalled catching them together in the supplies cupboard. I counted the absentees for the previous day and neatly wrote the number at the bottom of the column in red.

## Chapter 3

The bustle of noisy children and the startling school bells finally came to an end. The school day was over. Feeling dusty, dirty and fraught, I dragged myself to my car and sped through the school gates before I could stop and talk to anyone. The traffic roared and snarled as I edged my way home battling past impatient parents gripping the steering wheels of their BMWs and Audis. A glimpse of their taut faces was evidence enough that John and I had made the right decision not to have children.

Our familiar detached house finally greeted me and I swept into the drive. Balancing the heavy bag on my hip, I struggled with the door lock and finally staggered inside, slamming the door behind me. Panting, for a moment, I expected to see John, stumbling towards me, a stream of his words echoing in the hallway, but my heart sank. There was no one. The house was cold and empty    just as I had left it.

In one flickering moment I had hoped that last night was just a nightmare. The house was deserted. He was never coming home. I was alone.

I sighed and glanced at the mailbox. A familiar white envelope, my address neatly typed, lay on top. I grabbed the letters and struggled upstairs. I fell into the office and dumped the books on the table, tossing the

envelopes to the side. Heart racing, thinking the authorities were making more trouble for John and I, I took a deep breath and opened the white envelope. It was a false alarm – it was only an invitation from Anthea dated the day before Mark had died. Anthea's invitations were usually to cream tea parties on Sundays or to black tie dances – none of which ever appealed to me and since John had become so difficult in public, it would have been impossible to take him to any of these events. This time it was a cream tea. Would she still hold it after what had happened to Mark?

The answer arrived in an unstamped letter the next day. In her neat writing, Anthea explained she was not cancelling the cream tea party but was asking everyone to come to celebrate Mark's life. She said that the suddenness of his death meant there had to be an autopsy so she couldn't say when the funeral would be held. Poor Anthea, mystery though she was to me, I couldn't help feeling sympathy for her. Her husband dies suddenly and inexplicably, the police won't release the body, she's in a state of limbo. Ghastly – worse than my own situation. My husband's disappearance from the home reduced me to a nervous wreck so how could Anthea be so well organized at a time like this? With what little I knew of her it was typical. Mrs Perfection even in dreadful times. I blushed, momentarily shocked at my indiscretion, for I didn't really know her well. Mark's attachment, that's how we all saw her, but now that he'd gone she was proving her worth, whereas I – I wasn't coping well at all and my husband was still here, still needing assistance. I looked at my watch. Routine, routine, I chanted my mantra. I started marking the books. After the third, I threw my pen down. It was no good. I had to visit John at Gravesall Hospital.

The peak hour traffic was frantic as I drove around the outskirts of Cambridge. Feeling tired and frustrated I finally came upon the hospital. A tall Victorian fortress of a building loomed over me as I crawled along its narrow road, trying to find Allen Ward. My heart was heavy, oppressed by what felt like hundreds of sullen eyes staring at me from its dark interior – ghosts of the insane, screaming from crowded cells. It was easy to imagine that this had been a much-hated Victorian madhouse. An image of John broke the spell, John laughing as he joked that some day men in white coats would come to take him away to the madhouse in Gravesall. This was no joke now.

Still creeping at a snail's pace, searching the dull brick walls for some kind of sign, I turned the corner until a string of single-storey sheds came into view. They reminded me of the Nissen huts I had been forced to teach in when the school ran out of classrooms. Then, on the outside of the first one I read Allen Ward, a small stark sign that could have easily been no more than a traffic sign. This was not a welcoming home for people in trouble.

I pulled up into the car park immediately in front. As I got out of the car, huge ancient trees bowed wisely in a soft breeze. A gathering of rooks squawked overhead. The black outstretched wings of one of them spread above me symbolically. I knew that my husband and I were now doomed to a twilight existence. Routine, routine. Get on with it. After seeing John I could find a pub and have a meal. I slammed my car door and locked the vehicle. I walked along the worn footpath towards the building. At my feet were patches of dry soil trampled on by many footsteps of visitors and patients walking the grounds and yet, every now and then tufts of grass still struggled to survive.

There was an old intercom system on the side wall of the small porch. I pressed the button. There was no reply. I turned my back on the door and looked again at the restless rooks high in the old misshapen trees. I could see three of the dark creatures circling close now. I turned to the intercom again and pressed the button. This time, a harassed voice said 'Yes?'

'It's Sally Wilks to see John,' I said quickly. A buzzing sound clicked the front door open. I went in and opened a second door. Closing it behind me I looked into the room. It could have been a sitting room anywhere. A large crowd of people mumbled and moved aimlessly in the spaces between the heavy armchairs. Some of the patients stood still, awkwardly staring at the walls. Others talked to themselves agitatedly or rocked gently in their chairs. I couldn't see any staff at all until I realized they were dressed similarly to the patients.

A slim, moon-faced man approached me.

'Can I help you?'

'I've come to see John Wilks.'

'Oh, he's over there in the far corner. Let me know when you want to leave and I'll let you out.'

The entrance door banged loudly, the carer turned immediately and moved swiftly to the person making the noise. The patient's hair spread wildly over thin shoulders, shaking each time she yanked the door handle violently.

'Now, come on Doris. It isn't time to go yet. Come here. I have something to show you.'

I watched the carer persuade Doris to stop trying to get out and join him at the puzzle table. Pieces of a jigsaw were strewn across the white top and spilled onto the floor. An elderly man shuffled over some of the pieces, oblivious to their existence.

Suddenly I felt my arm being clutched.

'Help!' a loud voice cried in my ear.

My heart raced. I was out of my depth. John had been bad enough to deal with but I had no idea what to do with strangers. I turned abruptly to see who it was. The pale face of an elderly lady was only a few inches away. Her eyes were wide with fear.

'Can you help me please?' her urgent voice asked me again. 'I have to go home. Can you take me home please?' She gripped my arm more firmly.

Shocked, I said quickly, 'No'.

In my rush to escape, I grasped my arm, but she held it more firmly. In one huge pull, I yanked my arm out of her grip.

'Sorry,' I said, as I hurried towards the far corner where I could see the back of John's head. Heart still thumping, I pulled up a chair and swung it round to face him, glancing beyond to see if I was in danger of imminent attack again. The protagonist was quiet now, her expression perplexed as she grabbed another patient's arm.

John's head was bowed, his arms limp. He was like someone who had given up. His dull eyes reflected little more than a heavy sedative. It was as though his soul had been dampened, his vitality smashed.

'John?' I bent my head to look directly into his eyes.

He turned to me and his eyes met mine but there was no flicker of recognition, no response.

'How are you?' I asked, trying to eradicate the quiver that had crept into my voice.

Again, John didn't reply.

'Is there anything I can get you?'

Now I didn't expect a reply. Snatches of violent calls from disgruntled patients punctuated the general hubbub of the room. This was not a happy place.

John shifted in his chair and spoke, his words as clear as they had always been. 'I want to come home,' he said dully.

I was stunned. What could I say? If I told him the truth, he would be very upset. How could I tell him that he would never be coming home? If he was his old cheerful, fun-loving self, of course I would have him back, but the angry aggressive troublemaker that he had become was too dangerous. No, he could never come home. I paused for thought.

'When you're better,' I finally said, patting his arm.

'Never,' John said slowly and looked down at the floor despondently. A huge sense of sadness hung in the air, overwhelming us as we sat facing each other, our eyes cast down. We had reached an impasse – there was no way out for either of us.

Panic rose inside me like a raging force ready to sweep me away from this impossible situation. I wanted to run, run out of the room, out of the building and never return, but I knew I couldn't. I couldn't leave this vulnerable man. The silence between us was becoming unbearable. I must say something, but what? My responsibility to this man weighed heavily on me. Months, even years of pain loomed ahead like the slow but steady sinking of a huge vessel into a fathomless sea. How would I cope? John's problem was not going to go away. Routine. Try to find some kind of normality and stick to it, what else could I do?

I spoke in a matter-of-fact voice: 'Everything at home is just the same. When you are better you will be able to see for yourself. The garden is still full of roses, although some of your trees are changing colour. I'll clear the ivy from Silky's grave—' I stopped.

John stared at me as though none of the words made any sense.

I closed my eyes and allowed memories of Silky, our lovely grey and white cat, to pour into my thoughts. Silky was purring loudly as John stroked him again and again while the contented animal stretched across his lap, unperturbed by the awkwardness of the position as soft white paws hung either side, completely unsupported. A large glass of Guinness was clutched in John's free hand and from time to time he lifted it to his mouth drinking and swallowing immediately, unconsciously denying himself much of the strong syrupy taste.

Leaning back into the comforting softness of my armchair next to him at home, I waited for the turmoil of my thoughts to slowly dissipate as I gradually relaxed and let the stress of a busy day at school disintegrate.

But then, I was back in the cold reality of this room of lost souls. Out of the corner of my eye, I could see movement. John had become agitated and was pulling the edge of his jumper. I gently put my hand on his until he stopped. I forced myself to chatter to him as if the broken body before me was the person I first knew, as if he was alert, half listening but impatient to have his own say. Ignoring his cold, indifferent stare, I told him of the sudden death of the headmaster. As I took another breath to tell him more, he lifted his head, his eyes more focused and flickering with interest but the flicker was so brief, so undetermined, I must have imagined it, or, had I? The impassioned eyes that met me now told me nothing. He lowered his head again and I talked to the thick strands of hair on the top of his head.

Finally, I gave up chatting and sat in silence with him, my hand still resting on his arm.

'Good riddance!' John said.

I stared at him, but he did not respond.

Before I could try to elicit any more from him a huge ruckus exploded in the corner. A man in a blue T-shirt and jeans leapt up quickly and rushed towards the noise. A highly agitated female patient had grabbed the chair she had knocked down and was hauling it towards the centre of the room shouting an obscenity with each yank. He touched her arm, and spoke firmly to her. She stopped pulling the chair for a moment, narrowed her eyes and surveyed him as though she was weighing up whether a naughty boy in her charge was lying or not. Finally she let the man lead her towards another part of the room. He was still talking to her as she sat down, He spoke reassuringly, persuading her to join him in a long, deep conversation as he tried to bring her back to reality. As I turned my eyes away she was sitting more calmly, her thin arms dropped onto her lap. She had resigned herself to her fate.

At least John was in good hands, I mused, as I stood up ready to go. While I was walking towards another moon-faced member of staff, John got to his feet and followed me.

'I'm coming home.'

I hurriedly asked if I could be let out and one of the staff came with me to the door. John followed us all the way. As the door was opened, he tried to push his way through but the nurse was quick and forcibly prevented him from making his escape.

'Go,' he said to me, as he held John in a grip. My eyes filled with tears as I hurriedly opened the door, rushed through and closed it behind me. I could hear the scuffle still going on as I went through the front door and left the building. Tears fell down my cheeks as I returned to the car. I sat in the driving seat and wept for some time before I set off for home.

Chapter 4

'So, did he die of natural causes? What do you think?' Henry whispered into my ear as I was drinking my coffee.

'Pardon?' I was in automatic mode. Sticking strictly to my routine, I had hardly noticed Henry plonk himself next to me.

'I said—'

'Oh yes.' I realized I had heard him after all. 'Does it matter?'

'What's the problem with you girl? Of course it matters! It means one of us could have got so fed up with the headmaster that we finally did him in and now we're left with a murderer wandering free in our midst.' There was a wicked gleam in his eyes.

'Oh yes. I suppose so.' I stared at my mug. The garish design on the thick china did not suit my mood at all.

'So, what's the matter with you Sally? You're not your perky self.' Henry looked directly at me.

I held my mug close to me and glanced around the staffroom. There was no one in earshot. I looked down and sighed.

'I suppose I have to tell someone, sometime.'

'Yes?' Henry inched forward on his seat.

'Promise you won't tell everyone. It's bad enough as it is.'

'Promise. You know me, I won't tell a soul,' he put his hand on his heart in mock supplication, 'that is, unless I have to.'

I looked blankly at him. 'Well …' I hesitated, before reluctantly admitting the truth. 'It's my husband, John,' I moved my fingers nervously on the mug. 'He's been sectioned into Gravesall.'

Henry whistled softly. 'Well fancy that.' Then he turned to me, his face marked with concern. 'We knew the old boy was having difficulties, but we thought it was just temporary. I'm sorry. It must be awful for you.'

My eyes moistened. 'It is but it's better I don't dwell on it.' I put my mug down on the coffee table in front of us and stood up. 'I'd better get ready for the next lesson.'

Henry put his hand lightly on my arm. 'Now sit down girl. We've plenty of time before the end of break. You've had a shock. Take it easy.'

I sat down and sniffed. I put my hand into my pocket and pulled out a used tissue and wiped my nose. After three attempts I managed to push it back into my pocket.

'You'll have to tell Leonard, you know. Just in case. He might even give you time off.'

'Tell Leonard?'

I almost laughed. I thought of the letter that had been pushed into my hands when I went to see John at Gravesall. I had stuffed it into my handbag and only read it when I got home. It asked me to attend a meeting at Gravesall next Friday morning. I had dismissed the idea. I could never get time off school and besides, I'd long since decided that going to meetings, even before he was sectioned when we needed help but none was forthcoming, was a waste of time. I'd sit there trying to get help for John only to find no one was listening. They would all decide there was little they could do and because I was at the meeting, it was decided that I agreed with them.

As this was the first time, that maybe, just maybe, I would have a chance to know what exactly was wrong with John, perhaps I should try to see Leonard after all. I smiled cynically. 'Do you really think he'll give me time off?'

'Well, all right then. No time off but you must tell him.'

'OK. I'll do it after school on Monday.' But how, how was I going to tell him? How was I going to admit that my family was tainted, tainted with madness? Leonard was not nicknamed the 'Mean Machine' for nothing. He wouldn't understand. He would see me as a weak woman caught up in a maelstrom of family problems, a husband who was in a mental hospital.

Then another thought struck me. I had to face the fear, the real fear that was making my stomach churn; I would have to admit that I really didn't want to go to the meeting at all. And I struggled at standing up for myself. My mind flashed back to a previous meeting with Mark. 'So why do you think you should take precedence?' Mark's steady gaze shrank me to a quivering novice, just one of twenty people seated in the meeting room to discuss the school's budget. I stuttered and mumbled 'I don't know', when I should have stood up, looked at him directly and, speaking with the same confident authoritative voice I'd had to develop as a teacher, stated the reasons I had written on the notepaper in my hand, unequivocally, without hesitation. But this was not the classroom or a staff gathering; it was a meeting with one person, Leonard. My thoughts darkened just as the light in the staffroom dimmed when a cloud masked the thin sunshine that had penetrated the room. One way or another, like an indeterminate breeze whispering through the school, news of John's incarceration would eventually filter out into the open. My colleagues would become aware and even though they knew it should not make any difference, they wouldn't be able to help themselves, they would speak to me with a slight hesitation, avoid looking me in the eyes, and keep an inch or so away, as though they too would be infected with the illness that had stuck my husband down.

Perhaps Henry was reading my thoughts. 'It'll be all right. Your real friends will stand by you – me for a start.' He grinned. 'Look,' and his voice was more earnest, 'you mustn't think your whole life has to revolve around your sick husband. You may not have realized it, but I've noticed you've been having a hard time with him for quite a while. You've your own life to live.'

He was right, of course. 'Yes, I know, but for now I'll concentrate on sticking to the routine. Anyway, I can't abandon him. For better or worse it is.' I stood up. 'Routine, routine,' I said absently as I gave Henry a little wave and walked resolutely towards my classroom to prepare for the next lesson.

Saturday came. I went through the motions of my usual Saturday afternoon, at first pulling out the weeds in the garden and taking more ivy off some of the rarer plants. In a daze I flung open the shed door, dragged out the lawnmower, and struggled to start the engine. When the mower finally kicked into action I mowed the lawn as quickly as I could. I ignored the patches that I had missed, thinking that would have to do, and took the mower back to the shed. When I pushed the machine inside, it wouldn't go in completely; half of it was still stuck outside. I pushed it in one more time and it was blocked again. In a fury I shoved the wretched thing forward again and again, wriggling it, willing whatever was blocking it to shift, but the blockage remained obstinately in place. I swore, dropped the handle and skirted round the machine to look at the obstruction.

It was a lump of wood that had fallen from the pile that John had collected over the years. It was quite a large chunk of wood, paler in colour than the others. This one had a piece of string tied around it and a card attached. I bent down and read the label: 'Huon pine'. For a moment, I was transported back to Tasmania. I ran my hand over it, revelling in its smoothness, my fingers dipping in the natural holes that would create a challenge or delight for a woodcarver. I breathed in deeply, enjoying the faintly familiar aroma. Oh, how I missed the walks in the bush, the thick green foliage, the scent of the trees. I lifted up the hunk of Huon pine and put it back on the shelf. For a moment I couldn't remember how we'd acquired it, and then it came to me. It must have been when John was going through his 'wood' stage. He had always been interested in nature, but one time he had suddenly become obsessed with trees and their wood. He planted a copper beech, two silver birch trees and an ash in our garden no matter how much I protested that they would be too large for our little plot. He ordered more textbooks on tree and wood identification even though he already had a stack of them from his university days. He went to woodturning classes although he never came home with anything finished and was suddenly asked to leave the class midterm. He never did say why.

I stopped and thought for a moment. I still couldn't remember him getting this particular piece though. Then it came to me – he had often written to Dad and asked for weird and wonderful things. One item that John had requested was my old escritoire that he'd admired when we went out to Tasmania many years ago. I was very pleased to have it now, as it graced the spare room. It was when Dad came to visit us the last time; he had brought this wood with his luggage. Poor Dad, his case must have been really heavy. John was absolutely delighted with his trophy and took it to our shed to add to his collection.

I should do something about all this wood in the shed. Jumbled together in a forgotten heap, the pieces cried out for more experienced hands than John's to shape them into precious items for neighbours' mantelpieces. In time I would probably donate it to the woodturning club, or maybe Henry would like some of the bits but not now, not yet, not until John was no longer always with me in my thoughts. I could see him now, starting to talk enthusiastically about something he had found, proudly carrying it in one of his boxes. I had learned to be interested in the coupled worms, shiny bright beetles, or tiny spiders in his never-ending supply of discoveries.

I sighed, finally pushing the lawnmower into the shed successfully and started to close the door, but it was very stiff and I couldn't push it all the way in. I shoved it again but the door still wouldn't shut properly. I forced it as hard as I could, and then gave up. I could still see the contents of the shed through the thin gap I had left. John would have been furious if he knew I had abandoned the shed with the door ajar like this, but I was tired and really couldn't be bothered. Let him come and sort it out.

After a cup of tea on the back patio, I went indoors and faced the pile of ironing that had mounted up over the weeks while John was ill. Was there any point in ironing John's clothes? I decided I should. After all, he would need some in Gravesall. He'd always felt better in a suit and tie but now he would have to wear casual clothes only. The staff had asked specifically for his leisure clothes, ones that were easier to put on and survive the harshest of washes. I put away the final dress I had ironed and looked at the clock.

I felt exhausted. That night I flopped in the armchair and watched TV until midnight. I curled up in bed alone and cried myself to sleep. I would have the whole of Sunday off to do nothing. I willed myself to sleep, trying to let the numbness that engulfed me dissipate.

Chapter 5

On Monday, at the end of lunchtime, the reception desk was blocked by a crowd of pupils jostling to have their report cards stamped.

'Mrs Wilks. What can I do for you?' Betty, the amazing multitasking school secretary, smiled broadly revealing a line of scarlet lipstick on her teeth. The children lowered their arms and moved aside as I approached the desk.

'I would like to make an appointment to see Mr Hall after school today please.' I felt a mass of curious eyes look up at me.

'Well, he's very busy.' Betty put down the stamp for a moment and pulled out a large book from under the desk. 'I'm sure we can find space for you somewhere here, it's been so difficult since Mr King's—' she didn't finish the sentence. As she turned the pages of the book, a small frown developed on her pale forehead.

'It's very important,' I said firmly, blushing because of the children's sudden interest. 'I must see him after school today!'

Betty looked up, studied me closely, shrugged as if she understood, and slowly moved her finger down the page of the appointment book. 'If I juggle a couple of appointments around, he could be free at about five o'clock today. Would that do?'

'Yes, that'll be fine,' I said, and turned to go.

'Might I tell him what it is about?' Betty asked.

I gritted my teeth. 'It's very *personal*,' I said, so that the bevy of children had no doubt that it was none of their business. I marched purposefully back towards the staffroom.

The afternoon went very slowly. A strong breeze had blown up after lunch so the children were misbehaving more than usual.

'Quiet!' I'd shouted at 1C. For a few brief moments the children had made less noise but it wasn't long before Jerry tipped his chair over with a resounding crash. The class rose like a pack of monkeys, their chairs scraping noisily as they cheered and danced about the classroom in mock celebration. Their yells grew louder and louder as they egged each other on. I stared at them, open-mouthed, frozen, panic welling up inside me. I had to do something. Finally, without thinking, I picked up my own chair and threw it down hard on the platform, screeching at the top of my voice,

'For heaven's sake will you just shut up!'

For a moment, the children suddenly stopped what they were doing and stared at me for they'd never seen me so angry before. Taking advantage of the split second of silence I snarled,

'Now sit down!'

They scraped their chairs back into place, and started to sit down, but it wasn't long before they started being noisy again. I plonked myself down on my chair, glancing every now and then to see if any of the other staff had noticed and were peering through the window, but there was no one. I let the sound go over me, slumped down in my chair and despondently willed the end-of-lesson bell to sound.

The worst calamity came near the end of the afternoon with 4D, when Darren, a plump unresponsive but noisy individual always sitting at the front, decided he wanted special attention. With a voice like a foghorn he shouted:

'Miss, miss what do we do?'

'You've been given your work already,' I'd snapped. 'For the umpteenth time, DO the work that's been set.'

Daren ignored me, turned around, and stabbed his pencil at the boy behind him.

'Stop that!' I'd yelled but Darren had ignored me again. I'd stormed over to him, snatched the pencil roughly from his hand and shouted:

'Will you for once, just do as you're *told*!'

Darren, nursing his hurting hand on his chest, glared at me with one of those 'I'm going to tell my mum' looks. I'd glowered back at him defying him to do so, while I made a point of checking to see whether his hand was still red before he left at the end of the lesson. The clock had ticked forward and the afternoon lessons finally came to a noisy end.

After the last pupil tumbled out of the classroom, I followed him into the hallway slamming the door behind me, and went straight to the staffroom to slump in a chair. I was exhausted. Feeling dirty and dishevelled, I was first in the room and alone, so I slipped lazily right down into the armchair, not caring how it looked and watched the second hand tick slowly around the clock.

Finally, I felt recovered enough to struggle to my feet and go to the Ladies, wash the grit out of my hands, splash some cool water on my face, and pull a comb through my hair. When the comb got stuck in a tangle of knots, I winced. The face in the mirror looked more haggard than usual, the rings under the eyes were dark, the eyes themselves puffy and dull. At least Leonard would believe me when I said I needed help.

On the other hand, he might decide that I wasn't cutting it and think of letting me go. He wouldn't dare, would he? I pushed those thoughts to the back of my mind, checked myself in the mirror one more time, shrugged and left the room.

I returned to the deserted staffroom and slipped into the chair again. I watched the hands of the clock moving slowly towards five o'clock. There were only ten minutes to go. My heart started pounding. What had I to be so nervous about? After all, I was a fully grown woman for heaven's sake. I'd managed to see John through his worst, so what was I worried about now? I lay back in the chair and closed my eyes for a moment, willing my unsteady nerves to relax. Then I heard the staff door behind me open. I was too lazy to sit up and make my presence known.

'It's dreadful, truly dreadful,' came Teresa Evan's concerned tones. 'Dennis Dighton had been walking his dog when he found him near the canon on Palace Green.'

'Why there?' I heard Rita ask, her honeyed voice bringing to mind her smooth skin and sweet scent.

'He was apparently trying to meet Anthea outside the cathedral. She'd gone to the talk. He'd had some work to do in the office at school first, apparently.'

'How come you know so much?'

Teresa cleared her throat. 'My husband?'

'Oh sorry, I'd forgotten your husband is the undertaker.'

Teresa lowered her voice. 'I'm not supposed to say much, but we'll all be told soon enough. They have to have an autopsy – sudden death you know, even though it looks as though he'd either had a heart attack after the shock of being bitten by something, or someone had stuck a needle into him.'

'He was too young to have a heart attack, wasn't he?'

'People can have a heart attack at any age, you know. And there's nothing around here that could bite and kill a man. I've certainly never heard of any adders around Ely, have you?'

'No, no I haven't,' Rita's words slowed. I could imagine her moving her head, thinking. 'But then – going back to the heart attack – I remember once he said that he was feeling the odd twinge or two, but he put it down to indigestion. After all, he'd just had a huge meal at one of our dinners.'

'When was this?'

Rita hesitated. 'Oh, a few months ago. There was a group of us celebrating something or other – perhaps it was his birthday, I don't remember.'

'Mm,' Teresa said. 'I can't imagine anyone sticking a needle into him, surely not.'

'No, I agree.'

There was a moment's silence, then I heard Teresa speak.

'We'll all miss him terribly, won't we?'

'Yes,' Rita said, with a slight catch in her voice. 'Will you let me know what the autopsy says?'

'Of course. It'll take some time, I guess. More than likely it will be natural causes, like being allergic to whatever bit him although my husband has his suspicions.'

'Really?' Rita asked.

Their conversation lowered and their voices were drowned out with the noise of the kettle they had just turned on, to make themselves a drink.

I sat up, my eyes still glued to the clock. Teresa and Rita took no notice as they busied themselves with their coffee. It was five minutes to five, time to move. With my heart quickening, I stood up and walked towards the door. I might as well get it over with. One foot in front of the other – keep on with the daily routine.

Chapter 6

The reception area was busy with the end-of-day activities. A pile of letters was balanced  precariously on the edge of Betty's desk, her coat slung across the desk next to them. Betty, in deep conversation with a child clutching a satchel, glanced up and waved me to go straight in. I knocked gently at Leonard's door and feeling like a child about to be chastised, I walked slowly across the room to his desk where I waited for him to finish his phone call.

The dull walls seemed to ooze years of anguish, little children quaking in terror, parents weeping – their beautiful child had been expelled, staff staring sullenly after being dismissed. But there was something different – the room had changed. What was it? Then I saw it – the photo of Mark with his wife was no longer on the desk, it had been replaced by a grinning Leonard and his spouse. There was no doubt about it, Mark and Anthea were a far better-looking couple. Next to the photo was an open accounts book. I automatically glanced at it and noticed some entries at the bottom of the page. A list of girls' names were next to some account numbers written in pencil. Suddenly I saw John, standing talking at me as I was trying to get the vacuuming done. 'Vicky, Rita, Penny. Prostitutes, that's what they were,' he'd once said, after he told me he'd been to the school, couldn't find me so had spoken to the headmaster. I'd dreaded what John had said and now wondered if he, too, had seen these entries.

Leonard suddenly coughed, glaring at me and my indiscretion. He quickly slammed the book shut before putting the phone down and walked swiftly to the safe behind him, tossing the book into it, and closed and locked the door with one quick practised movement.

'Now, Mrs Wilks,' he said. 'Sit down.' He nodded towards the straight-backed chair opposite him. He sat down himself, pulling up the legs of his trousers to keep them in shape and surveyed me, his steely eyes drilling into mine. A piece of paper slipped from the top of a pile that was balanced on his desk and fell onto the floor. He ignored it. I sat frozen in the chair.

'What were you doing just now?' he tossed the question to me, as if it was of no consequence.

'N-nothing,' I stammered.

'You were looking at the papers on my desk.'

'Only glancing, I wasn't really looking closely. Was there something I shouldn't have seen?' I shouldn't have said that.

'Of course not,' he stared at me as if weighing up carefully what he was going to say. 'I just expect any staff of mine to have good manners. *Did* you see anything particular? You know my work is highly confidential and that it's very unprofessional to read anything that's not intended for you?'

'Y-yes, I know that. I didn't see anything – besides, it was all upside down.' Would he believe me? My heartbeat increased. Didn't he realise every teacher could read upside down? I slumped in my chair. I was done for now.

'Well, be that as it may. I can trust you to behave professionally can't I? and if you did see anything, keep it to yourself, understand?'

'Yes of course!' By now my heart was hammering very loudly.

'Now, to the matter in hand. What is so important that you have to see me?' he asked, his horn-rimmed glasses glinting.

'I thought you should know.'

'Know what?'

I blurted out quickly, the words spilling into each other, 'My husband has been sectioned and is in Gravesall Hospital.'

'Oh,' he said. 'That's got nothing to—' He glanced at me, suddenly smiled and said as soothingly as he could, 'I'm so sorry to hear that,' but his voice was cold. He was no more sympathetic than I was when he'd told me to do double duty because his wife wanted him to leave school early last week. He focused his blue-grey eyes on me. 'Is there anything I can do for you?'

'Well,' I shifted in the chair and cleared my throat giving myself time to summon up the courage to be direct. What could I lose? I took a deep breath. 'I may have to attend meetings about John during the day and I may need some time off.'

'Mm.' He glanced back at the cupboard he had just locked and having made up his mind, finally fashioned his features into another insincere smile.

'Well, Sally, we must do all we can to help you. So, as long as it is not too much and you make sure you have all the work set for the staff covering, it should be quite all right. See Mr Masters about it and tell him I have given you permission. I'll write him a memo too. All right?' He smiled as though he was making some kind of agreement with me.

I sat back, amazed. Was this the same mean deputy I had been wrangling with for years to get time off, for far more valid reasons than this? I smiled weakly, feeling uneasy inside. It had been too swift, too generous.

'Thank you,' I said, standing up to leave the room as swiftly as I could, before he changed his mind.

'Just a moment!' he called as I reached the door. I froze and turned slowly. 'Before you go,' he said calmly, his eyes never losing their steely sheen. 'I have something I would like you to do for me.'

'Oh?'

'Yes. Here, take this box of confiscated items to the staffroom and get the staff to return them to the miscreants or, bin them, will you please?' Then, lowering his voice, 'I think you might like to check them first though.'

I hesitated, my eyebrows raised in surprise. 'All right.' I took hold of the box and made for the door. What had come over Leonard Hall all of a sudden giving me time off so easily? Surely there was nothing untoward about the girls' names and numbers I saw in the accounts book? After all, they taught at the school. I shrugged, deciding that the new powers he had might be going to his head. I took the box to the staffroom and went quickly outside to my car. I would check the box tomorrow, for I couldn't imagine anything that was so important I ought to look today.

The next day, I put myself into automated mode again. The morning assembly was a bit of a disaster – the clarinettist kept squawking, the percussion got a bit carried away and the school's singing was diabolical. In the second lesson of the day I had another teacher claiming she had booked my room. We squabbled in front of two very restless classes until I won, so she finally went to the hall. I was very grateful for coffee break when it came, dashed into the staffroom, and sat down to gather my wits before I battled with the coffee queue. As I was taking my third breath to calm myself down, I could see Henry making a beeline for me.

'So, how did it go with the deputy?'

'Oh, that!' My mind was still whirring with the chaos of my previous lesson. I grinned. 'A piece of cake. I can take off any time I want – how about that!'

'Really?' Henry shook his head in disbelief. 'Are you sure?'

'Yes, very sure.'

He whistled. 'Never in all the time I've been here has the Mean Machine given anyone time off without a huge struggle. What did you do to him?'

'Nothing,' I said. 'Nothing, really, although—'

Henry leaned closer. 'Ye-es?'

'Oh it's nothing.'

By now his face was almost touching mine. 'There's obviously something, out with it girl! But then, of course he may be buttering you up before he gives you the chop.'

The shock must have shown in my face.

Henry laughed. 'Silly. Of course you're not going to get the chop. Of all the teachers here you are the least likely to go. Old Bill over there is bound to be the first.' We looked across the room at Bill, his rotund body squeezed into an armchair, his head on his chest, having forty winks.

'Come on. There must have been another reason.' Henry certainly was persistent.

'All right. It's probably just my imagination but, when I first went in, there was an open accounts book on the table.'

'There's nothing unusual about an accounts book – the headmaster and no doubt the deputy have to keep the accounts these days.'

'Yes, but it was the way he suddenly snapped it shut, and put it in a locked cupboard so quickly that aroused my concern. He'd just caught me looking at it while it was open on his desk.'

'Did you see anything unusual in it? Could you even read it? After all, you were looking at it upside down, I presume?'

'Have you forgotten – we teachers can all read upside down. Can't you?'

'Well no, not well,' he confessed.

'Really? Anyway there was something odd – there were three girls' names listed in the credit column – the names of young teachers here: Vicky, Rita and Penny. What do you make of it?'

'I suppose it could be their salaries.'

'Yes, but their names and the numbers beside them were written in pencil – the rest of the accounts were in ink.'

'Hmm. Interesting.'

'Oh and another thing.' I sat up, 'I'd nearly forgotten.'

'Yes?'

'He gave me a box of confiscated items to bring to the staffroom to give back to the children, saying that I would be interested in one of the items.'

I stood up and went across the room. The crowd of staff trying to grab their coffee had diminished by now and the box lay undisturbed and in isolation on the table next to the coffee machine. I pulled open the lid and screwed my nose up at the smell of dirty children's keepsakes, ones that had had grubby fingers holding onto them constantly, some dragged through the dirt and I didn't dare think of what had happened to the others. There were handheld toys, scraps of paper, cigarettes, matchboxes, penknives, rubber bands, a catapult, a steel letter opener and envelopes. Most of the envelopes were blank but one had writing on it. It was addressed to the headmaster. My heart stopped. I recognized the handwriting. It was John's! How on earth—? I grabbed it. The envelope had already been torn open and when I looked inside, the letter was still there. I suddenly felt cold. What *had* John written to the headmaster? I pictured him outside the headmaster's house again – I'll fix him! – John had ranted until I was finally able to drag him away.

I glanced around to check that no one was looking. Henry had stopped to chat to another teacher before coming to join me. I hastily folded the envelope and shoved it into my pocket.

'Right,' Henry said in his matter-of-fact way when he arrived and started sifting through the other items. 'What do we have here?'

He looked into the box. 'We'll never find out who they all belong to. I'll get the boss's secretary to put a notice up on the board and the pupils can come and claim what they think is theirs. They'll have to identify them, of course. In the meantime the cigarettes can go.' He threw them in the wastepaper bin. He opened the matchbox. It was empty. 'That can be binned too.' Henry cleared the rest of the rubbish from the box and closed the lid.

'Now Sally, let's get our coffee. We've got better things to do than sort out the headmaster's confiscated items.' Henry poured a coffee, handed it to me, then grabbed one for himself and we sat down again. I could feel the envelope scrunched up in my pocket. What could John have written in his letter?

Henry whispered into my ear. 'And what was that you secreted into your pocket?'

'Nothing.' Did the man miss anything?

'Now come on, Sally, you can confide in me. Promise I won't tell anyone.' His tone was gentle and persuasive.

My cheeks now bright red, I fingered the envelope.

'No, don't get it out, just tell me.'

I turned and looked at him. 'It was a letter of John's.'

'Oh. Why would John be writing to anyone at the school?'

'As he became ill, he started writing odd letters to people of importance. I found him writing to the Queen, the Prime Minister, you name it, so it was inevitable he would be writing to the headmaster. Goodness knows what he said in those letters. I managed to stop some of them, but he was very cunning and sometimes managed to get a stamp from someone and get them into the post. I knew nothing until I saw the replies containing weird comments about being mortified or highly offended and suggesting John desisted from writing any more letters and that he should contact his doctor instead. It was so embarrassing.'

'Ah.' Henry leaned back. 'I understand. It must have been very difficult for you. At least it won't be happening any more eh?'

My eyes moistened. 'No,' I said and took a drink from my mug. I couldn't wait any longer. I slipped my hand into my pocket and withdrew the envelope, my hands shaking as I fumbled to extract the letter inside. John's hard, angular script scrawled across the page. I held the letter close to me so that no one could see it, not even Henry.

*headmasters are jailed for abuse three little maids from school your day will come*

My mouth felt dry.

'So?' Henry was looking at me, keen to see the letter.

'Don't let anyone else see it,' I hissed as I handed it over.

'Mm, I see,' Henry said, as he gave it back to me. 'I'd keep it very safe if I were you.'

'Why would Leonard let me have this? Surely he should've handed it to the police?'

'Maybe. Mark'd probably only got it recently and there wasn't time, and now Leonard's put you in a quandary. You should hand it over to the police but that will get John into trouble. But if you don't give it in, Leonard knows about it and can dob you both in anyway. Either way, you can't win.'

I shoved the letter back into my pocket. 'Thanks for that. So that's his game.' I sat back and watched the busy staff chatting amongst themselves, worrying about various classes and pupils, living in a world that I had almost forgotten. 'I think I'll keep it for now and only hand it over if the police contact me. Meanwhile, Leonard knows I'll be on my best behaviour.'

'As always,' Henry said, grinning. I glared at him.

'Look,' he said, 'we only have a few minutes of our break left, let's change the subject. What are you doing on Saturday?'

I swallowed. 'Nothing.' I thought of our cold dark house, no John, no living being to talk with, to share the worries of the day.

Henry was speaking again. 'We would love you to come to dinner.'

I looked at him. His eyes didn't waver. The picture of Rita and Henry clasped in each other's embrace in the resources cupboard flashed into my mind. It was nearly a year since it had happened, but it was one of those images that haunted me. The simple course of action was to ask Henry what had been going on, but that was too simple for me, besides, what if it wasn't completely innocent? What then? I didn't reply.

Henry put his hand on my arm. 'Nothing untoward, I promise. Carol loves cooking and on Saturday nights, as you know, she likes to invite a number of friends to try out her latest concoctions.'

He smiled. 'No one has ever had food poisoning from her cooking yet.'

I relaxed. 'All right, I give in. What time?'

'Come at about half six. You don't have to bring anything except your pretty smile.'

The bell rang for the beginning of the next lesson.

'I'll see you tomorrow anyway eh?' Henry tapped me gently on my arm, let go, and crossed the room.

I stood up and watched him walk out.

'I wouldn't believe everything he tells you, you know,' a dark voice said in my ear. I turned to see Vicky, the latest trainee teacher and one of the names in the accounts book, standing next to me, her green eyes flashing.

I stared at her for a moment. What was that about? Surely not Vicky as well as Rita?

Chapter 7

I didn't see Henry again in the next few days. I was too busy with teaching and trying to get my lessons sorted for the following week. I needed to keep busy – anything rather than having to face going to the meeting at Gravesall and seeing John on the following Friday. Although I dreaded the silence of the house while John was missing, I was not looking forward to seeing him again, not the way he was now. An image of his confused, angry face staring into mine flashed into mind. I shuddered.

On Saturday, at a quarter past six in the evening, I closed my front door and, clutching a bottle of wine, got into my car. The traffic to Sutton wasn't too bad, much less than the seven thirty rush I always met on the way to my evening classes. As John had got worse, my one ray of light was my evening classes when I taught music theory to a small group of enthusiasts on Wednesdays and Thursdays. Janet, the gentle housewife, proud to spend most of her time keeping the home beautiful for hubby, had a special flair for the subject. It was so rewarding being able to teach without all the flack and disruption of my daytime pupils.

Eastwood Close was deserted as I pulled up outside the Matthews' house. I picked up the bottle of wine, stepped out of the car and locked it. I stood for a moment admiring the view of the Pepperpot – the fourteenth century church tower that dominated the village skyline. It seemed only a moment ago when John and I climbed the steps up to the bell tower. Tom, the leader of the bell-ringers, patiently showed us how to hold the ropes, carefully balance the huge tons of metal above, and feel the tremendous vibrations as the noise sounded across the fens. Tom's face was creased with sadness when he told us we had to stop. So many centuries of bell-ringing had weakened the tower until it had become unsafe.

I turned, walked round my car and up the path to the rather large bungalow. Thank goodness they didn't have any children. I had had enough of noisy youngsters for the day. I knocked on the door and it was immediately opened.

Henry gave me a lengthy hug. His aftershave was the same as John's. I let myself revel in the warmth of his arms for a moment, the wine bottle still held awkwardly in my left hand. He finally broke free.

'I could see you coming. Glad you made it. I thought you might change your mind.' He accepted the wine and stepped back inside the house. 'Come in, come in and see Carol.'

I hesitated. I had met Carol before and always felt shy and intimidated. She was one of those wonder women you hear about. Beautiful, friendly and everything she turned her hand to was perfect.

'Hello.' Carol gave me a peck on the cheek, her curly brown hair softly brushing my skin and her Chanel No 5 just noticeable. 'I'm so glad you've come. It's a long time since we last met. It was at the staff Christmas party I think, wasn't it?'

'Yes, that's right.' I remembered seeing her in earnest conversation with Mark King, while Henry and Rita stood very close together, their arms touching, pretending to be engrossed in the school pictures on the wall.

Carol led me into the sitting room. 'Come and meet the others. We're about to have dinner. Henry, can you see to the drinks? I think some of us need a top-up.'

'Sure.' Henry smiled at me, 'What can I get you?'

'Just a soft drink please. I'm driving. Have you got an orange juice?'

'Orange juice it is.' Henry turned and walked over to a well-stocked drinks cabinet at the other end of the room. There were signs of his artistic talent everywhere. A stunning oil of a semi-naked woman filled the wall above the mantelpiece. I wondered if it was Carol in her younger days. A pair of beautifully carved deer was either side of the perpetual clock, the soft wood of the animals glinting gold from the timepiece.

Carol cleared her throat. I turned to look at my hostess, who beamed.

'I think you know most of the people here.' She took my arm and led me forward. 'Leonard and Dorothy Hall,' she stepped back, leaving me plenty of space to acknowledge them.

I *so* did not want to spend my Saturday evening socialising with the deputy and his wife; what on earth were Henry and Carol thinking? I suddenly felt an urge to loosen Leonard's tie, but resisted. His wife was over-dressed with the bright pink flounces of her voluminous frilly collar around her pale, round features contrasting drastically with her bright red lipstick – making her look like one of those clown's heads at the fair. I had to stop myself imagining Dorothy's head moving from side to side, mouth wide open ready to receive a ping-pong ball.

Carol moved me gently on, 'And Anthea King, Mark's widow.' Anthea looked no different, her straight dark hair still shiny, her complexion faultless, except for her eyes that were now slightly dull with grief, and her smile that was more relaxed than usual. Carol spoke in softer tones as if her words were highly confidential. 'Anthea's being very brave and is determined life should go on in spite of her recent bereavement.'

I also knew that life had to go on in spite of my loss but it seemed irrelevant here. Anthea's situation was different, her husband had died suddenly and apparently in suspicious circumstances. John, on the other hand, was very much alive and difficult with it. I smiled weakly, accepted the cold glass of orange juice from Henry and sat in a stiff upright chair. Henry finished topping up the drinks and Carol asked everyone to move to the dining room for dinner. I found myself sitting next to Henry on one side and Leonard on the other. Opposite were Dorothy and the bereaved Anthea. I glanced at Carol and Henry. Thank goodness the lover, Rita, was not here.

'This is a new recipe I'm trying out – avocado with a lime dressing.' Carol swiftly served the first course and sat down at the head of the table. I lifted my spoon to start.

Dorothy took a mouthful and swallowed quickly. 'Delicious, absolutely delicious Carol. You are a marvellous cook, isn't she Leonard?'

Leonard nodded.

Dorothy put her spoon down for a moment. 'When you invited us to come, I mean it's only natural that you would want to have us here, I knew we would be in for a real treat. Didn't I say so Leonard?'

Leonard nodded again. I smiled to myself.

Dorothy wrapped her fingers round the stem of her wine glass. 'It's so brave of you to hold this dinner party, Carol and Henry, after such a terrible tragedy. It's affected us all.' She turned to Anthea. 'You don't mind talking about it, do you Anthea? After all, in times like these it's better to talk about things. Get them off your chest. Isn't that right?'

'Well—' Anthea held her spoon mid air while she tried to think of a reply.

Dorothy was on a roll. 'Never mind. You take your time. In spite of his little problems, Mark was a wonderful man and a wonderful husband I'm sure. You'll miss him a lot, but you just say the word and one of us'll be there if you want to talk. When you're ready, you'll let it all out, won't you?'

Anthea frowned and focused on her food.

The woman was insufferable. I stared at Dorothy. 'Mark's little problems?' My voice was more strident than I intended. I cleared my throat. 'What were they? No matter what we all thought of him, he always behaved impeccably, and he always takes, I mean, took, good care of the new staff, I'm told, so what could these "little problems" be?'

Anthea took a swift drink of wine. 'Exactly.'

I raised my eyebrows at Henry who showed no reaction.

Dorothy's spoon clattered as she picked it up clumsily. 'Well, there were his health problems. He had something wrong with his heart didn't he?'

Anthea didn't reply.

Unperturbed, Dorothy turned to me, 'And you're having troubles of your own Sally, aren't you?'

I looked at Leonard. His face was inscrutable. Then I saw Henry fidget in his chair. He mouthed 'sorry' and looked down at his half-eaten avocado pear.

'I suppose so.' What the heck. I had ceased caring. 'I guess you all know that my husband has been sectioned into Gravesall Hospital. He's unlikely to ever come out.'

There was an uncomfortable silence.

Dorothy took in a deep breath but before she could say anything, Carol spoke quickly and firmly. 'How awful! It must be dreadful for you. If there is anything we can do, you know you only have— however, tonight I think we should forget our troubles for the moment and talk about something else. Yes?'

Anthea and I nodded.

Dorothy piped up yet again, 'But—'

Leonard looked at his wife. Using his deputy head voice he said, 'Enough, Dorothy.'

She closed her mouth. He turned to address the rest of the table in calmer tones. 'Did anyone go to the talk the other night? You know, the one in the cathedral?'

Dorothy could not help herself. 'That was the night that—'

Again he glared at her and said hurriedly, 'Yes, all right Dorothy. That was the night that Mark collapsed. Now we are discussing the talk, *right*?' The emphasis he put on the word 'right' made everyone, even his wife, take notice.

Silence descended again.

Henry cleared his throat. 'Yes, Carol and I went. It was very interesting. The chap giving the talk was certainly a character. Maybe when I get old and grey I might be a bit of an eccentric like him too.'

Carol's eyes sparkled. 'You mean you aren't already?'

'All right, darling, have it your own way. I'm a bit of an eccentric already. Why else would you put up with me?'

'Indeed.' She lifted her glass to her husband. 'Even including your lovely friends of the female kind. Who was the last one? Rita, was that her name? and previously—er, a name of a queen—yes, Vicky?'

Leonard stared hard at Henry.

Henry coughed slightly. 'Yes, all right.' His eyes swept around the table. 'I only offered friendship, and you know that Carol.' Carol's eyes twinkled at him again. He squared up to the remaining enquiring eyes. 'Vicky was a new girl then. I was just showing her the ropes and as you know, Rita's the new drama teacher at school. She'd been having a bit of trouble with her own love life. Her husband's a bit of a bore. I only offered my friendship, until she made it up with him. Then I left them to it. All right?'

Leonard still didn't stop looking at him.

Anthea looked at Henry and then at Carol, 'I must have been mistaken. I thought you two had had a short separation because of Rita?'

Carol laughed, 'Rumour, I was away looking after a sick aunt, Anthea.'

Henry's laughter joined Carol's, 'And I always let you look after sick aunts, don't I my dear?'

Carol smiled at her husband. I thought I detected a glint in Carol's eyes, but who was I to question their relationship? After all, it was nothing to do with me and was never likely to be. It wasn't as if Henry and I were up to anything. Whatever I might like to think.

Carol broke the atmosphere and stood up. 'Finished everyone? Now I hope no one's allergic to nuts because there are some in my next dish.'

There was no answer. Carol quickly collected the used plates. Henry put his serviette on the table and prepared to stand up.

She said quickly, 'No, Henry. I'll manage. You stay and entertain the guests.'

He sat back down and she left for the kitchen.

Dorothy's grotesque mouth opened wide. 'It's amazing isn't? Another Fanny Craddock don't you think?'

Anthea smiled weakly, focusing on her wine glass, which she kept twirling round. 'Yes, I have to agree. She's an excellent cook. I hope it's my special nut roast. I've often used the same recipe but mine always tastes different to Carol's.' A slightly awkward feeling emanated from the others at the table as she said that.

Anthea took another large swig of wine and said rapidly, 'Of course, hers is always delicious.' She drained her glass.

An audible sigh of relief could be heard in the room and then, in the silence that followed, I felt obliged to add to the conversation. 'I never seem to have enough time to cook properly. John had his favourites and that was that. Most of them were grilled meat of some kind—very easy to do though—' I paused, a picture flashed into my mind of John throwing his plate across the room. 'It's overcooked!' he'd shouted. 'I'm not hungry, I'm going out!' I'd heard the front door slam as I tried to sweep up the pieces of the broken plate.

Dorothy's carping voice interrupted my thoughts. 'We prefer a grilled fillet steak, don't we Leonard?' Carol re-entered the room. 'That is,' she continued hurriedly, 'if we aren't having a delicious meal prepared by Carol!'

'How kind,' Carol said, as she concentrated on handing out the plates of food.

The evening went very slowly. Everyone was so polite that they were verging towards rudeness. The death of the headmaster hung in the air like a storm cloud ready to burst but no one made any attempt to touch on the subject again. No one looked at Anthea when she kept asking for more wine. When they had finished coffee and liqueurs, I stood up.

'It's late for me I'm afraid. I really must go.'

Carol glanced up. 'Really? Stay for a little while longer. After all it's Sunday tomorrow. You'll be able to sleep in.'

I sat down heavily. She had no idea what it was like for me. I'm very unlikely to sleep at all, especially with the prospect of having to go into the ward full of mad, or should I say ill, people at Gravesall again.

Henry put his hand on mine. 'Yes, stay. You need to lighten up.'

I stared hard at him, it was so unnerving when someone could read my thoughts and feelings so accurately. His face was expressionless.

Finally Leonard and Dorothy made a lot of fuss about preparing to leave, insisted on driving Anthea home and asked for their coats. I was able to follow. Leonard stopped a moment to let me catch up. He spoke softly, a tone that I didn't remember ever hearing from him before. Could someone change so much or was there something behind his newfound sympathy? 'As we live in the next village,' he said, 'if you ever need anything, even a lift into school, for example, I would gladly come over to Witchford, you know.'

Dorothy's chest expanded, pushing her fur coat aside to reveal her ample chest. 'How kind of you Leonard! In fact, you could drive through Witchford from time to time anyway, just to make sure Sally is all right.' She turned to me, 'It's going to be dreadful for you dear, in that big house all alone.' She pecked me on the cheek and stepped forward to say goodbye to Carol and Henry and waddled onto the path. Leonard followed and they left with Anthea, Leonard turning back very briefly to smile enigmatically at me.

An uneasy chill descended on me. I turned to Henry and Carol who were standing side by side, arm in arm. Henry's smile put an end to my unease. However, although cheered, I suddenly felt awkward in his presence. Keeping a slight distance between them and me, I shook Henry's hand. He laughed, let go of his wife, pulled me towards him and held me, finally giving me a light kiss on the cheek. I could detect his rapid heartbeat. I pulled away from him, my hands shaking, smiled at Carol, thanked her profusely, pecked her on the cheek and went swiftly to my car.

I couldn't get away quickly enough. I sat down in the driving seat, pulled out the choke and turned the key. The car wouldn't start. I tried again. Nothing happened. I slammed the steering wheel with the palm of my hand. Would nothing go right? I turned the key for a third time, but it was obvious, the engine was dead. Tears of frustration blurred my vision. A figure appeared at my window. It was Henry. He indicated to me to pull my window down.

'You've flooded it,' he said. 'Here, out you get and let me sort it.' He opened my car door. I stumbled out and let him take the seat. He put his foot down hard on the accelerator, revved the engine very loudly and finally it came to life. Sheepishly, I thanked him as he slid out of my seat. He put his hand on my arm. 'You are a pack of nerves aren't you?'

I fought hard to keep my tears from falling.

He helped me into my seat. 'I can drive you home if you like.'

'No! No!' I shrieked more loudly than intended. I dropped my voice and said, 'No, thank you. It was a lovely dinner and I'll see you at school on Monday.'

'You know if you have any more trouble with little Bumble, just call me.'

I wondered how Henry knew the nickname for my car and drove away quickly, conscious that he was watching my every move as I left Eastwood Close.

The drive home seemed to take ages. I blinked my tears away and concentrated hard on the road now cloaked in darkness. I would have to get used to driving in the dark alone. For a moment I wished I could rest my hand on John's slim knee. I longed to feel him, seated in the driving seat, concentrating on the road ahead, his head angled slightly, the proud husband looking after the wife. Henry was proud of Carol in the same way. When they stood close there was definitely a spark between them, one of those rare intangible auras of a powerful empathy that made them one, a couple which would never be separated, no matter how sorely their relationship was tested. I had to admit it, they were both far more empathetic than John or I – Henry could see right through me for a start. It was so unnerving. But if they were so much in touch with the world, why had they invited Leonard and his wife to the party, the

Mean Machine – Henry's own nickname for Leonard? He and his ghastly wife were party killers of the first kind, and Anthea? the poor widow shrouded in a cloud of misery and still in deep shock from the sudden death of her husband, starting to take to the drink – surely it was too soon for her? – but maybe she wanted, even needed people around her, maybe she too hated the cold silence of her home. Waifs and strays – that's what they were doing – collecting the waifs and strays together like the good neighbours they were.

A loud revving behind me interrupted my thoughts. A black Peugeot shoved its nose up the back of Bumble, far too close. I slowed a little and glanced in my mirror. The youth pushed his foot hard on his accelerator and screamed past.

And Leonard, was I being paranoid, or was he suddenly just too helpful? He'd never offered to help before, not even when I had pneumonia, so why now? Surely a glance at an accounts book couldn't be that threatening? Besides, it didn't matter what I said or did, he had the air and personality of a man at the top who could squash me as easily as treading on a solitary ant. A meeting from the past swam into mind, when once again he'd trampled on me. 'Forget it,' he'd said. 'There will be no coach trip for your choir. Taking the children out of class for so long is unquestionable. Your time would be better spent getting your reports in promptly for a change don't you think?' I shivered remembering his withering look at this last staff meeting.

An oncoming car dipped its lights. At least it would be daylight when I next had to drive.

## Chapter 8

At eleven o'clock in the morning the next day, Sunday, I closed my front door slowly. I was not looking forward to the journey to Gravesall Hospital. When I tried to click my car doors open, nothing happened. I put my hand on the door handle and pulled. It came open immediately. Oops, I'd forgotten to lock the car the previous night. I glanced around but the street was empty.

I had a sudden thought. Did I remember to turn off the headlights? I travel so rarely in the dark, I wasn't sure. With trepidation, I put the key in the ignition and turned it. The engine didn't respond. I turned the key again – nothing. I banged the palm of my hand on the driving wheel in frustration. I should ring the AA or I could try Gary at the garage – but no, the garage was shut. The AA would take ages. I flung open the car door, scrabbled in my purse for the front door keys, stormed in the house, looked up the number and dialled Henry. Henry had said, 'just call me', hadn't he? I listened to the phone ringing at the other end, and I wondered if I had done the right thing after all.

It took ten minutes for Henry to arrive in his Volvo. In a few minutes he had retrieved jump leads from his boot and my car was purring.

'OK?' he leaned into my open window.

'Yes, thanks.'

'Look, if you're worried about the car breaking down again, I could come with you.'

'No, no,' I put the car into gear. 'I'm going to see John. You wouldn't want to come. Besides, you should go back home to Carol.'

'Oh Carol doesn't mind. She has even said to me that she likes me to get out from under her feet sometimes. It would be no trouble.'

'No,' I said firmly. I gazed at his tanned hands that lingered on the door frame.

'I'll move my hands if you promise to come out with me on a picnic next Sunday. Carol's going to be away on a course until Monday.'

'Is this a proposition?' I grinned.

'It can be whatever you want it to be. The hand of friendship is what I'm offering. Say yes?'

'All right. Yes, if you don't mind me leaving by five afterwards to visit Gravesall.'

'Whatever you like. You're on!' Henry stepped back from the car. As I drove towards Main Street, I glanced in my mirror. Henry was standing beside his car, watching me. He looked pensive, his slim arms at his side, a wisp of his blond hair waving gently in the breeze.

The next day I arrived home from school to see a police car parked outside my house, with two people inside, waiting. My heart leapt. Had something happened to John? I'd only seen him yesterday. In trepidation I parked on my driveway, slowly pulled out my bag and went to the front door. Out of the corner of my eye I saw the doors of the police car open and two uniformed people got out. It was no good, ignoring them wouldn't make them go away. My heart hammered as I fumbled at the door.

'Mrs Wilks.' The man's voice was young but clear and assured.

I turned to see a tall muscular police officer, his hat jammed firmly on his head, his eyes expressionless but fixed on me, and his partner, a young policewoman, petite, sinewy and with soft dark eyes. My voice croaked, 'Yes?'

He pulled out a card from his jacket pocket and held it towards me.

'I am Constable Thomas and,' he jerked a finger in the direction of his partner, 'this is Constable Parsons. We would like to speak to you. Can we come in?' he demanded.

The three of us sat in my sitting room in silence. The woman who had been introduced as Constable Parsons reached into her pocket, slowly retrieved her pad, and her pencil was poised.

I coughed. 'Would you like a cup of tea?'

She looked at her partner. He opened his mouth to speak but before he could respond I leapt to my feet. 'I'm absolutely dying for one, so I'll go and make some eh?'

I nearly tripped over the bag I'd dumped at the side of my chair and scuttled to the kitchen. I knew why they were here. It was obvious. John had escaped and may even have died. I didn't want to know. The tea tray shook as I carried it to the sitting room.

Constable Thomas cleared his throat.

Before he could say anything, I lifted up the jug. 'Milk?'

'And we both take one sugar please,' Constable Parsons said. Her colleague glared at her.

Constable Thomas began. 'We are here to ask you some questions about the death of Mark King.'

I let out a sigh of relief, John was all right! The police officers stared at me. Then the implications slowly dawned on me – if it was foul play, I had no alibi, I was at home when Mark had died. I glanced at my coat hung up near the front door. John's letter was still burning a hole in the pocket. I smiled to myself, at least John had his own special alibi – even if it was being carted off to the mental home.

'It's no smiling matter young lady,' Constable Thomas snapped. 'Tell us, where were you on the night that he died? That would be Wednesday, the fifth of September?'

'I was at home alone.'

'Mm, at home, you say,' Constable Thomas sneered. 'Alone. Are you sure?'

'Of course I'm sure,' I tried to keep my voice steady. 'That's the night Gale came over to tell me that my husband—'

'Ah,' Constable Parsons interjected swiftly, 'so Gale saw you here. That's good.'

Constable Thomas glared at her, his thin lips cracking into an insincere smile. 'And the full name and address of Gale?'

I stuttered as I gave him her details, my cheeks getting hotter and hotter.

'Your husband John, I understand, was taken to Gravesall Hospital in the fine village of the same name – a fitting place for him, and my colleague here?' He laughed. She glared at him. He ignored her. 'Is that right? He was sectioned that night?'

'Yes,' I replied.

'And your husband, is he capable of murder? Do you mind telling us what he was—er—is like?'

I minded terribly, but I was not going to let him know. 'Not at all,' I said, trying to maintain an even, unemotional tone, wondering when I should produce the letter or if I should just leave it.

'What was he like then?'

To avert his eyes, I looked towards the window and started, 'He is a very intelligent man. He can—could—quote Oscar Wilde non-stop. He was interested in anything and everything. He was a rep for a pesticide and herbicide company.'

'Is he indeed?'

'No,' I said. 'Not NOW. He left years ago and certainly had no access to any of the herbicides and pesticides anymore, if that's what you're thinking.' I stared into the cold eyes of the constable; they were watchful and suspicious. He blinked and continued.

'And lately just before he was sectioned—'

I hesitated. The two interviewers stared at me, waiting patiently.

'Well,' I fidgeted in my chair. Suddenly I felt guilty, guilty of talking about my husband behind his back, talking about the worst side of him. It didn't seem right.

The two pairs of eyes held their gaze.

'All right,' I shifted position again, 'he was not himself. He was getting difficult —even— dangerous. That's why he was sectioned.'

'Yes?'

'No, not in any kind of way that made it possible for him to plan a murder. He would just get angry about the silliest of things and was very difficult to calm down. He rarely lashed out although it was getting more and more difficult for me.'

'Mm.' The questioners exchanged glances.

'Why?' I demanded.

Constable Parsons spoke with a warm comforting tone. 'Oh, it's all right. Mark King hadn't been in any kind of fight, so we don't suspect your husband of—'

'I'll lead this investigation if you don't mind!' Constable Thomas interrupted, glowering at his colleague. She looked down at her notepad.

'You suspect him of something, don't you?' I asked, my voice quavering with anxiety.

'Well, now,' Constable Thomas said, his tone becoming more and more patronising, 'don't worry your pretty little head about it. We're just tidying up the loose ends.'

'Loose ends?'

Constable Thomas smiled as if trying to appease a petulant child but it wasn't working. 'Look' he said.

'It was probably an accident, we're just trying to get to the truth and we're asking you to help us do this, all right? Now, was John diabetic?'

'No.'

'Did John have anything to do with poisons or have any exotic pets?'

I shrugged my shoulders. 'Not really,' I lied, remembering the time I managed to grab the bleach from him as he was pouring it into our teapot.

They stared. I had to give them something, I glanced at my coat again.

'He used to bring home all sorts of things when he'd been out on the road on his bicycle.' I frowned remembering his strange and random acquisitions from the roadside. 'He lost his driver's license when he had epileptic fits.'

'Ah, so he had fits. What were they like?'

'Just like any grand mal seizure. He would fall down, shake, and when he finally stopped he would sleep a bit and then he'd be all right. OK?' I was finding it difficult to keep my tone friendly and informative, when I really wanted them to stop questioning me and go away.

They surveyed me for a while longer. The atmosphere was cold and my fingers dug into my palms as I recalled how John could sometimes be in a fit for a whole day and never remember anything afterwards. Even at those times he could act as though he was perfectly normal. I refused to believe that he could have been in a fit, gone to Mark King and somehow, in some devious way, given him a kind of poison. It was not possible. I held their stare, thinking I should show them the letter now.

Constable Thomas cleared his throat. 'And tell me about the things he used to bring home.'

'Oh, they were just silly things, like rubber gloves, carrots and sugar beet that had dropped off the lorries, and various wildlife—'

'Ah, wildlife. Such as?'

'Nothing serious. We don't have anything dangerous here anyway. He certainly didn't bring home an adder if that's what you're thinking. He used to bring things like frogs, butterflies, ants, spiders, the occasional dead bird …' I shuddered as I remembered him bringing that wretched box to me and insisting that I looked at a dead pigeon he was going to bury in the garden for compost, so he reckoned.

Constable Parson's pen was scribbling fast.

'How did your husband feel about Mark King?'

'It wasn't a matter about how he felt about anybody, it was just that—well—he'd lost track of reality, so I couldn't say.' I wasn't going to tell them the times John yelled that he was going to do something to the headmaster, something spontaneous, something violent but I knew that he wouldn't. He never did it, he just threatened. The threats in the letter were insubstantial too, he never did any of the things he said he would.

'Well, is there anything else you can tell us that you think would help?' The constable followed my glance to the coat. I could feel his steady eyes piercing my troubled thoughts.

I paused. I was sure he suspected me and the more he stared, the more I hesitated and the more my cheeks reddened. There was no escape. 'Well,' I fingered the collar of my blouse, 'he did write people threatening letters, but,' I gabbled quickly, 'he never meant anything by them, they were just expressions of his wandering mind. He could never follow through on any of his threats. His thoughts were always disconnected. One minute he'd be talking about worldly things like the atomic bomb and the next he'd be chastising someone about smoking, suggesting they had something to do with Hiroshima. A lot of what he said didn't make sense.'

The constable raised an eyebrow.

By now my face was bright crimson. 'No,' I insisted, 'as I said, his mind wandered so much that sometimes he would change tack within a split second. One minute he would be a raving lunatic ready to attack anything that moved, the next he'd be a gentle, confused, lost soul wanting you to be there with him and guide him.'

'Do you have any of these letters?'

I swallowed and stood up uneasily. 'Just this one.' I stumbled to the coat, withdrew the letter and gave it to the male officer. He looked at it, grinned, and tossed it to his colleague.

'Yes, I see what you mean by disconnected thoughts. This will be most useful. Now, can I use your toilet please?' He stood up.

Nonplussed, I said, 'Yes, it's the first door on the right in the hallway.'

With that, he left the room, closing the door behind him. Constable Parsons cleared her throat but said nothing. The clocked ticked loudly as we waited.

Constable Parsons,' I began.

'Call me Wendy,' she looked at me, her eyes kind and sympathetic.

'Wendy, we're not in any trouble are we, really?'

'Who knows—' She looked at our picture above the mantelpiece. 'Sorry, I hope not, Jarvis does get a bit carried away sometimes.'

'What did he mean by Gravesall being a suitable place for you?' I digressed, wondering what Constable Thomas was up to in my house besides going to the toilet. I glanced at the piano stool. Thank God I kept John's worst letters in there.

'Oh, I live there, near Gravesall, unfortunately.'

'Why, do you get much trouble from the place?'

'It's not the place itself that gives me trouble, it's the families of the patients that keep bringing their complaints to me when I'm at home. It's as if I'm never off duty – even then, I don't mind – I do what I can, but it gets difficult.' She glanced at the closed door.

'I think I know what you mean,' I said. 'But, what's wrong with the place?'

'Oh, it's only certain wards. There are complaints of patients being treated badly and a couple of families say they are being harassed for money that they believe they shouldn't have to pay.'

I looked aghast. Was this what I had to look forward to?

'Oh no,' she said hastily. 'It's only about certain wards – there've been no complaints about the one your husband is in now. None at all – really.'

On a sudden impulse, she scrabbled in her bag and produced a card. 'Here,' she said glancing at the door again, 'take this. This is my home number and address. I'm not supposed to give it out, but if you need any help—'

'Thank you,' I said, stuffing it in my pocket. 'I really appreciate this.'

'In fact,' she said, 'why not come round to my place after you've visited your husband and when I'm off duty? We might be able to help each other.'

'Yeah, I'd like that,' I said slowly, wondering what she really had in mind.

'I'm off duty next Sunday – what about then? How about popping in for coffee? I'm on the main road as you go in, the house with the roses climbing up the wall.'

'Thank you. I'll come after seeing John, probably about six o'clock if that's all right. I'd like to—'

The door suddenly swung open. 'Having a girlie tête-à-tête? How sweet!' the male officer sneered. He glared at his colleague who averted her eyes.

'Well, we mustn't keep you any longer.' His pockets looked bulkier than before, or was this more paranoia?

With that, the two constables moved swiftly to the front door, and as Wendy crossed the threshold, she turned, looked expectantly at me and, checking first that her colleague was not in sight, I nodded. I would definitely be at hers for coffee after seeing John.

My hands were shaking as I closed the door. We'd never had the police call at our house before. I hoped Mrs Brown wasn't too shocked. No doubt the curtains would be twitching and it would all come out, John, Mark King and the fact that I taught at the school. My blood ran cold when I thought what Constable Thomas had seen and what he might do. I watched the police officers walk straight past their car to Gale's house. Breathing deeply, I tried to force my body to calm down as I went into the kitchen to make another cup of tea. I would be able to drink it hot this time.

Chapter 9

Friday came too quickly. There was a chill breeze as I climbed into my car to head for Gravesall and my first meeting about John. The sky was overcast and the clouds moving gently overhead were darkening. In spite of the depressive thoughts that lingered in my mind, there was a moment of exhilaration when I realized that besides missing four lessons in the morning, I would not have to suffer 4D after lunch either. While I could almost tolerate the remedial classes in the second and third years, the fourth year pupils were impossible. By then they'd become very secure – in their element in fact, and they knew how to wind up the weaker teachers well. Tussling with them was one of the hardest things I had to do. I groaned as I imagined the mob of angry youths gyrating round the classroom. I would be driving back from the meeting at about that time. After all, I had to have lunch somewhere before going back to school.

Bumble started first time and purred as I drove out into the street and headed for Gravesall. Who'd have thought that John and I would end up with a major part of our lives centred round the local mental hospital? John's sunny smile as we first went into our home in Sutton flashed across my mind. Then, our future was rosy. In our naive innocence we believed that the world was ours and ours for the taking. There was nothing we couldn't do. I suddenly felt old for my years. Our dreams were now nothing but a puff of smoke in the wind of change. John was a problem; he had been from within the first weeks of our marriage, but I had refused to see it. Now that he was incarcerated in hospital, I had to face facts. He was gone from my life forever.

As I drove along the main street of the village I glanced at the houses. On the left near the junction was a small thatched cottage with roses climbing up the wall and over a quaint little porch. That must be Wendy's place. Eventually, I chugged into the car park of the administration building at Gravesall Hospital, arriving at five minutes to eleven. The air was still, too still, as I locked the car. I breathed deeply to shrug off the oppression that threatened to overwhelm me. My feet thudded on the sandy pathway as I approached the flimsy box-like building of the administrative block. I hesitated. Nothing I could do would stop the fear creeping slowly inside me. Suddenly I was no longer the capable, confident teacher I'd learnt to be, I was like a whimpering child, weak, afraid and uncertain. Our future could depend on what was said today. I eventually lifted my trembling fingers, formed them into a fist and knocked, my knuckles thudding on the cheap wood of the door. I looked back at the trees. There were no rooks this time. I waited. Nothing happened. I took in a deep breath and knocked louder. Suddenly the door swung open and a pair of bespectacled eyes blinked at me.

I cleared my throat. 'I've come for a meeting about my husband John Wilks?' It was more of a question than a statement.

'Mm,' the woman paused for a few moments as if weighing up whether she was going to let me enter or not. She looked at her clipboard. Eventually she stepped back. 'This way.'

The door swung back firmly. I only just managed to catch it before it hit me. It was very heavy, surprisingly heavy for its flimsy structure. As the door smacked against its frame behind me, I glanced down the corridor. The woman was about to turn the corner at the end of it. I walked quickly, tripping over my feet as I hurried forward. I caught up with her and half walked and half ran as we moved swiftly along the corridors. She eventually stopped. 'Here,' she said, pointing to the door marked 'Meeting room 3'.

The spectacles on the individual before me glinted, while she stood her ground as if to say, 'Well, get on with it, I haven't all day.' I could feel my heart thumping. As the forced smile of my escort turned into a grimace of impatience, I tapped on the door three times, quickly glancing at her as if to reassure her I wasn't going to run away, which I was sorely tempted to do.

'Come!' a commanding voice bellowed from inside. With a sigh, the spectacles turned and disappeared down the corridor.

I turned the handle of the door and slowly pulled it back. There was an atmosphere in the room, not a welcoming one but one that caught the throat as strongly as if someone was squeezing their hands round your neck. Something had happened and that something was not pleasant. As I took a step inside, I detected another effect clouding the atmosphere, it was not the feelings of the people surrounding the table this time, it was something personal—a scent, a strong sickly sweet scent that added to the tension. I soon realized that it came from the plump figure at the head of the table, her pale jowls wobbling as she was attempting to recover from a moment of disquiet. I felt nauseous. I tried to close my nostrils to avoid the offensive aroma and swallowed, willing myself to become accustomed to the room. I prayed that my distaste wasn't visible.

The jowls stopped moving and the woman snapped 'Sit.' She indicated with a plump hand that I should sit at the empty chair next to her. The variety of people gathered round the table watched every step I took until I was seated and then all eyes were fixed on the oppressive chairwoman.

She glanced briefly at me. 'You must be Sally.'
I nodded.

'I'm Tamara Dighton, chair of this committee,' she stared at me, and then at each person in turn ensuring her unequivocal control. This was HER committee, no matter what some upstart had tried to manoeuvre. She looked vaguely familiar but I couldn't put my finger on why, and as soon as she spoke I had no time to think. This was going to be a battle.

'You may be permitted to listen to our discussion, but you are not permitted to speak. Understood?' She poured herself a glass of water and slurped the liquid noisily. I noticed that no one else had the luxury of water.

I shifted in the hard chair. 'Yes, but—'

Her glare was even more threatening than any I had practised on 4D. I closed my mouth, my heart beating strongly and waited. The tension in the atmosphere increased a notch.

'Right. Let's move on,' she moved the closed files in front of her, fingering the single page on top as she did so. 'I want to be out in ten minutes. Is everyone clear that *I* am in command here and that I have the final say. After all, we have to follow the guidelines we've been given, not some fancy idea of our own making. All right?' She glared at a slim figure on her left. His cheeks were flushed and there were beads of sweat on his forehead. He slowly nodded, his eyes glued to hers as if willing her to understand that their battle was not over.

'Good. Now we have to make cuts. There is no other solution.'

A suited gentleman further on her left cleared his throat and leaned forward. 'Yes, and as the Director of Finance, I should advise—'

'No!' Tamara Dighton interrupted. 'We've been over this ground before. We've heard your advice and it is rejected.'

'Yes, but there are one or two matters in the accounts that I want to talk about.'

'We've all seen the accounts, you've passed them, so we don't need to spend more time poring over them again.'

He sat upright, frowned, and tried again. 'It is my duty. Surely—'

'Enough!' she screamed. Again she stared straight into the protagonist's eyes and turned her head slowly around the table so that no one dared protest.

'Not here, not now,' she snarled at the finance director. 'Contact me later.'

No one moved. The tension had reached fever pitch.

'Now,' she settled more comfortably in her chair. 'Let's get on with it.'

She paused, held her sheet of paper up and looked around the room again. 'There is only one way to balance the books and that is to close wards.'

A murmur of dissension swept around the table. 'So,' she challenged, 'just who is prepared to lose their job?'

No one answered.

'Then we'll close the wards. I'll leave you to decide which ones,' she sneered at the finance director.

A curly-haired individual, dressed less formally than the others blurted out, 'But what about the patients?' He looked familiar.

Tamara Dighton lifted her huge chest above the level of the desk, one of the large buttons on her jacket clinking against the edge. 'What about them?' she boomed.

The speaker did not waver. 'Where will they go?'

'Edward Boulten, we've talked about this time and again. Where do you think they will go? Why, into the community, of course.'

'But—'

'There are no buts about it. It's cruel to lock people up, they are best served by their family and you know that!'

'But some—'

'Enough!' Tamara snapped.

Edward Boulten scowled and glanced at me. 'And John Wilkes?' he insisted loudly and firmly. I knew where I'd seen him before—he was the blue T-shirt and jeans chap in John's ward.

Tamara looked confused for a split second and then stared at me. Her plump lips shaped into an insincere smile, moving her massive jowls closer to her eyes which now became tiny, glinting with menace. 'Of course, people like John Wilks will be catered for in the emergency ward. I trust you will not be closing that one first eh?' she laughed heartily at the finance director who smiled crookedly in return.

She looked at her watch and moved as if to stand but before she could, Edward Boulten decided to take advantage of his small victory. 'Isn't Sally entitled to know how her husband is now at least?'

Tamara looked blankly at Ed then turned to other people at the table. 'I suppose so,' she clipped, settling back into her chair. 'But quickly, mind—a very short report from each should suffice—Dr Edwards?'

The slight figure next to Ed stirred, pulling his white coat around him as if in defence. 'Er, I've been told that Mr Wilks is fine. I have only just returned from holiday, so I have not seen him yet but—'

Tamara cut in, 'Thank you.' Her eyes swept past me to a tiny woman seated on my right. I couldn't help feeling sorry for her as she cowered into the desk as if praying to disappear. Her voice matched her diminutive figure as she spoke – small, inconspicuous and of very little substance. She looked down as she spoke.

'It's too early to say.'

Tamara smiled, a smile not just of satisfaction but there were undeniable traces of victory in the corners of her mouth, 'Thank you Heather,' and she turned to the next member of the group, 'Mrs Payne?'

'Ditto' she said, looking down at her notes on the table, glancing immediately at Tamara as if to confirm she had said what was expected.

Tamara smirked at Edward Boulten. 'Satisfied?'

Edward was about to speak, but before anything else could happen, Tamara looked at her watch again and noisily staggered to her feet. 'It's time to go. I declare this meeting closed. The date of the next meeting is to be determined, we'll let you know.'

With that, Tamara Dighton and her obvious skivvies, the two mice, Heather and Mrs Payne who had been taking notes, swept quickly out of the room.

The remaining people glanced apologetically my way and scuttled outside like a group of meerkats who had been frightened by an invader.

I sat alone in the room, my mouth open. I couldn't believe it. Then as I leaned down to retrieve my handbag that had dropped to the floor, I felt someone had come back and was standing near me. I looked up to see Edward Boulten. He looked repentant as though the meeting had been all his doing.

'I'm sorry about that,' he said.

I stared at him, unable to speak while I gathered my thoughts. 'Oh,' I said, 'it's not your fault.'

'Look,' he said, one hand stretching out as if to help. His features were smooth, open and honest, so different to the overweight blob of Ms Dighton's and the scrawny mealy-mouthed visages of the others. He beamed, revealing a fine set of teeth and the creases at the edge of his eyes broadened his smile into one of the most affable and charming ones I had ever seen. 'I'd like to help. Are you busy for lunch? Perhaps we could have lunch together to give you a chance to talk?'

I opened my eyes wide. Was he asking me for a date, NOW? My husband had only just left the marital bed! Then when I saw his eyes, dark and sincere, it was obvious that he really did want to help me. I looked more closely at this slim figure, his curly hair surrounding his kind, gentle face.

As if reading my mind, he suddenly said, 'My wife understands. I'm always having lunch with my clients.'

I raised an eyebrow. 'Clients Mr—?' For a moment I couldn't remember his surname.

'No, sorry, I didn't mean you were the client, I mean, I'm sure I can be more helpful than that committee was this morning – about helping you and John, that is. That was an awful meeting and you must be feeling dreadful. I'm sure I can help you honestly, please?' He paused, waiting for my response.

My eyes started to water. The morning had been a shock and his sympathy at this time was starting to affect me; perhaps he could ease some of the pain. Afraid to speak in case my voice croaked, I nodded quickly, blinking hard to try and hide my tears.

'Meet you in the car park at the pub, all right?' he asked. 'And, by the way …'

'Yes?' I managed to say with a squeak.

'For God's sake call me Ed will you?'

'Sure, Ed. Thank you,' I croaked, turning away from him swiftly.

I rushed out of the room, down the corridor and outside, keeping my back to him so that he wouldn't see the tears. I drove out of the car park as quickly as I could, narrowly missing a Mercedes that swept past the junction.

When I arrived at the pub, I sat in the car for a moment. The more I thought about the meeting the more angry I became. How dare that stuffed-up woman stop me from speaking! How dare she cut me out of a meeting that was supposed to be about John and me? What for? For nothing! None of them, except Ed, were even interested in John or me. I had to arrange cover for this? I fumed. I could sense someone walking towards my car. Ed's cheery face appeared.

We walked into the pub and sat next to the leaded window, the ivy throwing shadows onto our dark oak table.

I hissed softly enough so that the people around would not hear. 'So what was that all about? Talk about a rigged meeting! Why weren't we given a chance to speak?'

Ed grinned back at me, 'Don't be put off by it. It's all sham.'

'Too right it's a sham!' I snapped, my jaw rigid with anger. 'How do you know?'

'Experience – you've just got to beat them at their own game if you can.'

'Oh yeah?' I glanced around. 'And how on earth is one supposed to do that?'

'Well, it's pretty difficult, and we don't always win, but it's worth a try. After all, we can't let the likes of Tamara Dighton get away with it all the time. We've got to fight for the patients because they're in no condition to fight for themselves.' Ed paused, looked at me and took in the emotions that were raging inside me. His voice was quieter. 'If only—'

'If only?'

'Yes, if only we had real proof that what's happening isn't what the government's dictated at all, that someone or some people like Tamara are actually taking advantage of the situation for themselves. Then we could really do something about it.'

'Yes?'

'Yes, but no, we have nothing, no proof. The more I try to search the files, the more I'm hindered. However, for now ...' he smiled weakly. 'For now, what you can do is ignore what they say at meetings like this, although sometimes it's very difficult. You have to do something. When I need to take action, when I need to make decisions, I    consciously decide what is right for the patient, no matter what has been said or decided at meetings, and then I tell the committee in writing. They don't know what to do about that, for they know it could be used to prove that they are in the wrong, so they have to take some notice and let me do what needs to be done. They know I have a close friend in the press. They don't want any serious wrongdoings made public.'

'Mm, interesting. But I can't ignore them, John's in their hands. They'll be making decisions about him and I must have a say on his behalf.'

'Look, don't worry. I've been in the Mental Health Department for years. You can tell by my crazy personality right?'

I grinned.

Ed fingered the menu. 'I guess we should order. What would you like?'

Meals ordered and paid for, we continued our conversation over our drinks.

'Now about John.'

'Yes?'

'He really didn't want to be sectioned, you know.'

'I didn't think he would.' I suddenly saw his rigid expression, belligerently refusing to come with me to see the psychologist.

'But you do realise that he's quite dangerous.'

'I suppose so,' I looked down at the table.

'You know he suddenly wanted to break out of the ward and come home. It usually takes two of us, but it took six of us to hold him down to stop him escaping.'

I cringed. The vision of my John spreadeagled on the carpet, a pile of bodies on top of him holding his wriggling body firm petrified me.

Ed put a hand on mine. 'Don't worry. He's settled now although you might find him a bit drowsy when you see him next. We had to sedate him rather heavily.'

'That's what the doctor wouldn't do when I needed him to. It might've been all right if he'd helped us then – before John had to be forcibly taken in.'

'GPs can't give patients sedatives unless the patient agrees. I guess John was never willing to be given an injection or even tablets that might've calmed him down – right?'

'Right.'

He took his hand away and leaned back. 'You know, while I'm at Gravesall, I'll see that he's all right.'

'What do you mean, while you're at Gravesall? Are you thinking of leaving?'

'No, but I'm likely to get the chop any time soon.' This was the first time I'd seen the corners of his mouth turn down.

'Really? Why? I thought they were just closing wards?'

'No, jobs are going too. It's the times, but until it's official, I'm going to look after my patients including John, no matter what nonsense I'm fed from above.'

'Oh?'

'I've known Tamara Dighton for years,' Ed said between gritted teeth, his disrespect for her deeply entrenched in his tone. 'She and her darling husband live near me in Ely.'

'They do?' I sat back. 'I live close to Ely too! And I work at the private school there.' I paused and said quietly. 'I thought she looked familiar.'

'You've probably seen her around. What's to bet she's a governor of your school? She and her husband are on almost every other committee in town.'

'Ah, that's where I've seen her! Now I think of it, she's often been at the school asking to see the headmaster about something or other.'

'It's a small world eh?' Ed said, 'although maybe too small with the Dightons nearby.' He lowered his eyes and fixated on the small ball of froth that circled his half-empty glass. 'They've ruled the mental health service here ever since she arrived. She's taken over the committee and no one dares to question her, so much so that she brings her husband in even though he has no official role. It has nothing to do with her husband, yet there he is, sticking his finger in the works every day.' He looked up. 'I'm surprised he wasn't at the meeting.'

'Anyway, why did Tamara Dighton behave the way she did at the meeting? Why wouldn't she let me speak? Or you, for that matter?'

'Fear, that's all it is.' He tipped up his glass savouring the last few drops. 'The more she huffs and puffs, the more afraid she is. She's afraid of the likes of you and me questioning what she's doing, for she knows she's in the wrong. and the worse she gets the more certain I am something is seriously wrong.'

'Oh? But didn't she say her decisions are based on what she's been told to do?'

'That's what she says, but we've no guarantee that what she does is exactly what she's been told to do.'

'What'll happen to John if they close his ward?' I could feel the fear rising within me again. John shut out of the place that had become his new home, left to his own devices. I shook my head. No, it isn't possible. Fifty or a hundred miles would be easy for him to walk. He could arrive home, his smiley but confused and dangerous self. I couldn't cope! What would I do? I'd already rung the police in the past and they said they couldn't do anything until something happened and if something happened they could then arrest him. Great, I'd thought, they couldn't do anything until John had physically attacked someone – most likely me. My heart thumped noisily as I forced myself to look into Ed's concerned face.

He stretched his hand forward, his fingers just touching mine. 'Don't worry. It won't happen overnight. Our Tamara Dighton is right about one thing. They wouldn't dare close the emergency ward where John is now.'

'Thank goodness for that!' I took my hand away, sat back and tried to appear relaxed.

Ed leaned over, the furrows on his brow still showing concern. 'It's when they move him you might have some trouble.'

'Move him?'

'Oh yes, he'll only be in his current ward until he's been fully assessed.'

'But how long will the assessment take?'

'It should take about three weeks.'

'Three weeks! But that's nothing! and then?'

Ed shifted in his seat, and tapped his fingers on the table. 'Then they move him to another ward.'

'But if they're closing the wards?' I could feel the panic rising within me again.

Ed nodded. 'Exactly. There should be at least some wards still open for him, but it'll be no easy ride from now on.'

Elbows on the table, I stuck my head in my hands and closed my eyes for a moment, trying to blot out the darkness that was crowding my thoughts. We sat in silence, the contented noise of the pub in the background, a surreal backdrop to my visions of the impending doom.

I felt Ed touch my hands again. 'It's all right,' he said, his voice steady and assured.

'How can you say it's all right? What are we going to do?' I could feel my eyes watering with the frustration.

'Look,' he said, forcing me to lift my eyes and meet his. 'The problem is not yours. He's been sectioned into their care so they are responsible.'

I blinked profusely. 'But if there's no ward for him to go to?'

'Look,' he countered again. 'I'll be here to help you. Maybe I'll be able to get enough evidence to put a stop to it in time. In the meantime, will you let me give you a word of advice?'

I nodded.

'Just follow your instinct. Stand up to the likes of Tamara.'

'That's easy for you to say!' I snapped.

Ed dropped his eyes for a moment. 'I know. It's not going to be easy, but stand up to her and her minions. Put everything in writing and then, I promise you, if nothing else you'll have some evidence of what's been happening.' By now, his dark eyes were looking directly into mine. He meant what he said and for the moment I let myself believe him.

'I have one more question for you,' I ventured.

'Yes?' Ed's kind eyes maintained their steady look.

'Say if John had threatened harm to someone in a letter, would that mean that he would actually do it?'

'Is this about your headmaster's death, Mark King?'

'Why—yes how—?' I was a little shocked at Ed's ability to guess what was in my mind.

'Well it's like this.' He settled back in his seat. 'He may well write all sorts of things in a letter but a few minutes later, he would have forgotten about it. The only way John might harm anyone would be at the time he had those thoughts, if those thoughts were strong enough. Even then, it would be quick, certainly not the result of some grudge he may appear to bear. He would just do it and then a few minutes later wonder what had happened.' He paused and looked steadily at me. 'Why, do you think John's done something?'

'No, no, not really.' I took a deep breath. 'No, I think you're right, John certainly couldn't have planned anything.' But inside, I wasn't sure. His shadow hovered in the background of my uneasy thoughts, where John was concerned, nothing was certain. I looked at my watch, and scrambled to my feet. I didn't want to think about this anymore. As if understanding my reluctance to talk further, Ed stood when I muttered that I had to go quickly to get back to school in time. He gave me his card and made me promise to call if I needed to.

Chapter 10

The week went by without mishap. Henry and I had met intermittently over coffee at morning break times, I had remembered to thank him for the dinner and finally, on Saturday he reminded me of the picnic.

'I'll pick you up at twelve o'clock, all right?'

I nodded. 'That'd be great.'

'We'll use my car because we can't trust yours, can we?' and his eyes sparkled. .

I grinned. Like John, he had a comforting way of teasing.

He returned the grin, making a dramatic gesture with his hand over his forehead, 'At last, a smile from the ice maiden!'

'Not so much of that if you don't mind,' I replied.

True to his word, at twelve o'clock on the dot, Henry drove up in his Volvo, stepped out of the car briskly and was soon knocking on my door. I had spent ages deciding what to wear. We're only friends, so, I kept asking myself, why the fuss? I had settled on my best blouse and jeans. I felt relaxed and that was all that mattered.

'Houghton Mill, I think.' Henry drove off fast and after a few moments of panic as I adjusted to being a passenger again, I gradually relaxed as we sped past flat floodplains, through quaint Dutch-like villages and round numerous roundabouts until we reached the mill at Houghton. There's always something rustic, and comforting about a mill, even when it isn't working. Like a testament to an age-long past, it stands resolute, secure as if assuring us that our civilisation can always be trusted to survive no matter what changes take place.

'This way,' he said, having grabbed a picnic hamper from his boot. We were soon sitting on his waterproof picnic blanket looking at the cool river flowing slowly below the bank.

Henry lifted out a bottle encased in a cooling jacket and took out two glasses. 'Champagne, my dear,' he said in an exaggerated voice.

I grinned. 'Don't mind if I do,' and I took the glass crooking my little finger as I held it up to him.

He raised his glass to mine. 'It's all right—I'm only having the one. You'll have to finish the bottle, OK?'

'N-not OK,' I stammered. 'I mean I'm relieved you are only having the one since you are driving, but I'm not sure I should finish the bottle myself.'

He balanced his glass on the turf, opened the hamper and took out two brightly coloured plates, decorated with sweeping lines.

I accepted one and put it in front of me. 'This is a lovely design. Did you make it yourself?'

'With my very own hands. That's the advantage of teaching art. You have to show the darlings what to do and in the meantime you can get quite a few of your own things done. You like it then?'

'It's lovely.'

'I'll make you some if you like.'

'No, no. Don't worry. Our cupboards are full of stuff we got when we first married.'

He handed me some sandwiches which I put on my plate. 'You could always declutter.'

'No, a lot of the things are of sentimental value still. Especially the wooden platters my parents' friends sent over from Tasmania.'

'Yes, I'd heard Tasmania was THE place for good quality wood. Now, where did I hear that?' Henry put his head on his side, thinking for a moment. His eyes suddenly lit up as he remembered. 'Oh yes, that's right. It was your husband when he came on that memorable Open Day a couple of years ago. Do you remember it?'

'How could I forget it! It was the last time I brought John with me to any of the school functions. Did he annoy you, too? I hadn't realized.'

'Oh yes. He came into the art room and gave me long lectures on how to paint, how to sculpture and on how I should get my wood supplies from the home country of his good wife – myrtle, sassafras, black wood, Huon pine – he knew them all. In spite of his problems, your husband was certainly very well informed.'

'Yes, he was.' I looked down at the food now on my plate, no longer feeling hungry. I still cringed inside when I remembered how John had behaved on that momentous day and how powerless I had been to prevent him from being such a pain. As I relived that dreadful time, the guilt began to niggle at my conscience. All the people who met John must have noticed there was something seriously wrong with the man, but no one said anything – well, not to me. In my blind ignorance, or was it simply denial? I carried on ignoring the signs, hoping it was all a temporary aberration, but I knew it wasn't.

Henry patted my hand. 'There, there, my girl. Let's not dwell on the past. No one else's likely to call the fire brigade at another Open Day are they? Besides, you must admit, it was funny. The look on the headmaster's face!'

I nodded, remembering Mark King, imposing headmaster of our unsurpassable school, flustered for the first time in his life. The corners of my mouth twitched as I recalled the school entrance crowded with bright yellow firemen hats, the huge crush of children and parents trying to push past, splashing in the water, tripping over a large dripping hose, the headmaster's puce face, his sputtered speech as he vainly tried to calm the horrified crowd.

We laughed as the memories came back.

Henry pointed his finger at me. 'There, I knew you could do it!' he said, his eyes still smiling. We sat in silence for a moment, the air calm and cool by the river.

'So,' I asked dreamily, looking at the dark water flowing gently beside us, 'what do you think about the headmaster, his dying like that, I mean? It was a bit sudden. Surely it would have been natural causes in spite of all the speculation and gossip about it being murder? Even if they did find toxin in his system – couldn't it have come from some weird insect that didn't actually kill him, just shocked him?'

Henry finished chewing the sandwich he had just bitten. 'I'm not sure. He certainly did have a heart attack, there was no doubt about that and I vaguely remember him muttering about doctors not knowing what they were doing, suggesting he had some heart problem.'

'Mm, a heart attack sounds the most likely cause.' I nibbled at the cheese sandwich, I preferred Cheddar to the Stilton ones Henry had prepared, but I didn't dare comment.

'Although,' he waved a sandwich in the air, 'I heard Teresa reminding someone the other day that the autopsy showed that there was something else – that they'd found a small hole in the back of his hand – like a needle or the bite of an insect or spider so they're not calling it natural causes just yet.'

'They're not sure? A needle, insect or spider?' I thought of John and his collections of insects and spiders. Surely not John!

'Yes, they want to be absolutely sure so the funeral has to be delayed even further, because the pathologist wasn't happy at all. Because of the mark, he sent off blood samples to check for toxins. It came back positive for some kind of neurotoxin. They think he was injected with it, but how on earth could someone get near enough to Mark to do this – and why in the back of the hand, why not in the arm or leg?'

I remembered again John's 'gifts' that he kept giving people. Then there was the pile of wood in the shed that included the large piece of Huon pine. The holes in it could easily have harboured a small spider – maybe a redback. I shook my head. No it couldn't have been possible, it was such an incredible coincidence, wasn't it?

Henry peered straight up into my eyes. 'Hallo, hallo. Do I detect that you know something about this? Come on, tell me what you're thinking?'

Did I really want to say this? 'It's John.'

'You're not suggesting John followed Mark and injected him? I mean your husband had a fantastic memory, but as for giving injections I just can't see it somehow.'

'No, of course not, although—' I paused. Once again I had a gut-wrenching feeling that I was being disloyal to John.

'Look, I've told you before, ' Henry said, 'you can trust me, you know that don't you?'

'Oh, all right. If you must know, John kept giving people very strange gifts. You name it, beetles, spiders ... He could have left a dangerous spider for the headmaster to find.'

Henry laughed. 'Oh come on. In this country? There are no venomous spiders in this country so something more than that must have happened. Even then, if John had somehow got hold of a venomous spider – say from your country – a redback—' He paused, glancing at my pale face. 'No, even then, even if John had got hold of a venomous spider and handed it to Mark, Mark would've killed it straight away. And then, if it bit him, he would have gone straight to hospital. Even if he died from the bite, he would've died there or outside his home – not in the middle of the night outside the cathedral!'

I watched a lone ant crawl slowly across the grass. 'I suppose so. You know the police came to interview me.'

'As they have everyone.'

'I gave them the letter.'

'You mean the one John wrote to the headmaster? Why ever did you do that?' Then he saw the guilt in my eyes. 'No, I mean, good for you and, did they take it seriously?'

'They said it was important, although I think they were trying to scare me into telling them more than I intended.'

'Even so, it was probably little to do with Mark's death – a piece of paper and unkind words that ramble across the page can't kill anybody. Conscience clear now, OK?' Henry took in a deep breath. 'Anyway, more champagne?'

I shook my head.

He put the bottle back in the hamper. 'It's far more likely someone injected him. Messing around with insects is too risky.'

'Maybe, but why in the hand? Besides, there are antidotes to most poisons. Why didn't he call for help?'

'Perhaps he didn't have time. He did have that dicky heart, you know. Once he even told me not to tell anybody, but he had told other people and I guess it doesn't matter now. Anyway his doc would've certainly known about it.'

'Yeah. It doesn't answer how he got bitten or injected though, does it?'

'I guess not, but Mark had a lot of secrets, and who knows – it could've been self-inflicted, although I suspect we'd have heard about that. I never saw him trying to inject himself and if he'd been harbouring venomous spiders—' He shook his head, 'No, if it was a spider, it's more likely to have come from Vicky.'

'Oh yes. Vicky keeps a variety of them in her lab, doesn't she? But she'd never be allowed to keep lethal ones there, surely?'

'I guess you're right but she may have had access to one with all the contacts she knows – after all she and Mark did have—'

'Yes?'

'Well, I suppose, now the poor fellow has passed on, there's no need to keep his secrets. Of course, there's also no need to spread this information round. We do have Anthea to think about.'

'Come on, out with it!'

'All right, all right. You remember that dreadful moment when you caught Rita and I having a cuddle in the resources room?'

'Yes, I remember it very well,' I said firmly.

'There was nothing in it, really.'

I smirked. 'Oh yes? I find that very hard to believe. You weren't exactly shaking hands—'

His pale blue eyes met mine. 'Really, you've got to believe me.'

'Why?'

'The reason I was giving Rita a comforting cuddle was because she'd just been dumped by her lover.'

'I didn't know she had a lover as well as her husband.' I scanned the faces of the staff in my memory but gave up. I had no idea who it could've been. 'Who was it?'

Henry looked steadily at me.

A duck quacked loudly on the river.

I sat up. 'No?'

Henry's stare did not budge.

I shuddered. 'Not Mark?'

Henry nodded.

I sat back and whistled. 'Well, fancy that. Mark King, perfection itself, a stickler for everything to be just right, was a philanderer! Who'd have thought it! Wait a minute, did Anthea know?'

'No, well, I don't think so. We took no end of trouble to avoid her finding out.'

'We? What do you mean "*we*"?'

Henry's cheeks glowed. 'Yes, "*we*". You know all those meetings I had with Mark – the meetings that everyone thought were about me misbehaving?'

'Yes. We thought you'd been up to mischief. I think we decided you were having affairs yourself.'

'Not true! Let's not go into that, but what I did have to do, was pick up the pieces after Mark. He had a penchant for the young trainees but his interest was very short-lived. Once he'd bedded them, he didn't want to have any more to do with them. I guess he just enjoyed the challenge.'

I stared open-mouthed. 'And you supported him in this?'

'Well no, not exactly, but I did feel really sorry for the girls. What else was I to do?'

'So how many?'

Henry paused. 'I'd rather not say, but there were more than Rita and Vicky.'

'Penny,' I said abstractedly. I bit into a new sandwich, my mind racing. So that's what Henry was up to? I was now determined more than ever not to fall into Henry's arms. Attractive as he was, any relationship I had with him would be doomed. I looked into his disarmingly handsome face. I shook my head and forced myself to concentrate on the conversation. 'Why are you telling me all of this now?'

'Because I wanted you to know that my relationship with Rita was nothing serious. I want us to be friends. You're having a very difficult time at the moment and as you know,' he smiled, 'I'm a great healer – it's been part of my job description. So, finish your sandwich and we'll go for a walk, or we could drive on into the village for a proper cup of tea.'

We packed up the picnic, put the hamper into the boot of the car and went for a stroll by the river. The water was still and dark. The ducks were swimming slowly near the edge as Henry and I walked under a large branch that hung over the path. As we both lowered our heads, Henry took hold of my hand. I let him. It was only holding hands, after all, what harm could that do? I breathed in the cool air tinged with a mixed aroma of river and leaves. The sky was a beautiful dark blue. A few fluffy clouds moved slowly across it casting a shadow on the river for a moment. Neither of us spoke as we walked on, hand in hand. I decided I would cherish this moment – one of those special times that I would be able to recall when things got difficult with John.

Chapter 11

The sun was setting when I finally set off to see my husband. I felt warm and cosseted after my time with Henry. He was very kind and only pecked me on the cheek when I said goodbye outside my house. Thank goodness Bumble started without any problems this time.

I pulled into the car park at Gravesall and a large figure was just getting out of her Saab. It took me a few moments to work out who the woman was, but as I watched her waddling closer, I knew exactly who it was. Tamara Dighton, the chair of the disastrous meeting on that ghastly Friday.

I acknowledged her and started going towards John's building but she was obviously ready for a conversation. She wobbled her cumbersome body rapidly towards me, crossed the car park in no time and was soon within a few inches of me. There was no escape.

She smiled. 'Well hello.' Her make-up and scent were even stronger than I remembered. 'It's Sally isn't it? Have you come to see your husband?' Her voice was cold and condescending.

I could feel the fear inside me growing stronger by the second. I wanted to say, 'What do you think?' but fortunately, I had enough presence of mind to stop myself. Instead, I simply said, 'I try to make it most Sundays. I'm at work for the rest of the week.'

'It must be very hard for you,' Tamara's eyes were dull with insincerity. 'I've come to catch up on my office work you know. We are so busy. I'm having to come in when I should be at home keeping company with my lovely hubby.'

I stared at her, my car keys still in my hand. 'Oh.'

'Yes,' Tamara continued, 'there's no peace for the wicked. We've got to get on with closing these wards. It's a very difficult time for us but nothing we can't handle. Then at home, there's been all that trouble about Mr King. We'll miss him SO much. It was my husband who found him, you know.'

'Really?' I was having difficulty in remembering what Tamara's husband was like – picturing him finding Mr King's dead body was beyond my capability.

'Yes, he was so shocked I had to take time off work to look after him. He was only walking the dog. Our dog, Dusty, a beautiful collie – so intelligent. Dusty found Mr King. He kept barking and barking until Dennis went over to see what the matter was.'

'Oh.' I rattled my keys and stepped forward in an effort to remind Tamara Dighton that I had come to see my husband, not her.

Undeterred, she stepped forward to keep up with me and persisted. 'Yes, it was Dusty's last walk for the evening. It was very late. Dennis likes staying out late several times a week. He says it keeps him and the dog exercised,' she laughed falsely.

'Does he?' I could easily understand why Dennis needed to stay out late. I was surprised he didn't stay out every night of the week, he would certainly need some kind of break from this insufferable woman, but I decided against commenting further.

Tamara clutched my arm. 'And do you know what? When Dennis saw the police afterwards, they found something in Mr King's pocket. Do you know what it was?'

'No,' I carefully moved her hand from my arm. 'What was it?'

'Why, a letter to him from your husband!' she smiled smugly.

Not another one! Surely the one I had rescued from the box of confiscated items from the headmaster's office was enough. What could the letter have said? My stomach churned. Knowing John, it could have said anything. He could have written something even worse that brought on the heart attack that finally killed Mark. Maybe Mark could have survived the insect bite, if that's what it was. John could really have been the cause of his death! My knees weakened. I shook my head and squared my shoulders.

'Thank you for the information,' I said with forced calm. 'I hope you manage to get all your administration work done.' I turned and walked unsteadily along the narrow path towards the entrance to John's ward.

When I got home after seeing John at Gravesall, I made myself a pot of tea and sat in front of the television trying to relax. I ignored the slopped liquid in my saucer and let the cup drip on my blouse as I took a large slurp. It had been a tortuous visit. John kept asking to come home, but then started talking about the Prime Minister visiting him and finally I had a tussle with one of the other patients who decided they wanted my handbag.

The visit to Wendy's was much more fruitful. Although I was later than expected, I still drew Bumble up outside her home. I could see lights on in her sitting room shining briefly onto the edge of the rambling rose on the wall, giving the flowers eerie shadows. Fortunately the path was well lit by the street lamp and I made myself walk straight up to the door and knock before I thought any more about it, or gave myself time to get cold feet, change my mind and go home. An outside light suddenly lit me up reminding me of the powerful police lamps they use to reveal crime scenes and accidents. When I looked at the lamp, it was only an ordinary outside light. I was imagining things again.

A voice from inside called out, 'Who is it?'

'Sally Wilks. You remember I said I'd call?'

I could hear several locks being pushed back before the door swung open. Wendy looked much prettier than she had when she was in uniform.

'Glad you've come,' she said waving me towards her sitting room. 'I need a break. I'll put the kettle on.'

I sat down on her comfy sofa, the armchair opposite awash with papers.

As she put the tray of mugs on her table she said, 'We aren't supposed to fraternise with suspects, but I don't know how else we're to progress.'

'Your partner was a little difficult,' I ventured.

'Well, let's say, I think we'll find out more if we put on a friendly face, besides, I'm hoping you can help with some of the problems your locals and the locals here keep bringing to me.'

'Oh?'

'While I have no evidence, I can't do anything. I need someone who is on the inside, as it were, to help.'

'Yes?'

'Well, for starters, my niece goes to your school and her parents are on the governing committee. They have been saying that a lot of activities have been unexpectedly cancelled because of lack of funds. They suspect some of the school's funds have been appropriated, but they have no proof.'

I thought of the accounts book I had spotted in the headmaster's office, but she was right, this was not real evidence.

'I suppose I could try. What can I do?'

'Just keep your ears and eyes open and if you see anything out of the ordinary, let me know. My boss is very sympathetic to my situation and he will act on anything I can find out.'

'And the locals here? How could I help them?'

'They say that things are not right at Gravesall. Some wards are fine, but others—the people who bring their complaints want to be anonymous; they don't want to jeopardise their relative's care. Would you see what you can find out?'

'I'll see what I can do.'

'There's no need to bring anything to the police station – you too can remain anonymous if that's what you'd like. You could leave any incriminating evidence in my letter box. I suspect you like a bit of cloak and dagger stuff. Am I right?'

'Yes, I guess you are.'

Her coffee was the best coffee I had tasted. At last there was a glimmer of excitement and glamour on the horizon.

Now, in my sitting room, bringing myself down to earth, I was glad I'd done all my preparation for tomorrow already. I glanced at the sideboard. There was a pile of mail I had left there unopened. I picked up the handful of letters, sat down and began to open them,

There was one from Tamara inviting me to the next meeting about John, a card from Anthea thanking me (and everyone else) for their concern telling us that the funeral had to be delayed because of inconclusive autopsies but that she wanted everything to continue as much as possible so she would be holding a cream tea at her home the following Sunday evening. I sighed, putting the card aside. It was one that I would have to answer and I made a mental note to write the acceptance before I went to bed that night. I hated these so-called friendly staff get-togethers, and now a tense atmosphere had invaded the school while no one knew exactly how Mark had been killed and who, if anybody was responsible. We were all under suspicion. I guessed I would have to show willing and turn up. Besides, I might be able to find out something concrete for Wendy and I might discover more about what was in John's letter. I tried to reassure myself that, as Henry had said, Mark had coped with a lot of excitement including having affairs with the young teachers without having any ill effect on his heart. However, I couldn't shake away the tiny shadow of doubt that lingered in the back of my mind.

On Tuesday morning, I had a free period before coffee break and decided to relax in the staffroom for a while. When I opened the door, the room appeared to be empty at first, but in the far corner there were two people huddled together in deep conversation, their heads nearly touching, Vicky's dark head of hair contrasting with Henry's fair strands.

Still holding the door handle, I paused, 'Sorry. I hope you don't mind my coming in early.'

Henry turned to me quickly. 'No, no, we were just talking about things. Do come and join us.'

He pulled some newspapers off the seat on the other side of him and I sat down.

'We were just talking about—you don't mind Vicky do you?'

'Well,' Vicky's eyes were glistening. 'I suppose not.'

Henry smiled at her, 'Come on, three heads are better than two. She's going to find out eventually and Sally's a good friend, isn't that right Sally?'

I nodded enthusiastically. 'Of course I am. Can I help?'

'Well—' Vicky straightened her skirt, 'you know I had been finding teaching very difficult. The children were all over the place. I didn't know what to do, so when Mark – er the headmaster – asked me how I was getting on, I told him.'

I raised my eyebrows. 'You did? First rule of survival, never admit defeat, not to the boss, anyway.'

Vicky looked at me. 'I know that now. Just after I'd told him I realized the risk I'd taken. I thought I'd be sent home as a failure but Mark surprised me. He was so kind.'

I forced myself not to look cynical. 'Was he?'

Vicky stared hard at me for a moment, weighing up what she was going to say next, then said, 'Yes. He came round to my place quite often to give me advice and help me with my lesson plans.' A single tear fell down her cheek. She sniffed. 'I'll really miss him.'

Henry put a reassuring hand on her knee. I stared at his hand. He ignored me and gave Vicky's knee a gentle pat. 'There, there, Vicky. It's a shock to all of us and we will all miss him.'

She pulled a crumpled tissue from her pocket and wiped her nose. A torn envelope dropped to the floor. She picked it up hastily. 'The thing is, that's not all.'

I looked at the envelope. 'No?' It was a different handwriting to John's.

'No, well, you see, you know I live in Church Lane.'

'Yes, what's that got to do with anything?'

'Well, so do a number of other people, including staff members and children from school.'

'So?'

'Well, someone keeps leaving me horrible notes.'

'Really? What do they say?'

'Just awful threatening things like "I know what you are doing and you'd better stop it now or something will happen" – they're really upsetting.'

'Is there any reason why someone should threaten you?'

'No, not really.' She looked down. The three of us sat in an awkward silence.

I cleared my throat, 'Who do you think is doing it?'

'I've no idea. The notes are written in a funny kind of handwriting. They could have been written by anyone. I wish I hadn't opened them.'

'Well, as long as you haven't been up to anything bd, why worry?' I immediately wished I hadn't said that.

Henry broke the embarrassed silence. 'I'm sorry Vicky, but Sally already knows about Mark's affair with you—well, she had a very good guess.'

Vicky stared in horror at him. 'You promised!'

'I know, I know, but Sally caught me giving Rita a reassuring hug and I had to explain about Mark's wandering ways.' Henry observed Vicky for a moment then took in a quick breath. 'You did know Mark had other affairs, didn't you?'

Vicky covered her face with both hands. 'I may have,' she whimpered, 'but I didn't want to think about them. He said I was his only one and I let myself believe him. I had a feeling there could be others, but I didn't want to face up to it.' She lifted a tear-stained face. 'I was his only one when we were together.'

The tension in the air was palpable. She looked at each of us in turn. 'What?' she asked, pulling out another tissue and wiping her face quickly. 'You don't think I did anything do you?'

We looked at her steadily. Neither of us replied.

I eventually said softly, 'You'd better tell the police about the letter at least. I know someone in the police who could help.'

Vicky's hands shook. 'No! Why? I didn't have anything to do with Mark's death. I don't want our names dragged through the mud. I don't want to tell them,' her voice getting louder and more agitated with each word.

Henry patted her knee again. 'There, there. It would be better if you told them yourself than they found out later. We know you couldn't have had anything to do with Mark's death. We can vouch for you.'

I raised an eyebrow to Henry who ignored me.

Vicky grimaced. 'I've burnt the notes.'

'But you've still got the envelope,' I said pointedly.

'It's no proof of the threatening letters, though,' Vicky replied.

'Yes. Well, don't destroy the envelope. Keep it somewhere safe,' I said, wondering if Vicky really was this naive or was it for show?

Henry sat back, his hands on his lap, 'Not to worry. Keep the envelope and any more—'

'More? You don't think I'll get more do you?' Vicky said, her eyes wide with fear.

'Well, why not? Unless they had something to do with Mark's death, then the writer might like to lie low. Whatever, why not hand in the envelope and tell the police about them?' Henry's tone was firm.

Vicky looked down at her lap, the black writing on the envelope just visible beneath her trembling fingers. I opened my mouth to speak but stopped as the break-time bell resounded round the room, the door swung open and a crowd of chatting staff burst in.

The week was moving on and I would have another meeting to attend next week, I would have to prepare for my absence and set class work again. Meanwhile a visit to John at Gravesall followed by Anthea's cream tea on Sunday loomed ahead. I was beginning to dislike the weekends.

Chapter 12

Sunday finally came. Saturday afternoon had passed without mishap. My car had run smoothly and the lawnmower gave no trouble. I no longer felt guilty about leaving the shed door ajar. Things were going well, although the visit did not go as smoothly as I'd hoped. John, was high and off beam, not as bad as he could be I suppose, but I longed for the cheerful fun-loving man I once knew. At first he had looked at me, his eyes puzzled and unsure but gradually they lit up. He had recognized me. He asked if I had any stamps. I didn't answer. I couldn't see the point of trying to explain to him, again and again, that he hadn't been able to write any letters, so what was the point of a stamp? I sat next to him, letting him speak the crazy wandering thoughts that filled his mind. I avoided answering any questions, simply changing the subject, avoiding his gaze, looking round me, as I did so. The walls were a bland faded yellow, the windows high, only allowing a thin part of the blue sky to reach the troubled eyes of those of us ensconced in this depressing place. Oh how I wished I could have my John back again. I nodded benignly as he told me again that royalty had visited and that he had his collection of gifts the angels had brought him. Occasionally I would try to bring him back to reality.

'I think it must have been someone else very important who visited you, John. It wouldn't have been royalty.'

'The Duke of Edinburgh—' he continued, as though my words were only vaguely related comments that offered another tiny thread for him to follow. He now lived in another world, his own world that was the only one he could cope with now. He clutched my hand, holding on for dear life, as if this was the only contact he knew that might lead to the sanity he once had.

My heart hardened. Why should I have to put up with this? This was supposed to be my husband who supported me throughout our lives – but my coldness was only fleeting. For better or for worse, we had promised and what if it was me in his place? I shuddered. I suspected I would have been even more violent than the troubled man next to me.

Suddenly one of the patients screamed. She was tugging hard at a chair that another person was sitting in. The man in the chair was obviously a visitor and his eyes were round with fear as he felt his chair being jolted by a strange determined woman.

'Now Doris,' a cheerful carer rushed to her side. 'Someone else is in the chair, so you must leave them alone.'

Doris, her long grey hair waving with the effort, pulled again at the back of the chair. The carer put his hand on hers and then grasped both hands quickly. 'I've got a nice cup of tea for you, but you'll have to come with me to get it.' Doris hesitated, finally relented and went with the carer. The visitor heaved a sigh of relief and turned again to his wife at his side. She was picking at her jumper, hardly aware that he was there.

'Women wear wigs,' John told me matter-of-factly. This was one strand I could follow – Doris's grey hair had given him the link. 'It was black, no wig – thin tentacles.' He had lost me. As I left John, Doris, now subdued, curled herself up in one of the armchairs. No doubt things would flare up again after I had gone.

My visit finally over, I climbed into my car and headed towards Ely so that I would be in time for Anthea's cream tea.

There was only one parking space left along The Gallery. No doubt everyone had come, all showing willing and wanting to help Anthea in her difficult time. That was not all, we needed each other. It was as if we had unconsciously kept ourselves in a self-supporting huddle, shielding each other from the tension and doubt that would never dissipate until the true events surrounding Mark's death were revealed, if at all.

I glanced at the sky. The air was still overhung as I rang the doorbell. I heard its shrill trill inside. It was some time before Anthea opened it, her eyes dull, and her face pale. We walked in silence towards the babble of voices in the sitting room.

'And what's more—' Dorothy Hall was pointing her finger at the rotund chest of Bill Greenland who was eyeing a large scone smothered in cream on his plate. Just as he was about to have a mouthful of the scrumptious morsel, Dorothy's arm shot forward again and he had to put the scone down.

'What's more,' Dorothy repeated, 'you and I know that Mark was not perfect but he ran a very happy school. Everyone knew exactly where they were and what was expected of them, just as they do with Leonard.'

'Oh I don't know.' Bill stepped back a little. He fingered the scone.

'I beg your pardon!' Dorothy gasped.

'No, no, I didn't mean to slight Leonard. What I mean to say is that in every school there are people who are dissatisfied, no matter how happy the place seems to be.' He snatched a large mouthful of the scone and licked the cream that had spilled onto his chin.

'What do you mean? Are you talking about yourself? Was there something you were not happy about? If so, I can tell Leonard and he—'

Bill swallowed hard and looked at her. 'Now, now Dorothy, you know that Leonard doesn't like you interfering. It's not really your business. If there was anything I wasn't happy about, I would be talking to your husband and your husband alone. Now—' He turned towards the dining room table laden with food. 'Those buns look delicious.' He walked towards them, leaving Dorothy open-mouthed, her beady eyes watching his waddling torso.

'Is something the matter?' Even though I had overheard this conversation, I was obliged to say something, anything to blot out the recurring image of Dorothy as an open-mouthed, head-swivelling clown.

Dorothy closed her mouth briefly before opening it again to snatch a breath. 'It was just something Bill said. I always thought he was a very polite, quiet head of history, but he just snapped at me. I think he's been unhappy about something.'

I looked at her. 'That's strange. He's always seemed very contented.'

'Yes, I know but the death of the headmaster has upset everyone I think. It must've affected Bill, too.'

'Have you found out anymore about it?'

Dorothy glanced around the room. 'Do you think we really should be talking about it, while we are in his house? Anthea might hear.'

I could tell by the look in her eye, that Dorothy knew something and was dying to tell someone. I moved closer and spoke softly. 'She's in the kitchen. It's all right and we can easily change the topic if we see her come near.'

'Well, you know me. I don't like to stick my nose into other people's business, but,' she lowered her voice. 'I've been talking to Mr Dighton, you know he's a school governor, and he says that the death was suspicious, and that there was a strange letter in Mark's pocket that could've been a contributing factor. Did you know about it?'

'I'd heard something,' I said.

'Well, it was from your husband wasn't it?' She paused, waiting for her words to take effect.

I stood my ground.

Dorothy lifted her head slightly, her heavy mascara even more noticeable than ever. 'He was a difficult man, your husband, wasn't he?'

I didn't reply. Was? Did he only exist in the past tense now?

Dorothy continued. 'He wrote a lot of letters. This one was very strange. He threatened to do something to Mark. I think the police are  investigating your husband as a suspect but, now that he is declared insane, they won't be able to do anything about it, will they?'

I could feel the heat in my cheeks. 'My husband, a suspect? No, it's not possible.' But we both knew it was quite possible. My hands shook, rattling my cup of tea.

It'd been a phone call from Gale that had been the first sign that John could indeed be a serious threat. It must have been about three weeks before John went away. Gale had sounded more serious than I'd ever known her to be.

'I don't want to alarm you, Sally, but you ought to know.'

'Know what?'

'It's about John.' I had felt Gale carefully managing the conversation, giving the information bit by bit so that the shock was not too great.

My heart had leapt. 'He's all right, isn't he?'

'Oh yes he's fine, well he's fine physically, but there is something else.'

'What?' I'd felt the blood pulsating loudly. 'For goodness sake, tell me!'

'Well, he said he was going to stop you using the car.'

'Oh, you must be joking, why on earth would he do that?'

'Well,' Gale paused. 'You know how he is.' Then her voice had softened, much of the anxiety that had tinged her first words had now dissipated. 'I'm sure it's just some nonsense that's wandering in his thoughts. He's very unlikely actually to do anything about it, but best to be on the safe side, eh? Promise you'll check your car every morning?'

'But what for? What could he do?'

'Just check, OK. I'm sure it'll be all right.'

Chilled and pale, I had opened the front door, only to find John walking jauntily towards me. I had gone to lift the bonnet of the car but his wide-eyed stare had given me second thoughts. I had resolved to check the car when he wasn't looking. I had never found anything and I continued to drive the car safely.

Now faced with the idea that John had actually done something to someone else, an ice-cold chill crept down my spine. How could I live with myself if they found out that John, my husband, was a murderer? Besides, if the police were really suspicious, they would surely have questioned me at the station by now. Wendy seemed certain enough that I had nothing to do with it at least, and even if she suspected John, she hadn't said anything. After all, why ask me to find out more? She certainly wouldn't have asked if she believed John was the culprit.

Dorothy's voice brought me back to reality, 'You look so shocked dear. Was it something I said?'

I stared at her incredulously.

She patted my arm. 'There, there. It's nothing to worry about. I'm sure it's all a mistake. Now, I really must have a word with Leonard.' She turned and made a beeline for her husband.

I gazed after her and watched her put her hand on her husband's arm. Leonard glanced at me. I had the distinct impression that this was not the first time he had looked in my direction. Dorothy pawed his arm but he turned away from her and continued talking to Chris Masters, head of maths, genius at timetabling and arranging cover.

It would do no good worrying about John being a suspect now. I forced myself to stop thinking about the bombshell that had just landed and instead focused on the scene in front of me. I looked at the two men talking, Leonard and Chris—so similar yet so different. They both had razor-sharp minds, they both were hard-working and ambitious but they had one vital and conspicuous difference. Leonard Hall stood rigidly, his bodyline taut like an athlete, ready to spring into action. His eyes were restless, often sweeping briefly in my direction. Chris, on the other hand, stood straight, well balanced and was as tranquil as a sunbathing seal. His eyes remained steady, looking directly at Leonard's agitated face. I smiled. Leonard was obviously making new demands of Chris but Chris was not responding. I wondered if Leonard had something in mind for me too, the way he kept looking in my direction. Leonard's thin pale cheeks tightened. Chris's hands lay resolutely relaxed at his side. How did he do it? Remain so calm when so many demands were made as a matter of course in any school, let alone a school with a possible murderer loose.

'Well hello.'

I turned to see Henry grinning at me, Vicky close by his side.

'Hi,' I said. 'Is Carol here?' Why did I have to bring the wife into the conversation so quickly?

Henry shook his head. 'No, you know how my wife finds it very difficult to come to these cream teas when she's always behind on her getting her dressmaking contracts finished on time.' He nudged Vicky. 'Besides, I have Vicky for company, don't I?'

Vicky looked down. He stood between us. 'Shall I get each of you a sample of Anthea's lovely food?'

Without waiting for a reply he walked swiftly to the table, dodging neatly between the clusters of people.

I looked at Vicky. 'Are you having trouble with Henry?'

Vicky slowly looked at me. 'No, not really.'

'I remember you warning me about him some time ago. Is there something I should know?'

'No,' Vicky said. 'No,' she repeated.

I took a deep breath.

'Well,' she finally continued, 'if you must know, I've had a bit of a crush on him.'

'Oh?'

'I'd been having a very difficult time of it.' Her tone deepened. 'Mark—' she glanced in Anthea's direction. 'It's been awful. Henry is a really good friend – just a good friend,' she turned away and, under her breath said, 'more's the pity.'

I stared at her. So Henry wasn't lying. He and Vicky weren't lovers. But there was still a lot of emotion in her voice when she talked about Mark.

'Well, here you are, you two beauties.' Henry handed us each a plate full of food. 'And I'll have no complaints.'

'Thanks,' I said absentmindedly.

Henry smiled at Vicky. 'Now, come on, Vicky. Follow me. It's time you rescued Chris from the dreaded deputy head. Chris, the most eligible bachelor of the school, would much rather talk to you wouldn't he?'

The two of them left me with my thoughts and my large plate of food. As I lifted a scone to my mouth, I saw Anthea making her way unsteadily towards me.

'I'm sorry I was a bit preoccupied when you first came. There was a bit of trouble in the kitchen but it's all sorted now. I'm so glad you could come. It must be very difficult for you.' She came closer and lowered her voice. 'Now that you and I are virtually husbandless perhaps we should get together sometime?'

I had a mouth full of food so could say nothing.

'If you're not doing anything tomorrow night, could you come round for a glass of wine?'

I nearly choked on my scone. When I had finished coughing, I gasped and said, 'I am so sorry. Of course, I would love to come round tomorrow night. What time?' I hurriedly pushed away thoughts of books to mark, lessons to plan.

'At about eight o'clock. All right?'

'Sounds good.'

She grinned. 'That's settled then. I feel so much better now that I won't have to spend the evening alone.' She drifted away towards the centre of the crowd. I watched her graceful figure mingle with the murmuring people. I couldn't help wondering why Anthea suddenly wanted to see me alone. It wasn't as if we had ever been friends. I felt sure there was much more to it than Anthea merely wanting company. Perhaps she was trying to avoid drinking alone. As I looked at her I could feel a pair of dark eyes from the bay window at the side of the room looking directly at me. I turned towards the culprit. Leonard turned his head away quickly and said something earnestly to the person next to him.

'Well.' I turned to the cheery voice behind me. Henry grinned at me again. 'I've left the forlorn Vicky with Chris. They'd make a lovely couple don't you think?'

'Why, Henry, if I didn't know you better I'd think you were a matchmaker.'

'No harm in trying eh? Why not give Cupid's little arrow a nudge?' He stood next to me. I could feel the tension between us heighten, not a nervous worrying tension, but one I had experienced with John when we had first met. I moved back a little. He stepped closer. 'Have you been to see your hubby yet?'

'Yes.' I prepared to tell him all about John but Henry didn't ask the expected question.

Instead, he said, 'Come around to ours for a decent drink after this if you like. Carol won't mind. She'll be busy with her dressmaking. She's still got five costumes to get done before the show.'

I should have said no but found myself agreeing, a little too eagerly.

'Oh yes, please, that would be lovely.'

'You're on – eight o'clock – don't be late.' He winked and moved away to mingle with the crowd.

At precisely eight o'clock I knocked on the Matthews' door. Henry opened it immediately and gave me a quick hug.

Carol called from the distance. 'Come in, Sally, I hope you don't mind my leaving you but I need to go out to measure a couple of people so that I can get these costumes finished.'

Henry beckoned me into the sitting room, sat me down and handed me a glass of red wine.

'I'm driving,' I said.

'Oh one won't hurt.' Henry raised his glass to mine. 'You can have as much orange juice after this as you like.'

I relaxed back into the comfortable sofa, raised my glass to his and sipped. I could feel the tension of the day dissolve. If only I could relax like this at home. The door clicked shut as Carol left. We looked at each other.

Henry sat down opposite me. I drank my wine again. He put his glass down on the table in front of him, sat back and surveyed me. I trembled. The anticipation was overwhelming. I should get up, leave, go home and prevent anything from happening but I didn't.

'You think I'm going to make a pass, don't you?' Then he smirked. It was so annoying the way he knew what I was thinking.

'But you can rest easy. I am tempted, mind, but I never take advantage of a woman in distress. You must know that.'

I wished for a moment that it wasn't true. I jutted my chin forward. 'You're a bit full of yourself aren't you? For all you know, I might not find you attractive at all.'

We smiled at each other. We both knew that wasn't true.

'Now tell me all,' he said, picking up his glass again, and resting it on the side of the sofa.

I spilled out the whole story about how unhappy I was about John, Tamara and Anthea. I even mentioned Vicky. Henry fidgeted when I mentioned her. As we were talking about Anthea's cream tea, Henry sat very still for a moment.

'Talking about the cream tea, what do you think is up with Leonard?'

I was curious. Had he noticed how Leonard had kept looking at me? 'What do you mean?'

'Do you think he has a soft spot for you?'

'I think he may be having second thoughts about being soft with me.'

'Why would you say that?'

'Perhaps there was a lot more to the entries in the accounts book I saw. Maybe he is still worried I might have sussed what was going on and spilled the beans.'

'He certainly has been soft with you. Why else would he give in so easily when you asked for time off?'

'I don't know.'

'After all, he's given poor Bill such a hard time. Bill's had several interviews with him and with the headmaster, too, and by the look of Bill's face when he passed the art room each time, he was livid.'

'But Bill wasn't asking for time off, was he and he probably hadn't seen anything, had he?'

'Well, he said he'd asked for a lighter timetable because of ill health but Leonard and the headmaster wouldn't even consider it, so it's very suspicious the way Leonard has suddenly been so considerate to you.'

'I agree, although it could be because Leonard's more contented now that he's got the headmaster's job at last.' I paused. 'You don't think—'

'No I don't think Leonard did the boss in so he could have his job. Can you imagine that?'

I frowned trying to imagine Leonard planning to murder the headmaster but I couldn't. Leonard with his determination to do everything the right way, even if it defied common sense, would hardly extend to killing someone. 'Although he has always been very ambitious,' I said.

'Yes he has, but so has Chris and I can't see either of them doing anything so drastic as murder to get what they wanted. Can you?'

'But, remember, when I went for my interview to tell him about John, he was behaving furtively, wasn't he?'

'Just seeing a few names in an account book can't have been that serious, or could it? What could he've been hiding?'

'It was Mark who had the affairs with the girls. What happened to the other girls? What was Penny like?' I asked.

He looked puzzled.

I continued, 'I mean, the Penny that was on the staff before I came. Did she have anything to do with Mark too?'

'You mean an affair?'

'Mm.'

Henry looked around. 'Well, there could have been something for she left rather quickly. Mark told us it was a family matter but there was no telling.

She could've easily been one of his conquests as well I suppose.'

'Why would Leonard be so worried about it? Did he know about the affairs too?'

'I don't think so. Mark'd asked me to make sure Leonard didn't know. He'd sensed Leonard's ambition to take his place, so he didn't want to give him any rope to hang him with. It makes sense, doesn't it?'

'Yes, I suppose it does and I guess you, like the rest of us, didn't really want the Mean Machine taking charge, Mark was much more reasonable.'

'Too right.' Henry mimicked the Australian accent I'd had when I first arrived at the school. 'And you say that Leonard has been keeping his beady eyes on you a lot more?'

'It's just a feeling I get but yes, I believe so.'

'I think I'm going to have to keep a careful eye on you too my friend.'

'Now come off it!' I pulled a face. 'You don't really think I'm in danger do you?'

'No, no, of course not. After all, whoever killed Mark, even if it was Leonard, they didn't do anything like bludgeoning him to death. It was more like a woman's crime – sneaky, maybe even poison.' Henry's eyes sparkled. 'Come to think of it—'

'Now you're going to suggest I did it!' I grabbed my glass from the table, spilling some of the red wine on the spotless surface. 'Anyway, there's nothing to suggest he didn't die naturally. Maybe some weird spider escaped from some exotic fruit they bought so that he died naturally, or maybe something tipped the balance and his heart finally gave up.' I tried to put out of my mind the suspicions about John.

'On the contrary. Although he apparently died of a heart attack, there was definitely something suspicious about the bite and his blood results as we discussed before. Murder is definitely on the agenda.'

'How can you be so certain? After all, you didn't do the autopsy did you?' I only just managed to keep my voice level. 'And now you're trying to suggest that I did it? For goodness sake, Henry!'

The door opened. 'What's Henry done to annoy you, Sally?' Carol stepped into the room.

'Oh nothing,' I tried to remove the splash of wine on the table with my fingers. 'He's just making fun of me, suggesting I'd killed the headmaster.'

'He does have a strange sense of humour sometimes, don't you darling?' Carol put her arm around her husband. 'Any wine left for me?' Carol sat down on a chair close to Henry's, took hold of the full glass he gave her and told us about the trials and tribulations of measuring people who were the prima donnas of the local amateur dramatic society. I had never laughed so much in a long time.

Chapter 13

The next evening, I knocked on Anthea's door at eight o'clock. The street was almost empty. A solitary car drove slowly past and turned right at the roundabout in Barton Square. It looked familiar but before I could remember where I'd seen it before, the door swung open.

Anthea smiled broadly and gave me a peck on the cheek.

'I'm so glad you came,' she said. 'Do come in.' She stepped unsteadily back into the dark interior.

I went inside and followed her into the immaculate sitting room. I noticed the flagstones at the entrance had been freshly polished, the antique furniture glistened in the pale light and the large sofa had new cushions. Anthea had had the place spruced up. I wondered how I would react if my husband died. I knew that spring cleaning was the last thing that would be on my mind, but her circumstances were different, and, after all, she was a very different person.

'You're amazing, Anthea,' I said, sitting down on the sofa and crossing my legs, my wedding ring shining as I rested my hands on my knee.

She smiled, accepting the compliment as though she was quite used to receiving it.

I continued, 'You seem to be coping so well. I wish I had your stamina.'

Anthea sat opposite, clasping her hands tightly. 'I'm a bag of nerves, actually.' She moved her fingers restlessly as if to prove her point. Then she forced herself to still them, and spoke softly, 'I'm a good actress, aren't I?' She smiled briefly.

The clock ticked in the silence between us. She slowly eased herself out of her chair, straightened her dress and glanced at her model figure in the mirror behind the drinks cabinet. Pausing to pat the back of her hair, she walked smartly to the sideboard, her heels clicking unevenly. A bottle of red wine was already open and half empty and two crystal glasses waited beside it. She poured a generous glass of wine and held it firmly with both her hands as she offered it to me.

I looked at the glass gleaming in the muted lights of the sitting room and cleared my throat. 'I hope you don't mind, but have you any soft drinks? I'm driving.'

Anthea looked surprised for a moment but quickly composed herself and put the glass down beside her own chair, 'Of course, how silly of me. Tonic do?'

She opened the drinks cabinet door, slowly took out a crystal tumbler, dropped two pieces of ice and a slice of lemon into the bottom of the glass, and poured a full glass of tonic. I accepted the drink and Anthea slipped into her chair again.

'Cheers,' I said, taking a large gulp of tonic, the clink of the ice almost deafening in the awkward silence.

We sat still for a moment, each of us with our own thoughts.

Finally, Anthea shifted in her chair and said, 'I suppose you're wondering why I asked you here on your own?'

'It did cross my mind.'

'You know,' Anthea held her glass in front of her, inspected the colour in the light, and turned to look directly at me, 'I've been watching you.'

'Oh?' My mind raced with images of what she might have seen.

Anthea put her glass down. 'You seem to get on with all the staff very well. Everyone says how trustworthy you are. You,' she said, pointing a finger in my direction, 'you are the only person I can safely talk to.'

I wondered how many drinks Anthea had already had. I raised my hand slightly. 'I'm sure that's not true.'

'Well,' she said, taking a large drink of her wine, swallowing and breathing in deeply. 'It was always difficult with Mark, you know.'

I froze. Oh God, not a wifely confession. Please God she's not going into detail about her sexual exploits, or lack of them in the bedroom. She really must be drunk. Mark had been my headmaster, so I should never be party to such goings-on and more to the point, the poor man was dead and I especially didn't want to know about them either.

Anthea wriggled about as if she was unable to sit comfortably, 'I mean, it was so difficult for you with your husband being the way he was and yet you stood by him all the time.'

'What do you mean?'

'Well you must've known that he kept coming round here.'

'He did? No!' My stomach was gripped with a sudden rush of fear. What on earth had John said or done to them? I didn't want to think about it, but looking at the serious face before me, there was no option. I sat very still, holding my breath. Anthea looked as if she was waiting for me to comment.

I had to say something. 'I hope he didn't do or say anything too dreadful.' I smiled weakly, my insides churning, praying that she wasn't going to list a whole lot of belligerent comments that John had no doubt shared with them, or, perhaps it was worse?

'Well, he used to call in the afternoons when Mark was at school. He said some very unpleasant things, so I knew something was wrong. I didn't really think he would do anything. Sometimes he would park his bike by the fence and bring a box to the door and when I answered it, he would insist I admire rubbish he'd collected off the road. It was very embarrassing, but as he hadn't done any harm, I didn't want to embarrass you at school, by telling Mark. You both had enough to cope with in your different spheres.' She paused as if weighing up whether she should tell me what she was thinking or not. 'You know,' she looked more serious, 'he also used to post weird letters through the door.'

'Yes?'

'Your husband wasn't a well man, was he?'

'No.'

'And he'd been ill for quite a long time, hadn't he?'

'I suppose.' I put my glass down and crossed my arms.

Anthea drained her wine. The clock ticked loudly as she stood up and went to the sideboard. 'I've been thinking,' she said, as she filled her glass again.

'Yes?'

'Well, you know how they believe Mark may have been killed intentionally.'

I took in a deep breath. 'Murdered, you mean?'

'Well, I was just wondering, could your husband have done something that killed Mark by accident?'

I pushed myself up on my arms hastily, knocking my glass on the floor. I stood up quickly to retrieve it. Thank goodness it wasn't broken.

'Oh don't worry about that. It was empty anyway,' Anthea said hastily. Then her voice hardened, 'Sit down!' she commanded.

I fell back into my seat.

'Now listen,' she said, her voice still edged with a menace that I had never heard before. 'I mean, John wouldn't have known what he was doing and now he's in the mental hospital, everyone would understand.' Her voice softened. 'He wouldn't get into trouble. It would be so much easier if I knew what had really happened if you'd only just tell me.' She pouted her lip like a pleading schoolgirl, but I knew in my heart of hearts, in spite of her alcohol consumption, this was no innocent schoolchild sitting before me.

I could feel the indignation rising into my throat. How dare she! Was she calling my husband a murderer? I glared at her, but she did not flinch. Her dark eyes were glued to mine. Suddenly I looked away and stared at the floor. The strong lines in the wood stood after years of polish. The trouble was, I was uncertain. John in his right mind would never have done any of the weird and wonderful things he did after he became ill. Anything was possible, although – I rubbed my forehead with my hand. No, I was sure. Even at the end, there was always one tiny bit of John left, the one that stopped him from ever harming anyone, but when he was at his worst?

'I'm not sure,' I finally said, my eyes still fixed on the floor.

'I don't mean to upset you or anything,' Anthea put a conciliatory hand towards me, 'but it would really put my mind at rest.' She was using her pleading voice again. I almost wished she was back to the menacing tones I had heard earlier – at least she was more honest then. 'It's been tormenting me since the day Mark died,' she continued. 'If I only knew the truth.' Her voice softened, 'You know Sally, we don't have to say anything to anyone. It could be our secret. Did John ever say anything to you about Mark?'

'Well, he used to say all sorts of things, but it was all talk,' I said. 'I'm sure it was all talk,' I repeated, as if to reassure myself. Flashes of that walk along The Gallery one fine evening, John shouting loudly about what he was going to do to the headmaster kept reoccurring in my frantic thoughts. 'I'm going in there to get him. It's got to stop,' he'd shouted. 'They're in their castle, lording it over all. They need bringing down a peg or two, along with that pile of stones.' He'd waved a hand towards the cathedral. 'All that money should go to the poor.' He'd put his hand on the gate. It took all my strength and determination to lead him away from there and back to the car. I cringed at the memory.

'And?' Anthea's dark eyes met mine.

I looked straight at Anthea. 'Look Anthea, I have no idea if John did anything to cause Mark's death, but I'm sure in his sane mind, he would've been horrified if he had.'

Anthea persisted. 'Yes, I know. I agree, but John used to make all sorts of threats and it wasn't only us he brought his rubbish to, he kept going to the school, too. He was very persistent you know.'

I hung my head. 'Yes, I know,' I said softly.

'Did you know what he used to bring here?'

'No.'

'Didn't Mark ever tell you that John left us an axe one day? He said he'd been given it. Eventually we had to get our cleaning lady to answer the door when he came. Plants, insects, old pieces of wood, rubber gloves, empty cigarette packets or the odd carrot or piece of sugar beet used to be the kind of things he'd bring, saying that they had been left on the side of the road especially for him to bring to us.'

I shook my head unable to speak.

Anthea stared at her reflection in the glass. 'One of the last things I remember him leaving us was a matchbox with some berries.'

'So?'

She turned her head sharply towards me. 'They were deadly nightshade. They're lethal, you know.'

'Yes, but Mark didn't die from eating something did he?'

'Well no, but how do you know John didn't leave a lethal spider for him? I wasn't the one that answered the door every time.'

'But there's no proof of this. Anyway, he didn't die here, did he?' My words sprung out of my mouth before I could stop them.

Anthea blinked, unmoved. Her voice dropped to a whisper, 'Yes, but how do you know where it happened? Where he was found was only a short distance from here.' She mouthed the word 'here' as if in a melodramatic drama, leaned back and waited for the effect to take root.

I cleared my throat and suddenly had a thought.

'If it was here, you'd have known about it.'

She laughed. 'You must've known I was in the cathedral, not here. Mark was coming to meet me at the interval.'

'Oh.'

The atmosphere in the room chilled. I took a deep breath. 'Well,' I said, avoiding Anthea's eye. 'If you both knew my husband was unwell, you should have understood that whatever he said was nonsense.'

'It wasn't always nonsense, though, was it?'

'What do you mean?'

'On a very windy day there was a lot of rubbish on the road and he said he was going to get rid of it and he did – not by picking it up himself but by making pedestrians, strangers to him, pick it all up. He does have a very forceful personality, doesn't he?'

I sat up stiffly. 'You know Anthea, I'm terribly sorry, but I find all of this a bit difficult. If John did something I'm sure we'll find out in time. I don't know anything about any circumstances leading up to Mark's death, so can we talk about something else?'

'Of course, of course.' Anthea took another large swig of wine. 'I'm sorry. It's just that it's so troublesome being on my own and not having a true friend among all the staff.'

'I'm sure that's not true,' I lied.

'It is! Being the headmaster's wife is very difficult. You have to be perfect all the time and be nice to people you don't even like.'

I fiddled with my empty glass on the table.

Anthea watched me. 'Have another one. Help yourself. Some more glasses and more drinks are over there.'

I was tempted to leave but realized that in spite of the uncomfortable air that had crept into the room, here was a woman who had just lost her husband in a sudden death. She was probably too drunk to mean what she said. She obviously needed company and maybe I should stay a little longer. It wouldn't hurt me.

Suddenly, the phone rang. Anthea started. She stood up and walked unsteadily to answer it.

'Hello.'

I strained to listen, but couldn't hear what the other caller was saying.

'Why that would be lovely!' Anthea smiled. 'In a few minutes. I'll be ready.'

Anthea turned to me. 'The Friends of the School thought I might like to join them tonight after all. I'd said it was too soon after Mark's death, but they are celebrating Betty's birthday at the end of the evening and want me to go round for the cutting of the cake.'

She walked straight to the entrance to the hallway. 'Someone is coming to call for me in a few minutes and we'll walk over there together. You don't mind do you?'

'N-no,' I stammered, as I hurriedly scrambled to my feet and followed Anthea to the front door.

She held out my coat for me. 'You could come too, if you liked. I'm sure they wouldn't mind.'

'No, it's all right. I have so much to do tonight.' I slipped my arms into the coat. 'Thank you very much for the drink,' I said breathlessly.

'If you're sure then.' Anthea smiled broadly, pulled open the heavy door and held her face closer to be kissed. I duly pecked her on the cheek and hastily stepped outside. I stared at the closed door behind me. What was Anthea really up to? It wasn't simple reassurance, or just company that she wanted. As I walked along The Gallery to my car I saw a dark figure walking briskly towards me. A large collie dog trotted beside him. I raised my eyebrows. Tamara, that power-controlling chatterbox of a chairwoman had said something about her husband walking their collie dog at night. So, was Mr Dighton a member of the Friends of the School? About to collect Anthea? There was no reason why he shouldn't be. I glanced back at him as I unlocked my car and climbed in.

The drive home was uneventful, then, as I pulled into my drive I saw a large silver car turn the corner.

It looked familiar. Something about the shape of the boot reminded me of – yes, of course, Leonard was supposed to drive by my house to keep an eye on me. I was not sure I really wanted Leonard poking his nose into my business, but once his overbearing wife got an idea, there was no stopping her. As long as he was only just keeping watch and his constant surveillance had no other sinister motives. A flash of Leonard's discomfort when I had spied him in his office that time ran a chill down my spine. Now I was getting paranoid. It had to stop. I shrugged, opened the front door and went inside.

Chapter 14

The day of another meeting about John arrived. It was cloudy and cool as I approached Bumble. A heavy weight lay at the base of my stomach. Instinct told me this experience was not going to be pleasant. I drove slowly out of my drive.

There was one space left between a large blue Mercedes and a Range Rover when I arrived at the car park. I wondered which members of the administration team owned these cars. Salaries were obviously worth something and it looked as though they had some kind of life outside work. My heart sank as I thought about my own future. Nothing but bleak images of John's mental torment and days of sheer loneliness filled my mind.

The pine trees seemed darker this visit, the path more downtrodden. The flat-roofed box that was the administrative building looked more and more like the Nissen huts I once taught in. Stale atmosphere, steamed windows and an unstable, creaky floor had made my days with C4 even more unbearable.

Perhaps this visit I would finally know more about John's condition and get some kind of reassurance that he would be well looked after. As I entered the meeting room, all the members of the team were in place; Tamara's large frame dominated from the end of the table. Next to her, an empty chair waited for me, then her sidekick Mrs Payne, who straightened her back and pulled her skirt over her skinny legs ready for action. Mr Barker, the man in charge of the finances, tapped his clipboard impatiently, while Ed stared at Mr Barker's pen with a mischievous look in his large brown eyes. Dr Edwards sat stiffly, pulling his white coat around him as if seeking his own kind of protection, while Heather, the young newbie, sat awkwardly next to him, her eyes fixed to the table.

I slunk into the chair next to Tamara and glanced around the group of serious faces. Would I get a chance to say something this time? None of them were looking at me, they were all focused on the chairwoman. I glanced over to look at the papers the newbie was clutching. I saw the heading 'Agenda'. As I moved forward a little more, the newbie glared at me, shuffling the papers so that I couldn't see them. I frowned and sat back in my chair.

Tamara, her blousy pompous tones filling the room, opened the meeting. Without looking in my direction once, she checked that there were no alterations needed to the agenda and turned to finances.

'Mr Barker,' she said, 'your report on the progress of the changes please.'

I willed her to notice me but her tight lips and blank expression made no change. Mr Barker was wearing the same grey suit as last time and the clipboard and fountain pen were in position. He glanced around the room before he began, taking in a deep breath to puff up his already self-important chest.

'As you know,' his tone was emotionless, like delivering the results of a very boring budget, 'we're having to make huge cuts in our spending. We really can't afford to continue the way things are and as Mrs Dighton warned us last time, wards will need to be closed. I can now reaffirm that the Trust Board,' he suddenly looked down, avoiding the chairwoman's eyes, 'the Trust Board are closing down all the hospital wards, save one—the acute ward.'

I sat bolt upright. 'All?!' I asked involuntarily, feeling my head spin at those words. Tamara Dighton looked at me, pityingly.

Mr Barker ignored me. 'The board says that if we can do this before the next budget, we will meet our targets. That means we will have to act quickly. If we start on Monday, everything will slot into place perfectly.'

'But what about—?'

Tamara Dighton's hand was raised in front of me. I was to be silent. I looked at Ed, my eyebrows raised. Ed shrugged his shoulders and held out his hands, palms up. He had no control over these events.

'Has anyone any concerns?' Dighton shuffled her papers as she spoke, her eyes fixed downwards, daring anyone to speak.

Dr Edwards, his immaculate features altered by a small wrinkle on his forehead, cleared his throat. 'Some of the patients will suffer when we move them. They need to feel secure and stay in the same environment as much as possible.'

'Really?' Tamara Dighton's lips curled.

Dr Edwards persisted, a slight glow now on his pale cheeks. 'They rely on routine, that's what holds a lot of them together. Changing their daily activities and moving them into different surroundings with different people looking after them will be really troublesome for them and for the staff. You mustn't do this.'

'Oh?' Tamara Dighton looked at the doctor sharply. 'And who are you to say what we do and we don't do? Your business is to see that the patients manage the change well. If you aren't capable of seeing to this, perhaps we should appoint another doctor to this committee.'

No one moved. The tension in the room mounted. Finally Ed shifted in his chair, 'It's been a very difficult decision.'

Tamara looked at him suspiciously.

Ed focused on the wall behind her, carefully avoiding eye contact and continued. 'I know we're trying to work in the patients' best interests. The wards have become tired and grubby and there is very low morale in the staff, but perhaps we ought to consider lightening their load by making fewer changes and by improving the conditions in some of the more recently established places?'

'Rubbish! It's too late, you know it's too late,' Tamara snapped. 'The decisions have already been made and it has been decided, the wards start closing on Monday.' Her heavy breathing and wafts of her sickening perfume filled the room.

'But what about John?' I said.

'John?' She looked at me, puzzled, 'Oh, John, your husband. Well what about him?'

'Is he going to have to be moved?'

'Of course. What else did you expect?' Tamara eyes glared. 'He's in the acute ward at the moment, so he's all right, although he'll have to be moved anyway. After then—well—' she shrugged her shoulders and then turned to the next item on the agenda which was not so contentious and was nothing to do with John.

Ed's and my eyes met. He shrugged as if to say this was just what we expected. Then he mouthed 'lunch' to me. I would find out more over lunch with him. At least there was one person on my side. We both leaned back in our chairs, eyes down and let the meeting take its drastic course.

As the group headed for their cars, I noticed Tamara climb into the passenger seat of hers and lean over to say something to the driver and both of them laughed. So, her lovely hubby was here at the hospital again and they were obviously up to something, or, was this my paranoia again?

The pub was busier than last time. Ed and I eventually found a seat together right at the back. Then, after a few minutes of tedious waiting and shuffling at the bar, he ordered our lunches and, clutching our drinks, precariously weaved his way through the crowd back to me and finally wriggled his way into our hard-won seats that I had hung on to. We both took a drink and looked at each other.

The only change I could see in Ed was an almost imperceptible increase in the depth of his natural frown. 'You've been having a tough time of it too?' I asked.

He rolled his eyes.

'Do you want to tell me about it?' I prayed that he didn't, I was too impatient, I wanted to know about my husband. 'Can you tell me what's going to happen to John?' I said before he could respond.

His dull eyes told me all I needed to know before the words fell out. 'They really are closing the wards down,' he said angrily. 'Far more than they said they would. It's money, that's what's driving them. They want all the patients shunted out into the community or in homes as soon as possible. We've been fighting them at every turn but obviously we've failed.'

'Surely there's something we can do? What about the patients?'

Before he could answer, the waitress arrived with two ploughman's.

'Yes, what about them!' he picked up the conversation after the interruption. 'It'll be almost impossible to find other places for them and even if we can find somewhere, there'll be real trouble settling them in.' Ed stabbed a piece of cheese on his plate.

'And John?'

'He's too volatile to go into a home yet, they'll have to keep him in the hospital.'

'Thank goodness for that.'

Ed frowned. 'But we both know that he can't stay there forever. They'll have to find somewhere for him.'

'Well,' I said slowly. 'I guess if it's only one change it'd be all right.'

Ed sneered. 'I wouldn't be too sure about that. It'll be ages before he's ready for a home, and while they're messing us all about, it's highly unlikely he'll be able to stay in the same ward all the time. Heave 'em out and close 'em down, that's the motto today.'

We both ate in silence, neither of us wanting to believe what we were thinking. No matter what, John was in for the long haul, full of upsetting changes, a mere pawn in the hands of the likes of Tamara.

'Tamara,' I mused, 'there was something odd about the way she handles the meetings. It was as though she has her own personal agenda. Is something else going on?'

Ed took a sip of his low alcohol beer. 'Yes. You're right.'

'How do you know?'

'Well,' he paused. 'I've suspected her for ages. The meetings seem to run so quickly, all in her favour. I think Mr Barker's uneasy about the way things are run, but he doesn't do anything – did you see him look so uncomfortable when he talked about the Trust Board?'

'Yes, he did, didn't he? What could that mean?' I took a drink of my coke, my eyes never leaving Ed's.

Ed returned my gaze. 'The trust board are supposed to keep the committee in check but they haven't done a thing. It's like she's got them all in her pocket or they're all too frightened to stand up to her. Did you know she's one of the trust board directors?'

'No. How do you know that? You're not on the board too, are you?'

'No, of course not, but it's no secret, she mentioned it in a meeting some time ago, boasting about how important she is and how the board couldn't manage without her, or her husband.'

'But surely that isn't allowed? What's his involvement then?'

Ed sighed. 'I suppose he's an interested observer at meetings and he has other board-level experience. Plus, he's a doctor. So, he can contribute from his professional position. It's not illegal, but it's not right, and they know it and we know it, but nothing ever happens to change things.' He stabbed another piece of cheese.

The noise in the pub increased as another party of people spilled into the room. I watched them crowd the bar.

When the flush in Ed's cheeks had eased, I asked, speaking slowly. 'What else's been happening?'

He looked around, and satisfied no one was listening, came closer. 'Well, for starters, every time

I've come up with ideas that'd help our patients more, even ideas that we could do quite easily without costing much at all, and that would be cheaper in the long run, she's always steered the meeting against them. I don't know why, maybe it's just to be spiteful, though I think it's much worse than that.'

'Why, what do you think's going on?'

'I've no idea, but something's not right.' He sighed, thrusting his knife at the side of his plate.

'Well she's a pretty formidable woman,' I offered. 'Even I could tell that when I first saw her.' I paused and then had a sudden thought. 'Do you know? I've just remembered. Someone else said she was one of the hospital trust board members – and I think Mark, our beloved headmaster, was a board member too.'

'Really? What gives you that idea?'

'It's Henry, you know, the art teacher at school.'

Ed looked at me blankly.

I shrugged, 'Well anyway, Henry's very nosey. There's not a thing he doesn't know about school politics. He told me some time ago – I'd forgotten until you just mentioned it.'

'That fits, it's probably what she meant when she went on about a death amongst the directors. Wasn't it your headmaster that died suddenly recently?'

I nodded. 'And now they're saying his death was suspicious.'

'Really?' Ed looked interested. 'Does Henry know what happened?'

I shrugged. 'Well, it's common knowledge that they think he was bitten by some kind of insect or injected with a toxin that brought on a heart attack.'

'Very interesting. Then it could've been natural causes, couldn't it?' he said, speaking slowly, thinking it over.

'Not after the toxin results. If it was an insect it was probably a spider not native to this country, so it's a suspicious death at the least.'

I finished swallowing a mouthful of tomato. We both looked at each other and suddenly spoke at the same time.

Ed spoke again, 'You first.'

'I had nothing to do with it, you must believe me.'

Ed grinned, patting my hand and smiling. 'I know. I believe you, of course you didn't.'

I fingered the base of my glass. The dark liquid shone in the muted light of the pub. I looked around. No one was listening. The other customers were all in close-knit huddles, only concentrating on their own stories. I spoke under the noise, 'I worry that John might've done something.'

Ed raised his eyebrows. 'Really? You think he had something to do with it?'

'Well, couldn't he?' I held my breath.

'You know, we've been over this ground before and you also know it's highly unlikely. I've only known John a short time, but I can tell he's quite disorientated. He might lash out at someone but a carefully planned murder? No – that's highly unlikely. He couldn't do it. He's too far gone.

Besides, he didn't have access to exotic spiders – did he?'

I shook my head but as I did so, images of the shed and the wood from Tasmania flashed into mind.

'Well that settles it,' Ed sighed. 'You can forget all about John. He couldn't have had anything to do with it.'

But we both knew his words were only placatory; a shadow of suspicion hung between us.

'Maybe, but—' I couldn't leave it alone. 'Are you sure, absolutely sure? I mean, what if Mark had been shocked just before the heart attack, maybe reading one of John's horrible letters?'

Ed shook his head.

'He was a headmaster, for goodness sake. Surely he was impervious to the threatening comments in any letters. After all, not every parent was happy about how the school was being run. Beside, John's letters were confused, right?'

'Yes, but John said some very nasty things.'

'Look Sally,' Ed tapped the table in front of me, 'John didn't cause Mark's death, I'm sure of it. John would've been incapable of keeping any secrets, that's the nature of his condition. You may have noticed, he's quite uninhibited?'

The edges of my mouth twitched as I remembered that grand moment when John, still in his pyjamas, insisted on going outside to knock on a local councillor's door early one Saturday morning.

'So, if he'd done anything, it would have been quite obvious or it would have come out in his ramblings, verbally or on paper so you can put these thoughts right out of your mind, OK?'

I nodded, my eyes shining.

Ed said firmly, 'Well, now that's cleared up, let's finish this lunch.'

I grinned and tucked into the remainder of my meal. Ed slowly lifted his glass to his lips, his eyes watching my every move. As we left the pub, Ed took me aside.

'You know, I think we could do something.'

'Yes?'

He glanced around to make sure no one was in earshot. 'Every time I've asked to see the files I've been supervised by Mrs Payne – you know, Tamara's lackey? She nearly had a fit when I asked to see the accounts after some relatives of one of the patients asked me about them. It really is very suspicious. If you—'

'Yes, if I what?'

He shook his head. 'No, no. It's too risky.'

I grabbed his arm. 'No, come on, I'd like to help.'

'While there's a murderer on the loose, we can't take the risk.' He turned to walk away.

'No, wait! There's still no guarantee there is a murderer – even then I'm unlikely to be a victim – what do I know? Come on, Ed, I can't stand the suspense. What can I do?'

'Well,' he looked around again and lowered his voice. 'When you next visit John's ward, if you asked to see John's files as a carer – asking to read them alone because it was such an emotional experience, we might be able to get some evidence.'

'Yes, yes – anything, I'll do it.'

Chapter 15

As I turned out of Gravesall car park, I glanced at my watch. It was two o'clock. Rats! I still had time to get back to school and teach the last lesson. The traffic was mild.

Would I get the opportunity to get at the files? If Ed wasn't allowed near, how would he get the evidence? I certainly wouldn't have a clue what to look for. As for John, things weren't going to be easy, Ed had left no doubt about that, even though he tried to make light of it. At least he was convinced that John had nothing to do with Mark's death, but was John really that safe?

It had been late one Friday night when I had smelled smoke. Months before that night, our smoke alarm had started pipping when it needed a new battery. I'd taken out the old one and promised myself that I would replace it soon, but, of course, in the usual scheme of things, I had never quite got around to it. Then, that Friday evening, as I opened the door to the hallway, I was greeted with a strong stench of smoke and a large black cloud billowing from kitchen. I dropped my books and ran in. John had been standing, staring at a pile of newspapers burning on the stove, the flames racing to the ceiling, the smoke filling the kitchen. He looked puzzled when I pushed him away, grabbed a towel, dampened it, and smothered the newspapers. There had been another billowing of thick smoke but no more flames. I'd put out the fire.

I'd spluttered, 'John! What on earth were you doing?'

He'd looked at me blankly.

A car horn brought me up short. I screeched my brakes to avoid an impatient bike rider. I must drive more carefully. John certainly wouldn't have understood what he had or hadn't done and although the action may have been deliberate, it could not have been carefully planned. John was no murderer.

St Audrey's School was strangely quiet. I rarely arrived when the entire population was ensconced in the rooms mid-lesson. The eerie atmosphere unnerved me as I walked up the path to the front door. Betty smiled as I passed reception.

'Mrs Wilks.' She called me to her desk.

'Sally,' I replied, still worrying about the conversation I'd had with Ed.

'You look worried,' she said. 'I'm so sorry to hear about your husband.' Her smile softened. 'You know, my uncle went through the same thing last year.' I stared at her blankly finding it hard that such a cheerful, bubbly person could have any dark clouds in her background.

Betty folded the letter she had been holding and put it inside one of the envelopes piled next to her. 'If you're not busy after school on Monday, come round for a bite of tea?' I hesitated.

She sealed the envelope and picked up another letter. 'You know I had a special birthday just recently. After freezing my cake, I still have loads of it left. I really need you to help me eat it. After all,' she laughed, 'I don't need to put even more weight on.'

There were so many things I had to do, but a cup of tea and a chat with someone who might know what I was going through wouldn't hurt.

'I'd love to,' and I smiled at her.

'You know where I live,' she said. 'In Silver Street. See you about six on Monday?'

I nodded. I jumped when the bell rang loudly and the corridors were suddenly filled with staff and children spilling out of their classrooms. My stomach tightened as I thought of the boisterous individuals I would be facing in a few moments.

'You're back!' Henry raised his voice above the bedlam. 'I covered your last lesson. They were their same delightful selves. Jackie is especially on form – so watch out!'

'Thanks,' I said.

'Oh,' Henry touched my arm. 'How did the meeting go?'

'It was horrible. The chairwoman, Tamara Dighton, rigged the meeting from the start again.'

'Move along there!' A loud commanding voice pierced the corridor from behind us. Leonard was in his element.

Henry began to move on. 'I'll ring you later OK?' he called over his shoulder.

'OK,' I yelled, my lips set as I pushed my way through the bustling bodies of schoolchildren.

Henry didn't phone until nine o'clock that evening.

'Sorry I didn't call earlier, we've had visitors.'

I didn't respond.

'Well,' he said, 'I'm dying to know more about your ghastly meeting and I have something to tell you. There've been some developments. I've got to see you.'

'Oh?' What could he want?

'It's no good speaking over the phone. Carol and I talked it over and we agree that you've got to know. Can I come over now?'

'Now? I suppose so.' I looked around the room. It'd only take a few minutes to tidy up.

'Right,' Henry said, 'I'll be there in a few minutes.'

Worried, I shuffled my papers together and dashed down to the sitting room to sort things out there. As I was plumping up the cushions, the doorbell rang. I ran my fingers hastily through my hair and opened the door. Henry's face was pale and grave.

'Come in,' I said hastily. 'Sit down. Can I get you something?'

'No, it's all right. Sorry to jump this on you, but we thought you should know.'

'What?'

Henry shifted in his chair, 'Well,' his eyes fixed on the carpet. I made a mental note to do the vacuuming as soon as I could. Henry's voice was soft and confidential. 'We were visited by Anthea the other night.'

'Oh?'

'Well,' he said again, searching for words, 'you know how difficult it is for her.'

He cleared his throat.

'Tell me!' I pleaded. 'It can't be all that bad, just spit it out will you?'

'All right,' Henry looked directly at me. 'Anthea's been saying that your husband killed Mark.'

The sitting room clock ticked ominously in the silence.

'Bu-but—' I paused. 'That can't be right. John had already been sectioned when Mark died. He couldn't have done it.' I bit my lip knowing this was not wholly true. John could still have been responsible, even though he may have been unaware of it at the time. I suddenly remembered the letter found in Mark's pocket. Maybe that was the tipping point after all and Anthea knew it.

'I know, I know. Anthea's obviously stressed, she's drinking too much these days, but she's still trying to pin the blame on someone – anyone. It's so difficult for her not knowing for sure how her husband died. It's difficult for us too, we're all on tenterhooks. Someone obviously had it in for him.'

We exchanged glances. 'I know, it's awful. All that I know is that I had nothing to do with it and I'm pretty sure John didn't either!'

'Of course you didn't and neither did I, OK?'

We exchanged glances again and smiled.

'But if I think about it – maybe, just maybe John—' I looked out of the window for a moment. 'No,' I shook my head, 'John couldn't have done anything. The mental health nurse says that John must be innocent because he's so uninhibited that he would've told everybody what he'd done. He just can't keep secrets.' I shook my head again. 'No, I won't believe John was responsible.'

'Even then,' Henry thought for a moment, 'now that he is sectioned, it wouldn't make much difference if he were responsible anyway.'

I leapt out of my chair, 'That's a terrible thing to say!'

'Oh sorry, Sally,' Henry stood up and moved closer to me. 'I didn't mean it like that. He's in a safe place now. It's all right.' He put his hand on my shoulder. I was tempted to put my hand on his, but I clenched my fist at my side instead. I sat down crossly and folded my arms. Henry resumed his place opposite me. His clear blue eyes looked directly at me, warm and sympathetic. I could feel the tears gathering in mine. A car revved its engine outside.

'There's something else you might like to know,' Henry said.

'Oh?' I held my lips close together, my eyes blinking hard. I was not going to get emotional, not now.

Henry pretended he didn't notice. 'That Tamara Dighton you mentioned.'

I unfolded my arms. 'Carol and I were talking and she said she had the ghastly woman land on our doorstep and demand she alter a suit for her. Carol tried to refuse at first, but when the woman went on and on about how important she was and how she knew the headmaster of the school and was on the school board she gave in. She thought it would get me into trouble if she didn't.'

I nodded. I could easily believe Tamara harassing Carol this way.

Henry adopted his conspiratorial voice, 'Well,' he paused for effect, 'well, during their conversation, when Tamara learned that Carol's father was a stockbroker, she boasted about how much money she and her husband had made on the stock market. She said how Mr Alders, their stockbroker, had made so much for them that they were thinking of buying some holiday villas in Europe and America.'

'Yes,' I sat back, 'that could be true.'

Henry said triumphantly, 'Ah, but Carol knew that Mr. Alders had been out of business for years.'

I looked at him quizzically, 'Oh! That's different. What do you think's going on then?'

'Carol says the suit Tamara brought must have cost a bomb. They obviously have pots of money. Carol got the impression Tamara just wanted to show off, she could've easily got the suit altered at the shop where she bought it. Also, she kept asking questions about John and you.'

'Really?'

'Fortunately, Carol didn't know a thing and told her so. The woman wasn't very pleased. She's not a woman to cross.'

'No, she's not,' I agreed thoughtfully.

A car pulled up outside. I glanced out of the window but I couldn't see anyone. The letterbox in the front door rattled. Someone had posted something. I glanced towards the door,

'I'll get it later – someone's obviously trying to sell me something.'

Henry stood up. 'It's getting late. I must go.' He gave me a quick peck on the cheek and moved smartly to the front door. I opened it and he was soon gone. I stood for a moment looking into the empty street. The lamp opposite was flickering. With a sigh, I closed the door and pulled out the paper that had been thrust into the letterbox. It wasn't a leaflet, it was an envelope addressed to me; the handwriting was vaguely familiar.

I had to get on and sort out my plans for tomorrow. I tore the letter open, letting the envelope fall to the floor. There was a single page of folded paper inside. It was from a cheap pad – the sort I used at school to keep rough notes of what I planned for my classes. As I stood in the hallway my heart turned to ice.

*You evil witch! mistress, wife of a murderer – Confess now or face the consequences!*

As my eyes widened at the cruel words scrawled across the page, I remembered. This writing had the same unnatural shape that some of the children used when they tried to disguise their writing. This was the writing I had seen on Vicky's envelope. I clenched my hand. I was not going to let it get to me. I was not going to burn this one, oh no, it was about time something was done about it. After all, I had nothing to hide. I had done nothing – well, not yet, I flinched when I remembered the picnic with Henry. I felt uneasy about the looks Leonard had been giving me. Who was this nasty person? Not Leonard, surely! No, I dismissed the thought immediately.

If he had anything against me, he would choose a moment carefully and spell it out. If Leonard wanted to harm me, he would do more than write nasty letters. I'd be up before the school board. No, this was not the work of Leonard, power-crazy though he was. Could it have been a child? No, this letter had been delivered by someone in a car – although there was nothing to stop a child asking their parent to drop a letter off at their teacher's house to explain why some homework was delayed.

I was very tempted to suddenly screw it up and throw it into the fire grate but no, I mustn't. I must keep it and give it to Wendy – although, the guilt I felt on behalf of John made me reluctant to do this. Perhaps if I found the culprit myself, after all, there was no certainty that the poison pen writer was the same as Mark's murderer. I decided not to do

anything about it just yet. I went to the office, found a file marked 'John' underneath my pile on the desk and slipped it inside. Whatever the case, it had to stop. John's words echoed in my head. Was this what he was talking about? Then, I remembered, I knew John's writing and this was categorically not his. I would have a look around at school. Maybe I could track down the poison pen writer myself – be it member of staff or child. That would put an end to it. I would show the envelope to Betty first. I could easily say it had been empty and Betty, who saw lots of letters from staff and pupils, might recognize it. I slept badly that night.

At the beginning of the next morning – our school maintained the practice of morning lessons on

Saturday – I trudged towards the school's front door. I was dying for a coffee; my sleepless night had left me exhausted and the day hadn't even begun! My shoulder felt a sudden nudge.

'Sorry Miss,' a heavily built child pulled the satchel that had struck me closer to him as he marched on ahead.

Just as I was about to reach for the door, I saw Henry standing by his car, his whole body tense. I stepped back to let a large group of children through. Henry was facing Vicky, her hands gesticulating wildly. Should I intervene? I strained my ears above the hubbub of the children streaming into school but I couldn't hear what they were saying. I wasn't sure, but I thought I saw Vicky's mouth form the word 'Mar' several times. Could they be talking about Mark? Intrigued, I stepped forward. The school bell rang across the car park. I would find out later.

Chapter 16

After school the next Monday I realized I was glad of one thing. I didn't have to dash home any more to see what John had been up to. I could stay at school as long as I liked – until the caretaker came to lock up, of course, but that wasn't until six and today I could go straight round to Betty's for the tea she'd promised. I opened my purse. The poison pen letter was there ready. I sighed as I faced the pile of papers on my desk. Much as I hated the stuffy, sweaty smell of a recently abandoned classroom, the same heavy feeling always returned when I planned lessons, did my marking and ticked all the boxes that had to be ticked no matter where I was. I decided I would keep school at school. Home would become a place of relaxation. I could now sit down and watch TV at home without constant interruption. Although I missed John and his sunlit grin, I didn't miss his unending chatter. And the letter? Well, it was only a poison pen letter after all, and I wasn't the only one getting them. As long as I ignored its contents I was fine. But I knew, in my heart of hearts, that it unsettled me. Hate can creep into a person's heart so insidiously, and it can do so much damage.

I looked at the books and papers littering my desk. I sat down and opened the first file. Just as I was picking up my pen, suddenly, out of the corner of my eye, I saw a dark figure rush into the room and stand beside me. I looked up to see Leonard, his cheeks set, his eyes cold.

'Glad I caught you,' he said.

I resisted the temptation to stand up.

He towered over me. 'You know, you are a valued member of our staff, but you have a career to think of. It's about time you put in for a transfer isn't it?'

'A transfer? No, why?'

'As if you don't know. You won't have to wait until next May – I could sort it out earlier. I have decided. I want your letter of application on my desk by Monday.'

'But I don't want a transfer!'

'I think, when you've had time to reflect, that you do. Think about it. Your husband's behaviour has been bad enough, but—'

'Look, if I think about it, can't it wait until next May at least?'

'Put it this way. I could get you promotion to a head of a larger department next term, or you could be made to transfer to an inner-city school after next May. Monday!' he ordered and stormed out of the room.

I gaped after him. Within seconds there was a gentle tap on the open door.

'Hi,' Henry's cheerful frame filled the doorway. 'What's going on?'

I closed the file. 'You heard?'

He grabbed a chair and sat next to me. 'I did. He's bluffing – you're too good a teacher to lose or to mess about with. The responsibility of this new job is getting to him – he's already threatened a couple of other staff. They can't all go.'

'You reckon?'

'I'm positive. I heard that next term they'll be appointing a new head, a proper headmaster who is not Leonard, so then your so-called transfer will be irrelevant. Anyway. I've some other rather disturbing news.' I thought of Vicky's heated discussion with him on Saturday.

'Yes, what?'

'Anthea's at it again.'

'What do you mean, drinking?'

'No, besides that. She's now accused Vicky of killing Mark.'

'No!' I looked out of the window for a moment. A lonely seagull wheeled in front of the gathering clouds. 'You mean, she's decided John is in the clear?'

Henry shifted in his chair. 'No, not necessarily. I think she's still trying to put the blame onto anyone and everyone. Trying to stir things up so that she finally knows what happened and can be at peace.'

'She doesn't need to do that; it's up to the police isn't it?'

Henry ran his finger along the edge of the desk. 'Well, you know Anthea, a perfectionist to the end, in spite of her recently developed drinking flaw. She's always needed to dot the i's and cross the t's herself.'

I frowned. 'So why Vicky all of a sudden?'

'Vicky came up to me in the car park the other day. She told me that Anthea said that Mark had been helping Vicky because she was unable to control her classes. Anthea suggested that Vicky had been afraid of losing her job and had good reason to do away with Mark before it could happen.'

'Well, she certainly was having difficulty with some of her classes, she admitted it, and you couldn't help hearing the noise, but then, I can't really say that all of my classes are quiet and well-behaved.' Pictures of 4D and the dreaded Darren thumping his desk sprang into my mind. 'Even then, I'd never see doing away with the headmaster as a solution.'

'Yes, but we know Anthea is desperate and knowing that Mark had to help Vicky gave her some grounds for suspicion – and, of course, we know the full story, don't we?'

'Do you think Anthea knew Vicky was having an affair with her husband?'

'We'll never know, but there was something else Anthea went on about.'

'Yes?' I glanced down at an open file in front of me and decided it could definitely wait.

'Vicky said it was something to do with the keys Mark was supposed to collect as they had some plant-watering arrangement going on for Vicky. Anthea suddenly called at her house for them – Mark hadn't collected them after all. Vicky could hardly believe that Anthea was still expecting to water her plants the next weekend when she's away – not after all that had happened.'

'I agree. It does seem strange. However, it's right in character, I guess, but a bunch of keys wouldn't tell her anything.'

'When Vicky went to the cupboard to get them, Anthea pushed forward in front of her, opened the door herself and grabbed the box, shook it hard and took out the keys, turned and shouted at Vicky, saying how she knew she'd killed him and would have her revenge.'

'Anthea said this?'

'Yes, the once cool, calm, impervious Anthea. Do you think the drink is affecting her?'

'Maybe so. Well I never! I guess it's getting to her now more than ever.' I said. 'Poor Vicky.' I let my pen drop. 'You don't think—'

'No, of course not, I don't think Vicky would do such a thing. She was in love with the man for goodness sake!'

'A case of, "If she can't have him, no one else can"?'

'Vicky? Do you really *know* Vicky?' Henry put his finger round the neck of his shirt trying to loosen his tie.

'Well, perhaps not as well as you, but, yes, I have to agree with you, I can hardly imagine Vicky doing anything nasty, although there is no evidence either way.'

'Let me reassure you Vicky had nothing to do with it.' He slumped down in his chair. 'I wish the police would get on with it, find the killer and then let us all be in peace.'

'Me, too,' I said, glancing down at the page that needed my attention, thinking of Wendy.

'We can't let this go on.'

I thought of Leonard and suddenly felt cold. 'If only we could do something now.'

'You're right.' Henry paused. 'We must do something. But what?'

'Well, if we could get some evidence that explains Leonard's behaviour at least, I could give it to Wendy.'

'Wendy?'

'She's one of the police officers that interviewed me. She lives in the same village as Gravesall – John's hospital. I went to hers for coffee one time after visiting John. She says she wants to help.'

'Really? That sounds most promising. What if we got hold of that accounts book, made copies of that mysterious page and gave it to your police officer friend?'

'Sounds like a good idea, but how?'

'Let me think about it. But now, my lovely,' Henry stood up, touched my cheek and turned to the open doorway, 'now we must put our worries aside and go to our separate homes. Your car is still working all right, I hope?'

Henry walked smartly through the open doorway, his footsteps echoing in the silent corridor, gradually getting quieter until I could no longer hear them. I ignored the faint tingling of excitement I'd felt when he touched me.

I picked up the file again and starting making notes about the lessons I had to take over the next week or so. I fought back the inclination to think about our plan to get hold of the accounts. How would we do it? I shook my head. I had to prepare some work, now. OK, a worksheet on Musical Form. Binary, two parts, but I would have to compose something that would make it clearer for the restless listeners.

Finally, there was a neat pile of pages for Betty to photocopy. I was tempted to take them with me when I dropped round to hers for tea in a few moments, but I put them aside to deal with the next day. I opened my handbag and checked that the poison pen letter was there. If only I knew who had written the wretched thing. At least Betty would cheer me up, she always had this effect. She must be the most popular person in the school. I was looking forward to seeing inside her house too. Standing amongst some of the most ancient houses in the street, with its half-timbered uneven structure, and its pantiled roof, it had much to tell.

The sky was filled with billowing clouds tinged grey as I walked towards Betty's house, my elbow firmly pushed against my bag which held that dreaded envelope. Silver Street was surprisingly quiet at this time of evening. My footsteps echoing, I approached the half-timbered houses. They dominated the street, as if reminding us of their stable influence on an ever-changing and troubled world. Thick plaster walls and bowing pantiles told us that once, centuries ago, a different civilisation lived, breathed, and fretted in this same street, in these same houses and no matter what, these houses would stand the test of time, long after the inhabitants had gone. Betty's had a large solid knocker on its ancient door, now freshly painted black. As I lifted the knocker, my heart thumped loudly, the identity of the poison pen writer would be revealed.

Betty opened the door swiftly, her welcoming smile broader than I remembered and her arms wrapped around me as she pecked me briefly on the cheek. I stopped myself from wiping away traces of lipstick that she may have left. As I stepped into the well-lit room, I gasped. The place was huge – nothing like the medieval box I had imagined. The pristine white plaster on the ceiling was divided by a large trunk of an ancient tree. To the right of me was a brick fireplace big enough to stand inside, and to the left, a wall of faded grape vines graced the dull plaster between slim beams of natural wood. The warmth of centuries of loving families wrapped itself round me. Betty smiled. I thought how suited the building and Betty were to each other.

'Do you like it?' she asked.

'Oh yes,' I said, still in awe.

She spoke, her voice tender and warm. 'I do too. I've been here for five years now and I've loved every minute of it.'

I stared at the notches in the wooden beams, trying to take in every detail. How many changes had been made over the centuries?

'Upstairs is even more interesting.' Betty moved towards the doorway. 'Would you like to go up?'

'Yes please.' I held my bag close to me. I wondered when to bring out the letter, and decided to let our conversation flow naturally. I wanted some more time to bathe in the warmth of the moment.

'Mind how you go.' Betty stepped into a narrow staircase, the steps of solid stone curving sharply upwards. She only just fitted in the narrow opening. I watched my feet as I tentatively followed. When I finally stepped out into the light, my mouth gaped. This room was even larger than the one below. I looked up. The ceiling was so high, it was like the pinnacle of one of those ancient buildings I remembered seeing in the textbook for my music classes. It was the chapter about medieval minstrels, I remembered.

'This was once the ceiling to a great hall,' Betty told me. 'An extra floor has been put in,' she explained.

I nodded and then let my eyes be drawn upwards. 'It looks as though you could have bats,' I said craning my neck to observe the carving on the large post that stretched above me.

'It's not bats I get. I seem to get a lot of butterflies.'

'Really?' I said, wondering if Betty had a charm way beyond everyday friendliness.

'Well,' she said, taking a large breath, 'I'm getting a bit hungry. Are you?'

'Oh. Er, yes,' I lied, disappointed that I had been brought back to earth so swiftly. I followed her down the stairs, watching my feet on the narrow steps very carefully.

'Now,' Betty patted the sofa. 'Take a seat and I'll bring in the tea.'

'Can I help?'

'No, no, I'll be back in a minute.' Betty disappeared though the doorway and beyond.

I lay back on the sofa, drawing in the warmth of the room again. I understood why Betty loved living here. I wondered if there was some secret theory of life that people and buildings were somehow interconnected. Did the building draw in the warm, loving Betty or was it Betty who was adding to the warm and loving atmosphere the walls of this ancient building were emanating now?

'Milk?' Betty had put the tray down and was holding up a bone china jug.

'Yes please but no sugar.'

'Cake?'

I accepted a huge slice of Victoria sandwich. Tea dispensed, Betty sat down in the chair next to me again.

'Now,' she said placing her plump hands firmly on her knees, 'is there anything you want to ask?'

I didn't know where to start.

'I'm so sorry to hear about your husband. It must be awful. Do you want to talk about it?'

I could feel the tears welling up in my eyes. I shook my head. 'No, no,' I said. 'Don't be sympathetic, I might cry.' I forced myself to hold back the tears. Now was not the time.

'I understand,' she said, careful not to say or do anything more that would upset me further.

I pulled open my bag. 'Actually,' I took out the letter, 'there is something you can help me with.' I cleared my throat. 'This is confidential at the moment. I'm not sure what to do with it. I don't want to go to the police.'

'What is it?' Betty held out a plump palm.

'It's a poison pen letter,' I said placing it in her hand. 'I don't think I'm the only one to have got one.'

Betty paled as she read the nasty words. She looked up at me appalled.

'I'd hoped you'd be able to recognize the writing, even though someone has tried to disguise it.'

Betty looked carefully at the paper. 'Well,' she paused. 'It does look familiar. Now where—?' she leaned back in her chair, thinking.

I waited patiently, trying to ignore my thumping pulse, and willing myself to bathe in the comfort of the room once again.

Betty sat up. 'I know, it was when I was in hospital last year.'

'Yes?' I vaguely remembered a crazy month at the end of term when the secretary was away. I had presumed she was on holiday.

'Mark organized the staff to write something in a Get Well card. He was a great one for puzzles, so asked them to quote some of their favourite sayings and to disguise their writing so that I could try to guess who they were. I recognized everyone of course,' she laughed.

I wondered why I had been missed out of this little game. Then I remembered. I had been given leave to take John to hospital for check-ups for a number of days near the end of the same term. I also vaguely remembered being asked to sign a card for the secretary but had missed out. The card had been taken away before I got to it.

'Yes?' I asked, my pulse quickening again.

'I've got it in the next room.' Betty waddled quickly through the doorway again. The moments dragged by.

'I can't seem to find it.' Betty's muffled voice came from the next room.

I clasped my hands and waited. I concentrated, breathing in deeply as I did for the singing classes, trying to calm my racing pulse.

'I'm terribly sorry,' Betty's face was flushed. 'I can't find it at the moment, but I'll have a good look later tonight and tomorrow and when I find it, I'll let you know.'

I tried to hide my disappointment. 'Perhaps you could keep the letter and when you find the card, see if you can recognize who the culprit is and let me know then?' I was impatient for a result. I suddenly added, 'Don't say anything to the person yourself. Let me know first and then we'll take it to the police together.'

'Or do you want me to hand it to Leonard so that he can deal with it?' she offered.

'No, no, not Leonard,' I said quickly. Betty glanced at me. I forced myself to speak calmly, 'No, not Leonard, I don't think we should trust anybody. We should keep all of this secret.' For one quick flash, I wondered if Betty herself could be capable of writing the letters. I shook my head slightly. Ridiculous.

I slowly pulled myself out of the chair. 'I must let you have time for the search,' I said. 'Thank you so much for the tea.' I grabbed my coat and made for the door. Betty followed me, gave me a quick hug as though nothing untoward had happened and I stepped out into the cool air.

Chapter 17

On Wednesday afternoon as I climbed into my car to leave school, Henry opened my side door and slipped inside.

'I've thought of it!' he grinned.

'Yes? the accounts book you mean?'

168

'Yes, you arrange to have a meeting with Leonard right at the end of a school day on the pretext of discussing your transfer in private.'

'But I don't want—'

'Oh, you don't have to ask for the transfer. When you meet him, spring him with an idea about the end-of-term concert that you insist on discussing first – think up something that makes him leave the office to look up the files. I'll get the keys from Betty's desk, dash in, grab the book and I've got a copier at home – I'll take the copies and get it back the next morning. We'll leave it amongst Betty's files as though it's been momentarily mislaid.'

'Mm, very risky, but we've got to do something. I'll ask Betty to make an appointment for me for Friday when everyone's tired and wanting to go home.'

I slipped back into school and made the appointment.


Tonight I would not think about it, tonight was Wednesday, our girls' night in. The bottle of red wine stood open and the two glasses sat either side waiting for Gale. It had been a hard day. As I stood looking out of the sitting room window, the leaves on the beech tree quivered in the soft light of the street lamp. For a moment I was back teaching 4D, my nostrils filled with the dust and chaos of a troubled class. One of these days Darren, that loud-mouthed uncouth blob of a human being, was going to get his comeuppance, but it wasn't today.

Tomorrow I would go in early and look up his file. Maybe if I understood where he was coming from I could cope better? The house was eerily quiet. The permanent sense of unease that hovered in the back of my mind surfaced. Flashes appeared of John's contorted face peering into my eyes. He was demanding that I pay attention to something 'someone' had left on the roadside especially for him. He was holding his favourite box open and inside was a dirty industrial glove and a branch from a tree with a spider's web. I shuddered. No, I refused to think about this anymore. Now, I would have some 'me' time. I deserved it, I really needed it. I saw some movement outside. Gale was walking up my drive. The doorbell rang.

'OK?' Gale's dark eyes were duller than usual, her curly hair ruffled in the light evening breeze. There were deep circles under her eyes. She, too, was probably ready for a good night's session. She grinned, thrusting a packet of crisps at me.

I laughed. 'Thanks. I always forget, don't I?'

'Well, with the amount of wine I'm about to drink, we'd better eat something!' She slung her coat over the banister, went into the sitting room and slumped down into the sofa, her slim body draped like a forgotten rag doll. Her long legs shifted some of the crumbs left over from my TV snack last night. I should have vacuumed, but she didn't seem to notice or didn't care.

'Please?' She gestured towards the bottle of wine. I poured a full glass for her. As I carried it towards her, some of the wine splashed onto the carpet.

'Careful,' she said, looking up at my face which she read with pinpoint accuracy. I pushed my foot half-heartedly at the stain on the carpet.

'Crisps?' she prompted.

'Ah, yes.' I opened the cupboard door and clattered the bowls as I pulled one out. I tried to yank open the crisps but nothing happened. Muttering under my breath I pulled at the packet again. It still wouldn't budge. Grasping it with my teeth I tore it with all the fury I could muster. Suddenly the packet gave way and it rained crisps.

'Damn!' I shouted. I shook the remaining crisps into the bowl and put it next to Gale. She grinned.

'So, you've had a good day then,' she said, keeping a dead straight face.

'Yeah, right, you can tell.'

'Do you want to talk about it or shall we abandon all things to do with school and relax?'

'No school, right – I've had enough of school.' I gazed at the mantelpiece wondering if Henry and I would be able to get that accounts book.

'A penny for them.'

'Oh, nothing – it's secret, school stuff – you don't want to know.' I touched the side of my nose.

'The mystery of Mark King's death?'

'No, no, I couldn't cope with that either.' As an afterthought, I said, 'It wasn't you who did it?' I looked mischievously into her eyes.

'Definitely not. As you well know, if I was going to murder anyone, it would be that cow of a nursing sister.' Gale wriggled on the sofa. 'John then? How about John? How are things with him?'

171

I sat down, my fingers clasping the wine shakily. 'John seems OK, but it's all the other business to do with him that is driving me crazy.'

'Oh?'

'I sometimes think that those who are supposed to care for people like John have their heads stuck permanently in the clouds. They haven't got a clue what it's like for us poor mortals underneath. One minute a doctor is telling me that John should have continuity. He needs a consistent routine, he says. So, what do they do? They decide to move him! He's only just settled in the ward he was sectioned into and worse than that, they are threatening to close down all the wards anyway.'

'Really? ALL of them?' Gale savoured a drink of her wine.

'Yes, well, all but the acute ward that John is in temporarily. And do you know, besides this, I get a letter telling me to go to a meeting. When I get there, they hardly even mention John or me. It's as though we're just faceless things that get in the way of them having an easy time.'

'Tell me about it. It's the same with us nurses. We try to look after the patients, after all, that's what we're supposed to do, and what happens? Paperwork, nothing but red tape and paperwork. The patients don't get a look in.'

We talked well into the evening, both of us unwinding bit by bit. Gale was now sprawled lower across the sofa, and I had my arms akimbo, my hand clutching a half-empty glass. I was feeling more relaxed, the wine tasting better and better after every gulp and the tension in my shoulders gone.

After I'd opened a second bottle and our glasses were refilled, I slumped into my chair again, put my elbow on the arm and held the glass up to Gale. 'You know,' I said, moving the glass slowly to my lips. 'I used to think that when you needed help, all you had to do was ask.'

'Yeah,' Gale studied the light reflecting off my glass. 'I'm sure we all thought that once – when we were young and naive.'

'Young and naive. Gosh I can hardly remember what it was like.' I stared at the wall behind her. It was a pale blue, the colour of the sky when I was with John on the farm that warm summer when I first knew him and the colour that I had eventually painted it in spite of John wanting us to have it dark blue. Even then, he seemed obsessed with having everything dark and miserable.

'Me too.' Gale carefully lifted her glass. 'I was so certain that nursing was going to be the be all and end all. I would be Florence Nightingale curing the sick, saving lives, and now?' Her eyes glazed. 'Now, I'm just a skivvy, filling in forms, being nagged at all the time and trying to run a ward I'm not even qualified for.'

'I mean,' I splashed more wine on the carpet as I made my point. 'You'd think they'd want to make life easier for themselves. It's bad enough having to deal with people off their rocker, but then badgering the relatives to take their loved ones back into their homes when they know they can't possibly cope, it's just—' I searched for the word.

'Criminal?' Gale offered.

'Yeah, criminal!'

'It was great before,' I sat up a little. 'Before John was sectioned, before this murder –everything was OK. But now, now I find myself stopping and thinking, what on earth's the world coming to?'

'Yeah. What *is* the world coming to?'

We sat in a comfortable silence for a while, each of us thinking about our own problems.

Suddenly Gale spoke, 'You know,' her words were drawn out, while she was thinking of what she was about to say. She lowered her voice, 'I wasn't supposed to say anything.'

'Mm?' I forced my eyes to focus on her.

'What the heck. You should know.'

'Yeah, go on,' I roused myself.

'David overheard one of the policemen saying they're shelving the case.'

'You mean Mark King's murder?'

'Yeah.'

'Why?'

'Well he heard one of them say that their boss'd said that it could've been a rare accident or if not, the chief suspect was already declared incompetent and they had no evidence, so the case was not worth pursuing.'

'You mean they've decided it was John and they might *never* find out who the killer really was?' In spite of the heavy haze of wine that surrounded my thoughts, my heart froze. 'But that means—'

Gale said quickly, 'That means nothing. Don't you go thinking that it was John. They don't know anything for certain, John is just a convenient scapegoat.'

My eyes moistened. 'But that means, that means I'll never know, not for sure.' I put my glass down clumsily on the table. 'So that was what Wendy wanted to tell me but couldn't.'

'Wendy, who's Wendy?'

'Oh, one of the police officers who came to interview me. She lives near John's hospital and I go to her place for coffee sometimes. She's told me she'll help but she needs evidence – she says she shouldn't be speaking to me because I seem to be under suspicion too, but she wants me to help get her some proof. The last time I was with her, I felt she was on the verge of telling me something, but just stopped herself in time, so that must've been it.'

'Interesting, she could be very helpful, although she won't be allowed to tell you anything if she wants to keep her job.'

'Yes, I know. Even so, I don't know if I can stand it. It would be easier knowing that John *had* done it rather than all this mystery and uncertainty. Then at least we could all rest in our beds knowing that he is in the right place.'

Gale stretched a hand towards me. 'Now you know you don't mean that.'

I folded my arms. 'Well what else can I think?'

'You and I know that if it wasn't a freak accident and it was deliberate, then it was someone close to

Mark. It was personal, directed at him and no one else. Job's done. There won't be anymore.'

'How do you know that?'

'Well it stands to reason doesn't it? Anyway, I bet there's been more than one murder on my ward.'

I gasped. 'Murders?'

'Well think about it. On a hospital ward there are people in real pain, dying anyway. I'm pretty sure some of the doctors have given them more morphine than they should to put them out of their misery.'

'But Mark King's death is different.'

Gale and I sat in silence. My befuddled mind was still able to grasp the fact I might have to live with the uncertain knowledge that my husband could have been a murderer. I had to do something, but what?

Suddenly, there was a loud rapping on the door.

'Who can that be?' I looked blearily at Gale.

'Well it won't be David, he's not going to be back until midnight. Unless there's an emergency.'

I struggled to my feet and went unsteadily to the door.

'Check who it is first!' Gale called from the sitting room.

Too late. I'd opened the door. Leonard Hall's eyes gleamed in the pale light from the street. I stared at him, confused. What was he doing here at this hour of the night?

'Dorothy said I should check how you are,' he said bluntly.

'I'm fine.' I gave him a lopsided smile.

He stepped forward. 'I've got to speak to you.'

I wanted to say that I was busy, but even in my inebriated state his tall powerful presence made me pause. I stepped back.

'Why hello,' he said to Gale, obviously not pleased that I had company.

'This is my friend Gale,' I said coldly, 'Gale, meet Mr Hall.' Gale gave him a brief smile and raised her eyebrows to me. Yes, this was the mean Mr Hall.

Leonard eased himself into my chair. 'You know about Sally's husband, I suppose. It was such a dreadful thing to happen. Dorothy and I were talking tonight and we agreed we should keep a special eye on you Sally.' He patted the arm of the chair.

I stopped myself from saying, 'I wish you wouldn't'. Instead I leered in his direction hoping that it looked like a gentle smile of acquiescence and sat uneasily in the hard-back chair next to the sofa.

'I was really hoping to speak to you in private. These things are very difficult to talk about in company.' He hastily waved a hand at Gale, 'I didn't mean to be rude or anything, but time is so short now that I have these extra responsibilities. Now that the headmaster—' He paused as if trying to choose his next words very carefully.

'Now that Mr King is dead, you mean. Now that someone has murdered him in cold blood!'

For a split second, Leonard looked nonplussed, but he soon resumed his usual unswerving stare. 'Well, I wouldn't have put it quite like that. Now, back to why I'm here. Do you need some help with the little matter I discussed with you yesterday? Is there anything else we can do for you, now that you are on your own?'

'On your own,' I thought, a chill running down my spine. Why did these words suddenly sound sinister? After all, the fact was, I was happily on my own until now. What did the wretched man really want? I noticed that I had lost all of the luxurious relaxed feeling I'd had before he arrived. I was stone cold sober, my wine glass sitting abandoned on the table next to me. 'No, I'm fine thank you.' My tone was unwelcoming. Surely he would get the message.

Gale cleared her throat and moved to get off the sofa. 'Well, it's been a great evening, I must go,' and she stared at me. She too was a lot more sober that I remembered.

I looked back at her, my eyes pleading. 'No, no, do stay. After all you were here first.' I turned to Mr. Hall. 'Gale knows everything about me. You can say anything in front of her, I won't mind.'

He glanced at us both, weighing up the situation. 'Well, if you are certain.'

I realized I should offer him a drink but decided he could do without. It was our evening he was disturbing and after all, he hadn't been invited and he did plonk himself down in my chair.

He seemed oblivious of my neglect. He clasped his hands in front of him. Oh God, not another boring lecture, I thought. 'Well, besides the little matter you have to settle, you know Mrs Dighton is the chairwoman of the committee that oversees John's care.'

'Yes,' I said – allowing myself to continue in my thoughts – more's the pity.

'Well, we are very good friends you know.'

That figures I thought. I could see Gale's eyes flicker. She was reading my thoughts.

Leonard continued building his case. There was something he wanted from me, that was for sure. 'Dorothy suggested we offer to talk to Mrs Dighton so that your meetings can be arranged at a more suitable time for you.'

Yeah? This must be a first. I gave him no encouragement. I let him continue.

'John is in a very poor way, isn't he?'

Ah now we're getting to it. He wants to know more about John – why?

'Well,' he shifted in the chair, 'your John came to see me at the school on a couple of occasions, did you know that?'

'I guess he did,' I replied, determined not to give anything away.

'And one time he actually burst into Mark's office when I was there and when the receptionist was busy.'

'So?'

Leonard Hall sensed how unwelcome he was. 'I'm sorry to disturb you on your night off, while you are trying to relax.' He stared at the wine glass. 'But I really do want to help and we are all so busy at school there is little time for me to talk to you properly.'

I smiled weakly. The man was trying. I ought to give him some leeway.

179

Satisfied, he continued. 'John is a very intelligent man, isn't he?'

I stopped myself from saying that this had nothing to do with him or school.

He shifted in his chair again. 'I know I can trust you implicitly to keep counsel about school matters.' He glared at me, his eyes steady and unblinking, is if to reinforce the message. 'But what about John? Did he talk to you about anything he saw when he came to the school?'

'I can't really remember,' I lied. Flashes of John's intense features came into my thoughts. His agitated voice gabbling, 'That school is just a place for the children to be kept off the streets. That headmaster and his deputy need to be told a few home truths …' my heart thumped a little as I relived the fear and dread of John doing something drastic at my place of work.

Leonard Hall squared his shoulders, fixing me with a steely glare. 'You know, Sally, you are not helping. I've come here in good faith to help you. The least you can do is speak to me civilly. If you help me, we could even forget about our discussion yesterday.' The atmosphere in the room went down to zero. Gale sat inert, looking at her lap as if wishing she wasn't there.

'I'm sorry,' I said stiffly, 'but I really *am* all right. Please thank Mrs Hall for her kindness. It would be lovely if you organized our meetings at a more suitable time – perhaps on Friday afternoons so that I can get some work done with my morning classes –

some of them have exams coming up.' I purposefully shifted forward in my chair, ready to stand.

Leonard Hall ignored my words. 'What did John tell you?'

I sat back again. 'Nothing,' I said quickly.

'You know it's important to keep the memory of our headmaster pure. We don't want the school to suffer. If people start asking questions, rumours will start, we will lose pupils and you will lose your job. You do realise that, don't you Sally?' His dark eyes shone at me menacingly.

'I really don't know what you mean.'

'Well keep up this pretence if you will Sally, but I'm telling you, anything John told you or anyone else for that matter must not be repeated. After all, he would only be speaking the words of a madman. No one would believe him no matter what he said.'

Gale sat bolt upright. 'Steady on!'

'And what, may I say, has this to do with you?' he said to Gale.

She took a deep breath. 'It has everything to do with me!' she shouted. 'Sally is a close friend and anyone who upsets her will not only have me to deal with, but my husband is an influential lawyer. If you don't stop harassing Sally, he'll be pursuing the matter. Now that wouldn't be very good for the honour of the school, would it?'

Leonard Hall paled. 'Well, no.' He stood up. 'I didn't mean to sound threatening, but I'm just very concerned about the school. I shall go, shall I?'

Gale sniffed. I stood up.

When he reached the front door, he lowered his voice to me. 'Now you are on your honour, anything that John saw or has been saying must *not* be repeated. Do you understand me?' His acid tone cut through me. 'And, I want your response to the other matter by Monday, understand? Monday!'

I nodded briefly, closing the door behind him slowly.

Gale pulled a face. 'What was all THAT about?'

I grabbed my wine glass and drained it. 'Leonard is obviously frightened I'll tell on him. He's even demanded I ask for a transfer.'

'Really. Are you going to?'

'No, well not yet anyway. Hopefully he won't even be head next term when it matters.'

'Why? What do you know about him that he's afraid of?'

'It's just something I saw and something that John said to me. I thought nothing of it at the time, but now – especially after Leonard behaved so suspiciously when I went in to see him the other week, I think there's definitely something up.'

'What was it, did it make sense?'

'Yes, well yes and no. Promise you'll keep this to yourself.'

'Of course, I won't even say anything to David.'

'Please no!' I paused, uneasy about continuing.

Gale smiled reassuringly, 'There's obviously something troubling you and I've been a witness to your deputy's harassment, so the least you can do is tell me what it's all about.'

'Well,' I fingered my glass, 'all it seemed to me was a group of entries in an accounts book that were written in pencil – just girls' names – new staff. Then with John it's always very difficult to tell with him.

He was always so adamant about what he said, and some of the things he told me were absolutely ludicrous – like someone leaving carrots in the road for him to collect, but others made sense in the end, like when he told me the police had visited the house next door. I didn't believe him, but then when Jane came round to deliver a parcel, she told me they'd had to report her mum as a missing person when she'd wandered away. Their mum has dementia, you know – so the police came. They found her mum in the end, she'd invited herself for coffee at a house next to the petrol station near Ely and stayed on.'

'So what did John tell you that you think was suspicious?'

'It was about what he saw on one of his uninvited visits.'

Gale held out her wine glass. It was time for a refill. As I poured the wine, she said quickly, 'Yes?'

I filled my own glass and sat down. 'I remember once he said he saw the headmaster with a black-covered accounts book. It had girls' names written in pencil on the bottom of one of the pages.'

'That doesn't sound newsworthy. It could've easily been school accounts – the girls were just staff.'

I nodded. 'That's why I ignored John at the time. But now, after I saw it too, and after Leonard's visit, there must be more to it, surely?'

Gale smirked. 'You're not suggesting the high and mighty headmaster and his deputy were doing something underhand – like blackmailing the staff?'

'Well,' I replied. 'Think about it. Why else keep secret accounts?'

'Unless they were diddling the school?' she asked.

'Then why were there only girls' names in it?'

We sat in silence for a moment. I coughed slightly. 'You know Henry told me that Mark King was having affairs with some of the younger members of staff, now I think about it, they were the ones named in the accounts.'

'Really? Why didn't Henry report his behaviour to the authorities?'

'Who was going to believe him? Our Mr King had the whole school, the school board, in fact the whole city in his hands. No one escaped from his charm.'

'Well, you'd think it would come out somehow.'

'Well, it didn't. Henry helped pick up the pieces when the charming Mr King dumped the girls. Henry only did that to keep his job and because he felt sorry for the poor victims.'

Gale twirled the stem of her glass. 'So, if he was such a cad, he could've been blackmailing them.'

I stared at the crumbs under Gale's feet. 'Right. The good and upright Mr King and all his charm making all the girls swoon, was also a blackmailer – blackmailing his victims?'

'But why on earth would he need to do that? He had far more money than the rest of them.'

'Yes but he had to keep his perfect wife, Anthea, in the manner to which she would like to become accustomed or,' I wriggled forward, 'maybe it was his ego he was massaging. It would give him an even greater sense of power if his conquests paid him to keep quiet so they could keep their jobs.'

Gale took a large drink of wine and swallowed fast. 'I'm not sure. Anyway, what'd this to do with Leonard?'

'Leonard Hall's job was to do all the dirty work for the headmaster. He had to, if he was to keep his own head above water.'

She shuddered. 'Even covering up blackmail?'

'Who's to say that Leonard Hall wasn't getting a cut too? Would you believe a new staff member more than a long-standing deputy like Leonard? Did you see his withering look? I mean you've got to be pretty strong to stand up to him.'

'You're right. He was a bit of a so-and-so. You nearly buckled.'

'No I did not!' My voice was louder than I intended.

Gale smiled sympathetically. 'Well all right then you didn't, but you didn't exactly sling him out straight away when he started showing his nasty side.'

'I suppose not,' I admitted.

We sat in silence for a moment. Gale leaned back and closed her eyes, thinking. Suddenly, she sat up, her eyes springing open.

'Then it could have been one of the girls who had killed him.'

I pictured Vicky creeping up to a sleeping Mark and jamming a poisonous spider on his hand or Rita filling a syringe, creeping up to Mark and sticking it into him. The picture was surreal, impossible to believe – even Rita, with all her dramatic gestures, I couldn't see attacking the man she was in love with – even if their affair had finished – she had her husband, after all.

'Maybe,' I said slowly. 'But a special toxin from an exotic pet spider? It's more likely to have been an accident, isn't it?'

Gale shrugged.

I stared at my empty wine glass. What about the other name, Penny? Could she have slipped back to Ely and sought revenge? I knew she'd left the staff before I came. Hopefully Henry and I would be able to solve one mystery at least after our planned escapade. My heart thumped in anticipation.

Chapter 18

I'd had a sleepless night. In my dreams, the pudding-faced Tamara plummeted towards me, her mouth opening wide and coming closer and closer, the huge pink jaw slowly changing, Tamara's expensive false teeth turning into the vicious fangs of a shark about to engulf me. Just before her cavernous jaw clamped shut she changed into an evil snake-faced Leonard. As I could see the venom dripping and he was about to attack me, I woke up with a start. With my nightdress damp with sweat and my heart pounding, I sat up, slowly focusing on the familiar cupboard in the corner. Breathing deeply I waited until my heart stopped banging and I could see. I leaned over and grabbed my glass of water and took a few careful sips trying not to think about the empty space next to me. With a heavy sigh, I put the glass back, wriggled down under the bedclothes and willed sleep to come.

I was loathe to move when the clock's noisy alarm invaded my sleep. I dragged myself out of bed, hit the shower and while I was revelling in the warm refreshing water the phone rang. It might be about John. Dripping all over the bedroom carpet, a towel wrapped loosely round me, I lifted the receiver.

'Hello Sally.' Oh no, it was the penetrating tones of Tamara. Now she's invading my personal space at home, whatever next?

'Hello,' I mumbled, trying not to sound too disgruntled.

'I'm phoning to assure you that the rumours are untrue.'

'Rumours?' It was too early to play games.

'I'm just making sure that you know the meeting today is definitely on. Will I see you there this afternoon? I've very kindly changed the time for you – Leonard is such a sweety, isn't he?'

I held the receiver away from me for a moment and blinked at it in disbelief.

'So,' Tamara's voice boomed from a distance. 'This afternoon?'

'Yes,' I spoke into the mouthpiece. 'This afternoon.'

Ignoring the damp carpet, I moved into automatic mode, dressed and set off for school for another Friday morning's teaching.

The traffic was unusually quiet so I arrived earlier than expected.

On going to the staffroom, I found that there was an extra free period before morning coffee; Leonard was having his own assembly with the classes in that year in the school hall and said that he didn't need us. It was something about the inspection coming up. While I was a bit irritated that it was one of my exam classes and how on earth was I going to get through the curriculum before the exam, I was still very grateful for the time off and in view of the terrible night's sleep I'd had, or rather hadn't had, I decided a quiet cup of coffee before break was in order.

As I sat in the staffroom, I noticed that no matter how peaceful and comfortable the place was, there was still a tension and bustle in the air. It was not really a place to relax but it'd have to do. I sipped the steaming coffee, closed my eyes and let the distant sounds of a busy school wash over me.

The door suddenly swung open. It was Henry.

'Ah,' I said, sitting up. Henry's eyes sparkled just like John's when he was in one of his footloose and carefree moods. 'You're here too. You've come in for a coffee as well?'

'How did you guess?' Henry made his drink and sat down opposite. He looked straight at me. 'It's great to have some time off – what can have come over Leonard? It'll probably be him having a purge on behaviour, now that the inspection is due. Anyway, we'll worry about that later, more important things are on the agenda aren't they? I see that you're getting up your strength for another battle with the dreaded Tamara and you haven't forgotten why you'll be dashing back to school afterwards?'

I shook my head. 'I had a strange phone call at home from Tamara this morning,' I said, into my coffee. 'She said the rumours weren't true and the meeting was still on.'

'How odd,' Henry mused.

I coughed, forcing myself to focus. 'Why?'

'Where there's smoke there's fire. Something's definitely up. I've always been a bit curious about their business arrangements. No matter what huge income Tamara Dighton gets from some consultancy work, they seem to have much more money than they should. They're like a couple of spoiled rich kids spending like there's no tomorrow. I mean, have you noticed the clothes they wear? They've got holiday homes galore – one in Norfolk I know, a boat, and I'm surprised they don't have their own helicopter.'

'Jealous eh?'

He smirked, 'As if!'

I focused on his lips, avoiding those disturbingly lovely eyes. 'She or her husband could have inherited it all.'

'No, that's not possible. I believe the parents died well before the spending spree.'

'How do you know?' I asked.

'Because, I'm ashamed to say that my lovely wife is friendly with a cousin of Tamara's. Carol and cousin Delia often have coffee together so Carol gets the low-down then.'

'Yuk! Her cousin must be very different.'

'She certainly is! Carol says that Delia spends most of the time sounding off about Tamara. Delia can't stand her either. Apparently Tamara sets herself up as Delia's moral guardian and is particularly nosey about her relationships.'

'Why does Delia put up with it?' I asked.

'Deathbed promises to her mother, what else?'

'Do you think—'

Just then, the staffroom door opened with a crash.

'It's all right, it's only me.' Betty dumped the Times Ed on the table. I felt myself blushing even though Henry and I were sitting apart. She smiled at us and swiftly left the room. 'Besides,' Henry continued. 'Tamara is certainly telling porkies. Remember, she talked about getting extra funds from a fantastic stockbroker – one that Carol knows is no longer working?'

'Yeah, you're right.'

We paused in thought. I took a deep breath, now was the time. 'There's something I've been meaning to ask you,' I said, pausing to take another sip from my mug. The coffee was getting cold.

'Fire away. I'm already married you know.'

'Oh you!' I gave his knee a friendly push. 'No, I have an idea. What if something happens at the hospital meeting this afternoon?'

'Such as?'

'Oh you know what I mean,' I said. 'What if I get some evidence of Tamara's antics?'

'Why, what do you have in mind – nothing too risky I hope?'

I leaned forward and told him my plan.

He leaned back and whistled. 'Go for it girl, but take great care.'

Flushed with the anticipation of future success I said, 'Before I forget, I've got my appointment booked with Leonard today for after school. Are you still willing to help about the accounts book?'

'Of course. Have you worked out how to distract Leonard?'

'I think so. Today after school then. I should be back.'

'And—' but before he could say anything further, the school bell rang and our thirsty colleagues streamed in for their coffee break.

After lunch, I drove Bumble to Gravesall and to the meeting with Ms Dighton. What bombshell would she land on us this time? In the back of my mind I thought about what Ed had said. If only we could find evidence.

There was a chill in the air as I climbed out of the car. My feet thudded in the silence as I walked towards the administrative block. I hesitated, gritting my teeth. I was determined to quell the fear that threatened to overwhelm me. It was too late to turn back. I knocked firmly, sounding more confident than I felt inside and was soon entering the meeting room.

I was almost getting used to her sickly perfume and managed to slip into the chair next to her without wrinkling my nose or pulling a face of disgust. I was quite proud of my swanlike  demeanour. One way or another, this was going to be a meeting with a difference.

'As usual,' her all too familiar commanding voice pronounced, as Tamara glared at me, 'you may be permitted to listen to our discussion, but you are not permitted to speak. Understood?' She poured herself a glass of water and slurped the liquid noisily.

I shifted in the hard chair. 'Yes, but—'

Just as she was about to speak again, I coughed. I coughed like my lungs were clogged with the dregs of a huge polluted ocean. 'Wa-ater,' I croaked huskily and reached for the jug, my hand shaking so much that I knocked it over. Just before it spilled onto the table I dived for it, only to knock the precious pile of Tamara's files onto the floor. 'I'm SO sorry,' I gasped, in between hoarse paroxysms as I dived under the table, grabbed the files, and shook them until their contents scattered at my feet. On top of a pile of envelopes one was marked 'Vicky' and poking out of it was a cheque addressed to Mrs Digh … I grabbed the envelope and its cheque and stuffed them in my blouse as I massed the remaining files and papers and dumped them back on the desk in front of the fuming Tamara.

'Well REALLY!' she shrieked. I coughed apologetically and patted my chest, shoving the envelope down further so that it couldn't be seen. I didn't dare meet Ed's eyes.

Eventually I resumed my composure and her papers were reassembled so the meeting could continue. I only coughed slightly from time to time during the rest of the meeting, sometimes interrupting the chair mid-flow, but otherwise it was much like any of the other meetings. Wards were to be closed, John was to be moved and Tamara had to get away early. I couldn't wait to give the cheque to Wendy.

Flushed with success, I locked the cheque in the glove compartment in Bumble and drove confidently through the heavy traffic to make it just in time for our contretemps with Leonard.

The reception area was dark and unoccupied, Betty had gone and Leonard was alone in his office. I smiled. Detaining him gave me a slight flush of pleasure, although my hands were clammy with the prospect of what lay ahead. I glanced into the corridor and Henry poked his head round the corner and winked. I smiled back at him, knocked gently at Leonard's door and went in.

'So you've thought about your transfer eh? I could get you a plum job at—'

Heart thumping loudly, I held up my hand and said, 'Wait.'

He stared, 'Wait?' he echoed angrily. 'I don't think—'

'Yes, wait please,' I interrupted, blushing and forcing myself to speak steadily. 'There is another matter we need to discuss first. After that, then we'll see.'

Glancing behind him, he sighed. 'All right, what is this other matter? Surely it could wait.'

'You don't want to be prosecuted do you?'

He paled. 'What do you mean, prosecuted?'

'We need to know Fiona's professional arrangements.'

'Pardon? What ARE you talking about?'

'I want her to sing solo at our final concert. I'm told she is a professional singer and that we have to check her contract before we can use her. Her parents are adamant about this.'

'Professional contract? How on earth are we supposed to know about that?'

'Her parents swore they had discussed it with Mark when she first came and they insisted that a copy of her professional contract was put in the school files.'

'Humph.' Leonard stayed seated.

'You have a key to the files. I do not.' I stared straight into his eyes, my heart increasing its pace alarmingly.

He sighed, stood up, took out his keys, rattled them while feeling for the one for the filing cabinet and we left the room, me blocking his vision on his left so he wouldn't see anything that Henry got up to.

'What's her name again? he asked as we entered the filing room.

'Fiona,' I said blandly.

'Yes, but Fiona what? What's her surname?'

I blinked. 'Do you know, I've suddenly forgotten. I knew it this morning. Fiona—' I made as if trying to remember, 'Fiona—I think she's in year one or is it year two?'

'Really, woman! You're exasperating! We'll have to leave this until you know all the facts.' He slammed the filing cabinet shut.

'No, no, it's important,' I flustered. 'Fiona Cartwright. That's it. Fiona Cartwright.'

'Fiona Cartwright,' he said as he glanced at me, opened the cabinet again and started leafing through the files. I saw someone dash past the window. I moved to obstruct Leonard's vision. He glanced around at me for a moment but turned and resumed looking through the files.

'There's no Fiona Cartwright in year one.' He looked at me steadily, an angry flush appearing in his cheeks.

'Year two, I'm sure it's year two,' and I smiled weakly.

He leafed through the files again. 'No Fiona Cartwright in year two.'

I stared at him in disbelief. 'But there *is* a Fiona Cartwright in year two, a professional singer—I remember hearing her in my class.' Suddenly I struck my forehead with the palm of my hand. 'Oh sorry. So sorry, Fiona Cartwright is her professional name—she'll be in our files under her real name.'

'Her real name,' Leonard said through a clenched jaw.

'Yes, yes. Her real name is Iona.' I stuttered. 'Iona—'

Leonard folded his arms, knocking against the keys in the filing cabinet that jangled just as I thought I heard a door opening inside his office.

I coughed and smiled. 'Yes, Iona,' another cough. 'Iona Barns,' I announced triumphantly.

'Iona Barns it is now, is it?' he growled as he leafed through the files again. 'Ah, this is it!' He whipped out the file.

'Thank Go—' I stopped myself in time. 'Yes, that's it.'

'A contract you say?'

I nodded.

He sighed. 'Look, I've got to get home. We'll leave this until next week.'

I could see Henry's reflection in the picture frame beside us. 'No, no.' I panicked and starter to jabber. 'Look now you've got the file, you've only got to look. If we can use her, our concert will be the talk of the town—who knows, world famous. She's a real star and the parents said she could sing for us—wouldn't that be a terrific bonus—a real feather in your cap, whether I'm here or not? All you have to do is write to the firm that holds the contract and ask permission. It won't cost the school a thing—promise, although it needs to be done soon so she doesn't get booked up.'

'Hmph.' He paused and then leafed through Iona's papers. 'Ah, this must be it.' He withdrew an impressive copy of a contract. As we pored over it I saw Henry flit past the window again. Leonard stopped reading and looked up. 'What was that movement?'

'What? Nothing that I saw. A fly, a moth?'

'Right,' Leonard said, taking the contract, replacing the file and slamming the cabinet shut. After locking it, he turned to me. 'And your transfer?'

'Yes. I agree to ask for a transfer. I'll give Betty a letter as soon as I can. What I wanted to ask you, was, does it matter where I want to be transferred to? Could it be somewhere like Cambridge?'

'Wherever you like, but just do it!' He started to go into his office. Just then Betty's phone rang. 'Look, lock that office door will you, while I get the phone?'

He watched me closely as I pulled his office door to. The cupboard which held the accounts book was firmly closed.

Chapter 19

On the Sunday, I steeled myself for the weekly visit to see John. I hadn't had time to see him on Friday. Newspaper, chocolates, what else could I take? How would the other patients be? Would he know that he was going to be moved soon?

I smiled as I realized that at last I would be able to do something to help him. I had the photocopies of the accounts and the cheque in the car ready to deliver to Wendy. She was on duty this Sunday so I would just slip them into her letterbox, she would know who they were from. I had my camera with me too, I'd long decided to have it with me at all times since Henry and Ed and I had decided we had to do something.

My mood changed as I pulled into the car park in my usual space. The rooks wheeled and squawked in the watery grey sky. This fitted the way my mood felt exactly. I had to ring three times before anyone would answer the door. When I eventually went in, closing the second door swiftly behind me just in case, I felt the tension in the air. I looked around for Ed. He wasn't on duty today. One of the patients was rocking violently in an armchair, another banging their head against the wall and then I saw John stumbling towards me. His face suddenly appeared a few inches away from mine. His eyes were wide with anger.

'They've got to stop it,' he shouted. He had his 'run for cover' look. My heart thumped, there was nowhere to run to, although at least there were some staff who could rescue me if needed.

'Yes, you're right,' I said as convincingly as I could, although I had no idea what he was going on about. I continued, trying to sound as if I agreed. 'They HAVE got to stop it. Come and sit down and tell me about it.'

I forced myself to look calm and in control, while inside I was panicking. I sat down in the nearest chair and patted the arm of the one next to me, hoping that John would automatically sit himself down next to me, in spite of this sudden outburst of anger. He ignored me and stomped off towards the corner, and started pulling at a patient's arm.

'John,' I called firmly. He still ignored me and got hold of both arms of the patient trying to move her. She cried. He took no notice of her cries. A member of staff rushed over to salvage the situation.

'Now John, let her go. Look, your wife has come to see you. Come on John, come back to the chair and sit next to her.'

John faltered, and let the nurse remove his hands from the other patient's. Still holding firmly onto John's hands, the nurse persuaded him to be brought away and walked him kindly but forcibly to a chair near me.

She stayed with John until he was seated. 'Ah Mrs Wilks.'

'Yes,' I smiled.

'I'm so pleased you've come.'

'Oh?' I looked at John and then back at her. What was up now?

'You know you said you'd like to be there when we move John?'

I nodded.

'As you know, we are moving him tomorrow morning. Can you come?'

'Tomorrow?' I gasped.

'Yes, tomorrow.' The nurse looked at me blankly. 'You should have received a letter in the post.'

'Sorry,' I said quickly, seeing in my head the pile of letters that had gathered over the week. Most of them were bills, so I had decided to put off dealing with them until I had time, perhaps at the weekend. Letters from the doctors and hospital rarely reached me in the past so I was used to their silence.

While sitting in this claustrophobic room I suddenly had a thought. John had never accepted his illness; he would never agree to come to talk with the psychologist. Somehow, in spite of his confusion there was part of him that was still very much intact. His survival mechanism had made him crafty, cunning enough to spin a web of lies that he probably believed, and that in his mind explained why he behaved as he did and why he couldn't understand the fuss.

Just as he had hidden the strange treasures he had picked up on the road in odd places about the house, newspaper scraps dragged out of the gutter and placed on his writing desk, a dirty empty beer bottle in our drinks cabinet and the bird's nest amongst the pot plants on our dining room windowsill, so in the past he may have put any letters in a safe place – a place away from my prying eyes and the fuss they would cause. I cringed as I thought of the trouble we had caused. More than once I had shouted down the phone about their disastrous communication but then, they should have realized that this would happen, shouldn't they?

John suddenly shifted in his chair, leaned over, grabbed my hand and squeezed. I ignored the pain. I turned to the nurse. 'But I won't have time to arrange lesson cover. What can I do?'

She saw my agitation and said, 'I'll see, now that you're here, maybe we could move him now?'

I looked at John who was studying my face. It was obvious that he was as settled as he could be here. The staff knew what his behaviour was like and were trained to deal with it. It would have been better if John wasn't moved at all. He hated change, so why force it on him now? Even though it had been explained to me that this was the norm, I still did not feel that it was the right thing to do – not if you were really thinking of John. The nurse was waiting patiently for my answer.

Now that John had recognized me, perhaps it would be less upsetting if I was with him when he was moved. Besides, this would be the only change, they wouldn't move him again, surely. I reluctantly nodded to the nurse and put my other hand on John's trying to ease some of the pressure. As I glanced around the room at this group of poor souls living in their worlds of confusion, a feeling of unease crept over me. Nothing was guaranteed, especially after that awful meeting when it was clear the powers that be had only one intention, and that was to close the wards and get rid of the patients. How could they? A gentle woman, hair untidy over her elderly face, stood by John stroking his shoulder.

'Madge?' the nurse called to a plump, cheerful staff member who was just walking through the ward. The nurse and Madge went to John's room to collect his belongings. I sat with him willing him to stay with me, praying that his face would not change into a stranger's. He needed to understand that I was here, I was his wife, here to support him. He was not on his own. However, I also knew that I hated the feeling of being left alone with him. What if his anger returned? It could happen so quickly. I glanced around. There was still one carer left in the room – she would have to rescue me. My hand was really hurting now, so with considerable force, I finally extracted it from John's unbelievably strong grip. John didn't seem to notice.

An elderly gentleman suddenly padded towards me and leaned right over.

'Have you come to take me home?' John asked.

'No,' I replied opening and closing my hand to get the circulation back. John stared at the intruder as if he wasn't there and then gazed at me, his eyes now calm. I was so relieved that he still knew who I was and that his anger remained dormant for the moment. The intruder's face came an inch closer.

John frowned and in an angry voice asked, 'Well who *is* taking me home?'

'You'll come home when you're better, not now.' We both knew that this would never happen. I forced myself to smile. 'But you are going to a new home today and I'll be coming with you. You'll have some new hot and cold nurses to look after you, won't you?' I waited longingly for him to share the joke. I could see him now, early in our marriage when we went on a weekend break to a hotel in Jersey, he had joked that he was looking forward to the hot and cold running waitresses.

Now, he simply stared at me in silence, his expression blank, his eyes losing focus. We were no longer connected. He had no idea what was happening.

The carer and nurse arrived with a wheelchair. John suddenly recognized me again and we had a little tussle while I made sure my hand was on top of his this time. With seasoned experience, the helpers manoeuvred John into the wheelchair. His bent frame and his frailty were so disheartening to witness, after years of knowing this highly energetic man, capable of climbing mountains, doing marathons and walking miles in the fields of his farmer friends. I let John hold my hand firmly again, his lap covered with his travel bag and on top a file of papers. Madge, the nurse and I negotiated our way out of the building. As the wheelchair bounced along, I looked at John's travel bag, his black leather writing case visible through the gap in the open zip. He had broken the zip when he first came in. Could he still be writing? Even if he could, his words must be poorly shaped, still heavy, wandering over the page and reflecting a confused and angry mind, although he did have moments of insight when he knew where he was, he knew that he was this confused person inside an annoyingly frail body. Maybe he was still able to keep some form of diary and I would understand better what was happening and how he felt. Maybe he'd left some clues about any part he may have played in Mark's death.

The wheelchair suddenly came to a halt. Madge gritted her teeth and pushed it hard until it slid over the bump in the way and we were able to continue trundling along the rough path. I looked again at the pathetically small pile of John's possessions and I had an uneasy feeling that something was missing. What was it? I couldn't quite put my finger on it.

Madge said, 'I like it when family support their relatives when they are moving. It can be so distressing for the patients.'

'Why do they move them, anyway?' I asked.

'We ask that too. There's something going on that's really worrying. We keep telling them not to make so many changes. The patients don't like it. Once they've settled into a ward, they're so much easier to handle when they get to know us.'

The nurse put in her pennyworth. 'It's getting harder and harder for us. Not only are they disrupting the patients, they're cutting down on staff so we're always working under pressure. I'm not sure I can stick it much longer.'

Madge cut in, 'Don't say that. We really need you.'

'I'm not sure I'll have a job much longer anyway. I've heard the board have decided to close down all the wards they can and get rid of as many staff as possible. They claim there is a financial crisis.'

'Really?' I asked.

'The doctors are up in arms. There's been a letter in the Cambridge Evening News, didn't you see it? They're furious but still the board won't take any notice.'

We continued in silence, deep in our own thoughts. I looked down at John. He was very pale, staring blankly ahead while still holding firmly onto my hand. The only sounds we could hear were the scrunch of wheels on the path and the occasional bump as Madge negotiated over tree roots. The rooks started cawing as we came nearer to the building.

It was depressing, its brown walls and windows squat beneath a plain tiled roof. There were no flowers or flower tubs, only unkempt grass that was sparse and neglected. I could sense that John was sharing my mood of despondency.

As if to ease the situation, Madge said softly, 'Not long now.'

At least she didn't put on that tone that some people do when they try to communicate with someone with dementia – you know, that sarcastic one that tells the person you think they are stupid or subhuman.

We eventually found a concreted path that could take us to the front door. The worn sign at the front door said 'Teveran Ward'.

Once we were inside we were met by a tall authoritative man obviously in charge.

I smiled at him. 'John'll be staying here for good? There'll be no more changes, right?' I asked.

He stared at me blankly, patients wandering aimlessly behind him. 'I should think so. Thank you for coming. We'll see to him now. Patrick, will you show John to his room?'

The nurse handed her files to the man in charge and she and Madge left. Patrick, tall and calm, took hold of the wheelchair and we went along a dark corridor to a room with two beds. One of them had a picture of an old man and the name Richard above it.

'He's sharing,' I said bluntly.

'Yes, he'll be all right.'

I held my peace. Even if his neighbour was one of the violent types, John seemed to have a way about him that made him impervious to the anger or animosity anyone had towards him. I remembered an angry neighbour yelling at us over the fence. As he ranted and raved about our oil tank giving off smells that were harmful to his family, John simply stood his ground and stared. The neighbour tried again but could do nothing when John simply did not respond. The complainant finally gave up and stepped down from the fence. Yes, John would probably be all right, I thought.

I suddenly noticed what was missing from John's things. 'His picture, where is his picture? I bought it for him specially – the one of our beach in Tasmania. The one with the myrtle frame that Dad had sent over specially – oh and his diary, that's missing too.'

'Don't worry.' Patrick smiled. 'They'll bring the rest of his stuff over tomorrow.' I nodded, pretending to be reassured.

John let go of my hand and held on to Patrick firmly as he struggled out of the wheelchair. Patrick turned the chair and took it away. Suddenly, a voice snarled behind me,

'Go away!'

I turned swiftly to see an old man, tufts of whiskers still on his cheeks.

'I don't want you here!' he shouted.

'It's all right,' I said, my heart pounding. 'I'm going.' I swiftly walked away. glancing behind me before I went round the corner. John stood awkwardly and stared at what must have been Richard. There was no communication between them, just two lost people standing close, each with their separate troubled thoughts.

'Hello.' It was Ed. 'I've just come on duty.' He came closer to me and whispered. 'Glad I've found you here. Now's the time. Are you ready?'

Chapter 20

I looked at him blankly. Of course, the notes – more evidence that Tamara was up to mischief. If only we could really *prove* what she was doing, we might even get her removed from her position of chair of the committee that was deciding John's fate. It seemed so obvious that she was the cause of all the financial difficulties. Get rid of her and maybe fewer wards would be closed, more patients would get the care they needed and carers like me wouldn't have to go through the same hell. If only—

'Er Patrick,' I concentrated on keeping a sincere look. 'Did I see John's notes come with him? May I see them?'

'Well—' Patrick glanced behind at a patient shuffling towards him.

'It's OK,' Ed smiled, 'I'll take her,' and he took my arm and we walked swiftly towards the office. I glanced back at John who was still staring blankly at Richard.

There was no one in the office. Ed rapidly unlocked the door and we dashed inside. He turned on the printer. I could see John's name on a file on the desk. Ed grabbed the file, 'I'll be quicker?' I nodded. He rifled through the letters. 'Aha! I know he should have continuing care and yet here is a letter signed by Tamara herself – demanding money. You probably haven't got it yet.' He took it to the printer. 'More info is in here,' and he unlocked the filing cabinet. 'Now what was the name of those carers? Ah yes, Evans and the others, ah Peterson.' He whipped out the files. 'Stand guard will you?' he asked as he leafed through the files. 'Here they are. This one confirms continuing care and this one is demanding money.' He kept the two files open on the desk as he took photocopies.

I stood nervously at the door, my heart hammering. I saw a shadow in the corridor. 'Someone's coming!' I hissed. Ed froze. The owner of the shadow gradually revealed himself – an old man, a patient, shuffling aimlessly in his confusion. Seeing us, he came up to the door and started tapping on the window. Tap tap tap. Tap tap tap.

'Hurry up Ed!' I called.

'It's OK,' Ed said as he replaced the page on the printer and set the machine in motion again. 'It's just Adrian – he'll do that for hours.'

He shoved the original pages in the files, replaced John's file on the desk, stuffed the others back into the cabinet and locked it. 'Now for the administrator's hoard.' He dashed to the desk and fumbled with the lock on the bottom drawer until it opened.

'I didn't think you'd have a key for that,' I said, watching Adrian carefully. His eyes were blank as he tapped. Glancing behind him I could see the corridor was still empty.

'I don't,' he said, quickly rifling through the contents. 'This'll do,' and he shot over to the printer.

Tap tap tap. Adrian put his nose up to the window, his beady eyes now watching Ed closely.

A voice called from outside, 'Adrian? Where are you? What are you doing?' Tap tap tap. I could see a large round shadow moving in our direction. My heart's pace increased alarmingly, thumping loudly, out of sync with Adrian's tapping.

'For goodness sake, Ed, QUICK!'

'Done!' he said as the printer ground to a halt. He was about to shove the papers under his shirt when I said, 'I'll take them if you like. I can give them to a policewoman I trust. I'll do it – I'd hate you to lose your job.'

'Well, we can't stop now.' He quickly gave me the papers and I shoved them down my blouse. Tap tap tap.

We dashed outside. 'Now Adrian,' Ed said smoothly as he locked the door, 'what are you doing here? Let's take you back to the sitting room where we can keep an eye on you.' He turned to me, 'And then I'll let you out.'

There were tears in my eyes as I finally walked into the fresh air – tears of relief that we hadn't been caught and tears of pity at John's situation. I quickly shoved the copies into the glove compartment with the others and the cheque and sat back in my seat. It was only then that I realized I had forgotten to give John his paper and his chocolates.

I pulled up outside Wendy's place. The roses around her doorway were past their best, but provided a bright contrasting colour to the stark white of the walls of her little thatched cottage. The street was empty. I tore a page from my diary, hastily scribbled a note, took out all of the photocopies, and folded them. There was quite a thick wedge. My feet scrunched on the gravel on her drive as I walked to the black letterbox on the side of the house. The lid squawked as I lifted it, and my fingers trembled as I shoved the papers, cheque and note inside and banged the lid shut. I turned and smiled at the empty street; no one had seen me. I should have taken them home and tried to get extra copies, but it was too risky and we had to move quickly. The letters should still be in the files for the police to find if they were swift enough. For my part, my mission was successfully accomplished. I grinned all the way to the car.

I was latc. I grabbed a bottle of wine from the cupboard and dashed to Gale's. I was looking forward to a relaxed evening, dinner with her husband David and then our usual girlie session afterwards, while he worked upstairs.

'She's in the kitchen,' David greeted me with a smile and took the bottle of wine. His strong jawline, his angular frame and his direct approach to life made him one of the most attractive and dependable people I knew. He did not have the spark that John and Henry evoked in me so Gale knew she was on safe ground. This evening was going to be a lovely, tension-free time, a time with real friends who understood what I was going through. I needed this break after the fractious day I'd had at school.

I found Gale frantically putting the finishing touches to a prawn cocktail. Her face flushed, she gave me a hug and handed me the one she had just finished. I picked up another and took them into their dining room. The shine on the mahogany table reflected the candles perfectly. I could never understand how Gale was just as busy as I and yet she somehow managed to keep her house sparkling and everything in order AND on time. No pile of newspapers strewn on the floor here.

We were soon at the table, David filling our wine glasses with a dark red wine. I was too tired to worry about where the wine came from, and anyway, I knew it would be good. David took his wines, like life, seriously.

'So how are you?' David's brown eyes looked straight into mine. I felt like one of his clients being given the cue to tell all, but stopped myself in time.

I shrugged my shoulders. 'School's horrendous, so I'd rather not talk about it, John's getting worse, and is suspected of murdering Mark King and the hospital's now making life difficult for both of us, otherwise, everything is fine.'

'You too,' Gale said.

I raised an eyebrow.

'You're having trouble with the hospital management.' Gale glanced at her husband. He nodded. 'We're all being threatened with redundancies.'

'No! But I thought you said you were short-staffed?'

'Exactly. How they have the gall to cut down the staff we've got beggars belief. Sandra and I were just saying how if only Leonie had stood up for us at the meeting the—'

David interrupted. 'While they are legally entitled to reduce staff, it does have ethical considerations. No doubt you two will be able to talk more about your personal experiences after dinner,' his voice was calm and sympathetic.

Like a couple of chastised schoolgirls we grinned at each other.

David continued, 'You both might like to know, I have been looking into the way the hospital management at John's hospital have been behaving and one of the names on the board stood out.'

'Yes?' I asked.

'I'm sure I've come across the name Dighton before, in addition to what Gale has been telling me, it's something to do with a case a few years ago.'

'Really?' now I *was* interested.

'Yes, I didn't have time to look into it, but would you like me to?'

'Yes, definitely. That would be great.' I thought about the cheque and copies of letters I'd given Wendy and nearly said something, but as I didn't know how or when Wendy was going to use them, I decided not to say anything about that, not yet. I didn't trust her partner.

'It'll take a lot to shift things. The board and especially the chair of the committee, Tamara, seem so determined to do what they want and will do it whatever the circumstances. I'm not sure any of the members have any morals at all and whatever you find out may not stop them anyway,' I said.

'There are ways—' David nodded to me, raised his glass and took a sip. 'I'll look into it tomorrow afternoon and while I'm at it, I'll find out who is recommended as the best lawyer for dealing with NHS cases – just in case.'

'Oh thank you, David, but I know I couldn't afford to pay a lawyer.'

'Don't you worry about that – I have my contacts – so I'll ask around will I?'

'Oh yes please, thank you!' I raised my drink to him, Gale joined me and we touched glasses. I could hardly wait to know what David could find out. That would be one in the eye for the pompous Tamara and the chequc. Surcly the cheque would bring about her downfall. I so wished Wendy could tell me what was happening, but I knew she couldn't, not if she valued her job. I knew there was no hurrying her or David, for that matter, I'd have to bide my time and be patient, which was definitely NOT one of my characteristics.

The dinner passed without any other revelations. Gale and I behaved ourselves and joined in the talk about the law, the legal profession, David's golf handicap, their proposed holiday in Spain and events on at Ely Cathedral. They were friends of the cathedral and I agreed to go with them to an evening talk there the following month. I had realized by now that although I needed every hour of the day to keep up with my marking and school paperwork, the after school activities and evening classes, I also needed a life if I was to remain sane. A picture of John, his angry stare and the depressed atmosphere of his new ward flashed into my thoughts. I sighed and forced myself to focus on the conversation we were having about the cathedral.

The meal over, David kissed Gale and went upstairs to work. Gale and I began to clear the plates and started the washing-up.

We filled the dishwasher and Gale was scrubbing a pan in the sink. I held a tea towel ready. 'No need to dry these,' she said. 'I'll leave them to drain on the draining board. You can go and open the bottle of red waiting for us in the sitting room if you like.'

We eventually sat down and relaxed, a full glass of red wine each in our hands.

'So what *IS* happening at your hospital?' I gave Gale the cue to continue the conversation her husband had dissuaded her from having at dinner.

'Well, as I was saying, we've been told there will be a lot of redundancies and Leonie looked straight at me when she was telling us all. If only Sandra had stood up to her.'

'But would it've made any difference? If they've decided to give out redundancies there's nothing you can do to stop it. I guess complaining won't do any good.'

'Why not? We can at least make things difficult for them. Our union is on our side.'

We sat in silence for a few moments. I suddenly had a thought.

'Maybe David will find out enough incriminating evidence on the dreaded Tamara and the board that they'll be forced to resign.'

'Even better,' Gale's eyes sparkled. 'Maybe one of the Dightons, or perhaps both, will be discovered as the perpetrators of Mark King's death. That would certainly put an end to their connivance. I can just imagine the scheming Tamara planning some elaborate scheme to cause his demise, although I'm not sure how or why she would want to do such a thing?'

'Maybe they have some dark secret that Mark King discovered, so they had to keep him quiet.' I grinned mischievously and then, suddenly felt queasy. What if she'd seen me grab the cheque? Would she realise what had happened when she couldn't find it?

Gale, for once, hadn't noticed my sudden change. 'But surely it would be another board member, one who was closer to them, who may have discovered something about them.'

'Who knows? The Dightons are on all sorts of boards, they were on at least one that Mark King belonged to as well. Health, education, who knows?'

Gale looked serious. 'Yes, but they would have no real hold on him, why should he care what they knew or thought? Unless—'

'Yes, unless—?'

'Unless it was so bad that it would have ruined his career.'

'Well he did have affairs with some of the new staff.'

'That wouldn't be enough – it might've caused a divorce, but there are lots of headmasters who are divorced these days. It's almost part of the job. He didn't carry on with any of the children? That would certainly end all hope of keeping his job.'

'No,' I shook my head. 'No chance. He wouldn't have been that daft.'

'Well, if David manages to find out something it may stop me being made redundant – that would take the weight off my mind at least.'

'And if he finds out some juicy bit of gossip about the Dightons that would stop Tamara in her tracks, there may be some hope for John and the other dementia patients. They may be able to stay where they are at least and not have their lives shattered by being dumped from pillar to post as their wards are shut down.' I shivered. 'I still have the niggling feeling John was somehow involved in Mark King's death. It's a pity we can't charge the Dightons just because of our suspicions or that we know they're an evil, conniving couple of misfits.'

'Then half of Ely would be put away.' Gale grinned but then became serious again. 'Well, it was Dennis Dighton who found Mark. It's always the first person on the scene that is a major suspect.'

'Do you know what?'

'No.'

'This is all wishful thinking. We really have no idea – let's hope David finds something concrete. It could have happened some time ago, if at all, so it will probably have nothing to do with Mark King's murder, but it may stop the health service messing up people's lives so much.'

'Let's hope so. Drink?' Gale stood up and refilled our glasses.

'What will you do if you are made redundant?'

'Try to find another job, I guess. I could always become an agency nurse. They're paid much better.'

'Well, why not?'

'The hours can sometimes be dreadful and you never know if and when you'll get your next job.'

I took another drink of wine before continuing. 'I suppose so, but it'd be much better than supply teaching.' Flashes of an angry young boy having a tantrum because he couldn't ransack the instrument cupboard came into mind. I'd made my mind up then to avoid supply teaching at all costs. I shook my head. 'I mean, if your lot keep on getting rid of staff, they'll finally wake up and have to employ people back so you might be all right after all – redundancy money plus temp rates – it happens all the time.'

'Yeah, but it's the tension that's getting to me.'

'You? Really?' I laughed but Gale just looked down.

'There's a limit. The atmosphere on the ward is terrible. Everyone's looking over their shoulder. You daren't do anything that's not within the rules. It gets ridiculous sometimes and the patients are suffering.'

'It must be awful and I thought I was the only one with problems.'

The room felt heavy with our depressed thoughts.

'Come on, we're supposed to be cheering ourselves up. Let's talk about brighter things.'

'Agreed. So, what about this holiday you've planned?'

We talked well into the night, even after David announced that he was going to bed. We ignored the hint and after our second bottle had been emptied, I glanced at my watch and scrambled to my feet. I was a little slower than expected. Gale hung onto her doorway and watched me stagger home safely. After I had finally got the key into the lock and opened the door, she waved and I stumbled inside. I ignored the cold and lonely atmosphere in the house. Tonight I wasn't going to feel sorry for myself, I was going to focus on setting the alarm, going to bed, and only remembering the good parts of our conversation. I would worry about everything else tomorrow.

Chapter 21

I dragged myself through the next morning. The lead violinist in the orchestra for assembly forgot his instrument, the bass line was missing because the players were all ill and I lost my free lesson because I had to supervise 3B in the history room. Bill Greenland was ill.

Still feeling jaded I checked my pigeon hole for more missives from Leonard who was letting everybody know that he was now very much in charge. There was a handwritten envelope. I recognized the writing. It was from Henry. Why on earth would Henry write to me when he could say what he wanted to face-to-face at school anytime? My heart skipped a beat. Maybe it was a love letter. Now I was getting silly. I tore the envelope open. It was a jazzy invitation to Carol's birthday party this Saturday. I glanced along the pigeon holes, most other staff had one, except for the odd, obvious omissions. Ah how tactful. I would write him a reply tonight.

I didn't see much of Henry before Saturday as the school was in a bit of a panic about the inspection that was coming. I tried to tell myself that inspections shouldn't make any difference. They should see us as we are, for if we are doing our jobs properly, everything would be fine. However, I knew this not to be true and I joined the rest of the staff in doing a lot extra to catch up with the paperwork and tidy the classroom.

Saturday finally came and with Sundays taken up with seeing John, I was determined to have an afternoon and night off. The lawn and the ironing could wait for once. As I tried to make up my mind what to wear I felt nervous. Why on earth would I feel nervous when it was Henry and Carol!

In my heart of hearts, I knew why I was nervous but I also knew nothing would come of our relationship. I didn't do that kind of thing, but it didn't stop me feeling that way, did it? But I would still have to face John the next day, and even though I was never sure he fully understood what was going on, there was something between us that would never die.

Sometimes John hardly recognized me, but at other times he seemed to understand me and seemed to know exactly how I was feeling, so I didn't trust myself. Besides, I couldn't be unfaithful. John had been good to me in the years we were together, when he was all right. I'd really let rip once, when things were getting on top of me and instead of reacting and letting a whopping great argument develop, he just looked at me and when I had finally wound down, gave me a huge hug. He knew me, he knew how to deal with me.

My heart was thumping when I knocked on the door. Would it be Carol or Henry who would open it?

Leonard's chiselled face stared at me. 'Oh,' I let slip. I gave him a weak smile and held my bottle of wine forward for him to take, but he ignored it.

'Come in,' he ordered, a tinge of his daytime bossy tone remaining.

'Thank you,' I said, using my formal voice. I made a beeline for the sitting room, stopping in the hallway to hand the bottle to Vicky, whip out the birthday card, and sling the coat on top of another one on the pegs.

'Carol's in the kitchen,' Vicky said, still holding the bottle.

Carol looked resplendent, her face animated as she chatted to Anthea. Anthea had lost some of the haunted look she had since her husband had died, she seemed more relaxed and was enjoying Carol's idle chatter. Anthea's black dress was almost formal, expensive and in perfect taste, while Carol's was a close-fitting, colourful affair that showed every asset. Henry was standing next to her, his arm lovingly around her waist. I had to admit it, I was certainly no competition for Carol.

'Happy birthday!' I kissed her on the cheek and put the card into her free hand. Her other hand was clutching a glass of bubbly.

'Why thank you,' she said, raising her glass. 'Have some champagne.'

I said hello to Anthea while Henry poured me a glass. 'Here you are and you *can* drink it all at once! Everyone's in the sitting room. Come and say hello.'

Still clutching the bottle he shepherded me forward. The room was packed. The partygoers had grouped into separate packs – girls one side, boys the other.

Henry whispered in my ear. 'Glad you've come. Our mission seems to have been successful – book safely returned, nothing suspected.' He coughed and speaking louder said, 'We need to liven things up a bit. For a start you sort out the fellows and I'll chat to the girls.'

'Is that wise?' I grinned, but walked up to the men's group nevertheless. I stood between two of the shortest members of the party. On the left was Paul Barker, but the one on the right, although he looked familiar, I had forgotten his name.

'I'm Sally Wilks,' I said holding my hand out to the one on my right. He turned to me, his podgy paw gripping mine and said, 'George Evans, married to the best speech therapist in town.'

'Ah yes, of course. I think we've met before.'

'I joke when I say she's the best in town – she's the only one. She is so dedicated to her work, she never changes – even her way of speaking makes me feel like I'm one of her pupils. I tease her about it. Does it annoy you too?'

I didn't dare answer. Paul Barker, on my left, spoke quickly clipping his words as though they were being shot out of a machine gun in rapid succession, 'As you know, I'm Paul Barker, Financial Director of Gravesall.' He smiled coolly as he held out his hand.

'Oh yes, of course,' I said, concentrating on gripping his hand firmly. I inwardly sighed. This was going to be hard work. How on earth had Henry and Carol made friends with this character? Wasn't he responsible for all the ward closures and redundancies?

As if reading my thoughts, Paul said, 'I met Carol through her father. He was my stockbroker in the early days before I took on this job. I'm also a friend of your school's bursar, we trained together.'

'Oh,' I drank some of my wine. We stood in silence, searching for something to say.

At last George spoke. 'I have to give Teresa her due. She's in great demand these days. She was thinking of starting her own business as an independent as well as working for the education authority. Can you suggest someone as an advisor?'

'Well I certainly can't do it,' Paul said.

George cleared his throat. 'It was just a question, no matter. How's Gravesall these days?' he asked, in desperation.

'Fine. Everything is ticking over nicely, the changes we are making are having a great effect. We're managing to avoid making any redundancies in our management team.'

I swallowed and looked down at my feet. I would not rise to the bait. However, maybe now was my opportunity to find out a bit more about Tamara and her antics? I raised my eyes and looked at him. 'So Tamara Dighton will remain as chair of her committee?'

'Of course. She is one of the best chairpersons we've had. She's taken on the whole responsibility for her area. She even helps me with their accounts where the patients have to contribute. I just have to approve them.'

I stared at him.

'Tamara Dighton?' George asked.

'Oh, she's the chairperson of the committee that's dealing with my husband,' I said quickly, my eyes still glued to Paul Barker's.

'Oh?'

I turned to George. 'My husband's been sectioned into Gravesall,' I said, my tone harsher than I intended.

George paled. 'I'm *so* sorry.'

'It's all right,' I said, my eyes smarting. 'We're at a party now, let's change the subject.' I had an inkling that I should know what he did for a living, but I asked anyway. 'What's your line of business?'

Before he could answer, raucous laughter filled the room. We looked across. Henry had certainly livened up the girls.

'Tell you what,' said George, 'Teresa seems to be having fun, let's join them. We could all do with a few laughs.' He whispered in my ear. 'I'm an undertaker, you see.'

I gave him a quick smile in recognition before he and I hurried towards the group. I looked back to see Paul remaining where he was. He obviously had no time for frivolity.

'And remember that time we were supposed to be having coffee after school in the cafe over the road and the daredevil Wayne decided to come over to us and make mischief?' Teresa said, her voice light and feathery.

'Yeah. The look on his face when I invited him to sit down and told him he would be paying,' said Henry.

'He soon sloped off,' she giggled, her broad smile lighting up her elfin face.

'Ah,' George broke in, smiling. 'So you two have coffee together after school eh? Is this what you get up to?'

Teresa rushed to her husband's side and took his arm. 'Yes, silly, and that's all. I know you have coffee with your colleagues too—the live ones I mean.'

Henry and Vicky looked puzzled for a moment.

'Oh,' I said quickly, 'George is an undertaker.'

'Ah,' said Rita, 'you buried my mother. It was a very good service.'

George bowed. 'I thank you.'

Vicky said, 'Are you going to do Mark King's funeral when they release his body?'

Teresa and Rita spoke together. 'Vicky!'

Vicky shrugged her shoulders. 'I'm only asking what everyone wants to know.'

'As a matter of fact, I am,' George said in his rich calm voice, 'and I think the funeral is going to be scheduled soon. I heard the police are going to give up looking for the murderer. Rumour has it that they think they know who did it, but they don't have any proof,' he turned his head, avoiding my eyes, 'so, they'll probably be releasing his body in the near future.'

'Oh,' Vicky said. 'That must be worrying for Anthea – I mean that they haven't found the murderer, although she will probably be pleased to have the funeral over and done with.'

So they still thought John had done it, but couldn't prove it. Perhaps they'd decided John was responsible and I'd have to live with that for the rest of my life. Would John ever confess in his ramblings? Would I have to wait on tenterhooks until he did? Would he be believed?

'Stop digging,' Henry said to Vicky. 'Anthea's here somewhere.' He looked around. 'Oh. Maybe not, she's probably in the kitchen with Carol still. Let me top up your glasses.' Henry left the group to go to the sideboard for another bottle.

'I don't know why I always seem to put my foot in it,' Vicky wailed.

'Join the club. I have the same problem,' I commiserated. 'Although sometimes you can use it to advantage, you know. If you get a reputation for calling a "spade a spade", when you've got to stand up to bullying and the like, you get some leeway when—'

Suddenly, above the murmur of the party guests the strident tones of Tamara Dighton rose.

'I'm SO sorry we're late,' she bellowed. There was a moment of suspended silence in the room.

'Oh God, not that insufferable woman,' I said to Vicky. 'Why on earth did they invite her?'

'I think Carol has been doing some dressmaking for her and isn't one of her friends a cousin or something?'

'Oh yes, that's right.' I snatched a drink from my glass. 'I hope to God the cousin is here to entertain her.'

Vicky looked around. 'No, if I remember what Henry said, the cousin couldn't come today.'

I looked closely at Vicky. She was obviously still in close contact with our Henry. How close, I wondered? I shook my head – more paranoia setting in.

Suddenly, Tamara's voice was right behind me. 'Why Mrs Wilks. Fancy finding *you* here.'

I choked on my drink. She tutted impatiently while I coughed.

'You have a troublesome cough, don't you dear?' she said.

In the last paroxysms of my spluttering I noticed her green dress, obviously highly expensive, but doing nothing to hide her bulging body. I frowned, ignoring her barbed comment, praying that she hadn't worked out that it was me who had stolen her cheque. I decided to brazen it out. 'And fancy finding *you* here too,' I retorted.

Ignoring my comment, Tamara opened her large mouth and let the words spill out. 'It was SO good of my cousin to ask if we could come instead of her. After all, Carol did some lovely dressmaking for me. The least I could do is come to help celebrate her birthday. We have been SO busy lately; I wasn't sure we could come but I felt we just had to squeeze it in somehow.' She looked me up and down. 'I hope you are now happy that we have changed our meeting to a time on Friday that suits you Sally, for it took some doing. But then, I've always been considerate to those in trouble, like you, and I was finally able to rearrange it, thanks to my excellent organisational skills.'

'Yeah, like the way you organise the accounts,' I muttered, expecting her not to hear.

'What do you mean!' She glared at me. 'You're talking about something you know nothing about. It's none of your business!'

'Ah,' I said. Oh God, I'd done it now.

'You know, Dennis,' she said to her husband as he came to her side. 'Here's another person poking their nose into something that is none of their concern.' She turned to me. 'If you're not careful my girl, you'll be getting yourself into some serious trouble.' She took her husband's arm. 'Come Dennis, we have better people to speak to,' and they marched towards Paul.

Vicky had stood inert through our conversation. 'Goodness,' she said, 'what was that all about?'

'Well Tamara chairs the committee that handles my husband's care. You know he's been sectioned into Gravesall?'

She nodded. 'Yes, I know. I'm SO sorry, but why did she react so badly when you mentioned accounts?'

I leaned forward. 'Why indeed? The Dightons have more money than they could possibly earn. The other day, I overheard her boasting about all their second properties they have in Norfolk, France and even one in Australia. How can anyone afford that?

Paul Barker told me she helps keep her own committee's accounts, so I was just wondering—'

'Yes. You might have a point—' Vicky paused, glancing towards the subject of our conversation. Tamara was in fine form, her voice rising above the general hubbub as she talked at a small crowd trapped in the corner of the room. 'But even so,' Vicky said, lowering her voice, 'if she's that dishonest, are you wise in saying anything? I mean Mark King probably didn't die of natural causes, did he? Someone was responsible. We don't know it wasn't the Dightons, or one of them at least. Maybe he found out that they were diddling the accounts and so he had to go.'

'It's possible,' I mused, as a slow chill crept up my spine. 'Tamara's husband was the first on the scene. He could've easily arranged to meet Mark to have a drink together and done the deed then. All it needed was to inject a dose of the poison.'

Vicky nodded, her face pale and set. 'Maybe.' Her eyes were moist.

I spoke softly. 'You knew Mark quite well, didn't you?' I continued, 'Perhaps Mark told you something?'

She shook her head and said, 'Must go and see Carol,' and made a dash for the doorway.

I watched her slim figure retreat, her long black hair swinging with each swift step.

# Chapter 22

As I glanced over at the crowd in the corner, I saw Paul move swiftly towards Tamara. He caught her on the arm and she swivelled round, her body fat still wobbling as she faced him. After his first question, she gave a cry of indignation, but I couldn't quite hear what she was saying. Their discussion was becoming heated, Tamara's flabby cheeks flushed and Paul's jaw was set, the tone of his words sounding more hard-edged and sinister than I'd ever heard before. I moved towards them and as I was just about close enough to hear, I felt a hand clamp onto my arm.

'How are you?' Anthea's perfect features were marred slightly with a looseness to her jaw, her eyes duller than usual as though she had found the solution to soothing the acute pain she must have suffered with the sudden death of her husband.

I was tempted to answer her truthfully, but only replied, 'All right, thank you.'

She waited, forcing me to continue the conversation. 'You look much better, since—' I'd done it again. Tact, whenever would I learn to be tactful?

'It's all an act,' she said, still holding firmly onto my arm. 'I'm actually finding it very hard, living in that house alone with all those memories and with the uncertainty about how he died, who did it, how and why. If only I knew.' She stared hard at me, willing me to provide answers.

'It must be awful,' I said, trying to sound sympathetic, but all I wanted was to hear what Tamara and Paul were saying. Their voices were now raised and I could hear the odd word or two like, 'dare you' and 'later, not now', the pitch and tone of their voices agitated and tense. Anthea's grip tightened, bringing me back to our conversation. 'I'm sorry,' I said, 'I can't give you any answers. While John did some strange things before he was put into hospital, I'm certain he couldn't have harmed Mark, not really.' She gazed at me disbelievingly.

'Look,' I said, feeling exasperated. 'You'd better ask the police, after all, they're the ones that are investigating. Why not contact them tomorrow and ask them?'

She released her hand. 'I suppose I could.' She looked vulnerable and puzzled.

'I must have a word with Henry,' I said quickly, seeing him standing beyond the rowing couple. I arrived just in time to hear Paul say, 'I'll be round your place tomorrow night. Make sure you are both in.'

'Well—' Tamara started. 'I'm n—'

'Tomorrow!' he snapped. 'Now where's this Leonard you told me about?' She stood open-mouthed as Paul stormed towards the kitchen. This must've been the first time I'd seen Tamara beaten.

I came closer to Henry. 'What was all that about? Did you hear?'

'I couldn't help hearing. I think the wool has finally fallen from Paul's eyes and he's asking to have another look at Tamara's accounts. She didn't like the idea one bit. Now he thinks something fishy's going on and not only that, it looks as though Leonard is also going to have a pasting, although I'm not sure why. What had Leonard to do with Paul?'

'Maybe the accounts book John and I saw,' I suggested, and the more I thought about it, the more I thought it was the key to what might have happened. 'That's it!' I cried. Suddenly softening my voice, I whispered into Henry's ear, 'The girls' names on the bottom of the page, written in pencil were pseudonyms for people receiving money from the school funds. That envelope that I'd snatched from Tamara was labelled Vicky but the cheque was addressed to Tamara.'

'You're right!' Henry said but then frowned. 'But Leonard, why Leonard, he's surely not in the same bracket as Tamara?' he asked.

I smiled as I imagined the hard-nosed Mean Machine and the domineering blob, hand in hand. It just didn't tally—but then—

'Did I hear you taking my husband's name in vain?' Dorothy Hall butted in, holding out her empty glass to Henry. He blushed, took the hint, and bowed as he accepted her glass. He then raised an eyebrow to me, but my glass was still half full, so I shook my head. Henry headed for the kitchen. As soon as his back turned, Dorothy hissed to me, 'What've you been saying? What's going on?'

'Nothing, nothing—well nothing important,' I gabbled quickly, 'and I don't know anything about what's going on.' In desperation, I smiled and said,

'Leonard's making a good job as a substitute headmaster, isn't he?'

Dorothy's expression immediately changed. Her eyes lit up and her resolute cheek bones stood out more firmly as she raised her head with utter conviction saying, 'I think you'll find he'll soon be appointed as permanent headmaster, it's only a matter of formality.'

I cleared my throat. 'Well that'll be wonderful.' I tried to sound enthusiastic, but I knew that I'd made a poor job of it. The thought of the Mean Machine fully in charge of our school filled me with unease. While he was certainly efficient and a strong leader, there was a hidden side to him that, if allowed to flourish, could wreak havoc. Wasn't it him who'd made such a fuss about the film the education department wanted to make? Leonard, who'd been teaching history at the time, suddenly shouted at the staff meeting that he wanted nothing to do with it; he wasn't prepared to have anyone film him in class. Mark, never one for confrontation, just shrugged, and changed the subject. What had Leonard to hide then? And what special relationship did he have with the head that stopped him being chastised at the meeting?

'Dorothy, I must have a word with you.' Leonard suddenly arrived, grabbed Dorothy's arm and led her towards the empty corner of the room. Making sure no one could hear them, they leaned towards each other, their heads almost touching and launched into a deep discussion. Something was obviously wrong and Leonard kept looking over at Paul. Mid-conversation, Henry arrived with Dorothy's drink, saw that she had moved and made a beeline for her. As he caught up with them, the couple stopped talking, lips compressed, waiting until Henry left them and came back to where I was standing.

'It's hell in the kitchen,' he said, taking a sip from his replenished drink. 'It's a real struggle to get to the drinks, Carol and her cronies from school are reminiscing. They'll be there for ages.'

'So, what were Leonard and Dorothy saying when you got near them?'

'Oh,' Henry took a moment to recollect. 'I couldn't hear all of it, but Leonard is definitely in Paul's bad books for some reason.'

'I thought as much. So, Leonard was in on something too do you think?'

'Not for us to know,' Henry said out loud and then leaned towards me, 'I'll find out later,' he said softly. Then he stretched his neck to see where everyone was placed. 'It's getting a bit dull at this party. Let's liven it up again. Now where are the girls?'

Chapter 23

The weeks passed without mishap. I pulled the blankets over me firmly every night, willing myself to sleep and forget the cold, lonely feeling that threatened to overwhelm me now I was finally alone, truly alone. The visits to John were as traumatic as ever, but even though I was now used to seeing him in his new ward, the fear and sorrow that invaded my

234

feelings as I approached the place on each visit, never faded. Tamara still held boring, useless meetings and I reported to Ed that nothing had changed.

Then, one day as I was putting some copying for Betty to do on her desk, she whispered to me to come and see her after school. I raised an eyebrow, but she simply repeated what she'd said, her expression stolidly unchanged, 'After school.'

I spent the rest of the day wondering what it was about and why the secrecy? Perhaps she'd found out who had written the poison pen letters? Or did she want to warn me that I was in more trouble with Leonard? The classes helped me forget momentarily. Darren had started shouting again in his lesson. As I was writing the heading for our work on symphonies on the board, I asked,

'Darren, you're good at spelling, can you spell the name Haydn?'

As I feared, he ignored me, and shouted to the boy next to him, 'You've got my pen. Give it to me!'

I swung round to see Darren grabbing at the hand of the boy behind him. I yelled at the both of them, 'Stop it! Alan, give back the pen!' Alan glared at me for a second and then reluctantly threw the pen onto Darren's desk.

'Now, can anyone in the room spell 'Haydn? Darren, are you sure you can't?'

Again Darren ignored me, sorting his pens into his pencil case.

'Come on Darren, stop being so awkward. You're one of the most unhelpful children I know. Just answer the question will you?' My voice was bitter and angry. I hadn't meant to be like that. It certainly wasn't going to help. 'I'm waiting,' I continued.

Daniel, a scrawny boy just behind Darren, gave him an almighty shove. Darren fell forward smashing his face on his desk. He suddenly rose, roaring like a wounded bear, grabbed hold of Daniel by the collar and in one swift movement head butted him. Within seconds there was a heap of writhing bodies rolling on the floor, the rest of the class yelling and banging their desks, 'Fight! Fight! Fight!' Panic rose in me like a tidal wave.

'Stop it!' I screamed, my voice hardly distinguishable in the ruckus. 'Class, stop this noise NOW! You don't want more detentions do you? Now stop!' I may as well have screamed at the wind. My heart beating ten to the dozen I threw myself into the melee, wrestled with the first body I came across and yanked him to his feet. He stood flushed and panting.

Heart still pounding, I yelled, 'Now pick up those chairs and straighten the desks!' Still panting profusely, I glanced at the classroom window. No glaring face of Leonard appeared, thank God. I turned to the class. 'Now SIT down and pay attention.' Both boys reluctantly sat down, their flushed faces scowling and after a lot of chair scraping and noisy banter the rest of the class was also in some sort of order.

Taking a deep breath, I began the lesson again, 'Haydn, is spelt H-A-Y-D-N, notice there is no 'e' in his name.' The lesson had calmed down enough to hear me by now and I glared at the pupils while they wrote in their books. I remembered my mysterious assignation with Betty and looking at Darren's scowl, I realized I could also see Darren's file at the same time. Perhaps I would be able to find out just what was wrong with the boy. It was hard to concentrate in the next few lessons before the final bell rang.

As the last pupil left the classroom, I grabbed my bags and rushed out. Henry was coming towards me. I hastily waved to him as I joined the stream of pupils heading towards the exit and I heaved a sigh of relief when I finally reached the reception. Betty was busy with a long queue of miscreants wanting their report cards stamped.

'Come round to mine for a cup of tea later,' she called above the bevy of youngsters. 'In about half an hour? I should be finished by then.'

I nodded reluctantly, but stood my ground waiting until I could gain access to the pupils' files. When there was a gap between pupils I called, 'Can I have the key to the filing cabinet please?' I thanked God I didn't have to ask Leonard for it, he was still waiting for my letter requesting a transfer and I was starting to run out of excuses.

'Oh yes, of course,' Betty leaned under the desk and retrieved the key.

There was no one in the room when I entered. I soon found Darren's file and was about to open it.

'What are you doing here?' I jumped at the sound of Leonard's voice as I remembered our last encounter in the filing cabinet room. 'Look,' I said, 'I'm so sorry about the letter – it IS coming – I keep forgetting to bring it.'

'Be that as it may, what are you doing here now?' Even though I had a perfect right to be there and to look at the pupils' files, a flash of insecurity and guilt swept through me. I turned, and making a conscious effort to steady my voice I said, 'I'm looking up Darren Hart's file.'

'Why? He's been here for so long, you should know all you want about him by now.'

'Yes, yes I do, but I just wanted to check?' I forced myself to stare straight into those unyielding eyes. Leonard shrugged and went into his office, glancing briefly in my direction before he closed his door.

I was expecting the usual split family, Darren adopted or in a one-parent situation, probably with the father, hence the lack of nurture and the need to lash out. His written work was usually surprisingly up to scratch, so I expected his IQ to be perfectly all right. Had he seen a psychologist? This report would give me what I wanted.

My mouth swung open as I read the contents of the file. He was the child of middle-class parents who were still married and who had made appointments to see the headmaster on a number of occasions, expressing concern about their son. They wanted to make sure the staff understood that although Darren had already learnt to speak well, since an accident on his go-kart at home, he had suddenly become deaf. Mark King's writing advised us to sit Darren at the front of the classroom and make sure he could see our mouths when we were speaking. I leaned back on the filing cabinet. So THAT was what it was all about! I cringed as I remembered turning to the board while asking him question after question. I remembered my anger rising, my barbed comments to him cutting across the classroom when he hadn't replied. It had all been my fault and my fault alone. Why didn't I guess what was wrong? What kind of a teacher was I?

My confidence at rock bottom, I carefully replaced the file, locked the cabinet and left the room. Head down, eyes on the floor, I slipped past Leonard's office to the reception. Betty was still very busy, but in her usual multi-tasking magic, she extricated the key from me, put it away and mouthed, 'See you in fifteen' and smiled at the next pupil, his grubby hand pushing a piece of paper at her face.

I put my bags into the back of my car, grabbed my handbag, locked the car and decided to take a leisurely walk in Ely before knocking on Betty's door in fifteen minutes. It had been raining, so the ground was soaked, puddles of water gathered on the path, reflecting dull grey clouds that looked as if they had finally spent all their contents.

The city wore a shroud of stubborn austerity, rows of tiny bricks packing centuries-old walls. My worries paled into insignificance as I thought of the thousands of monks, nuns, church dignitaries, craftsmen and families who had worked, lived and loved in this city for centuries. I walked towards Barton Square. A watery sun crept out for a moment, the pools of water in the gutters and on the road glistening. The square was unoccupied – too cold and damp, too dark for it to be the gathering place for the locals.

My thoughts were interrupted as a car sped past the Porta and went straight down Back Hill. Now everyone was in a hurry, busy with no time to linger. No matter what mood the city evoked there was one treasure, besides the cathedral itself, that stood out. It was the Porta, the ancient gateway to the abbey. It was easy to imagine horse and cart trundling beneath its towering vaults, the cart awkward and bowed from its heavy load of food and wine, but today cars swept through, seemingly oblivious to its history, nothing mattered but the now, the immediate moment when something very important had to be done, something that in the whole scheme of things, was nothing.

What did it matter that I'd failed a student? No one else shared this knowledge and in years to come, no one would worry whether Mrs Wilks had faced the deaf child when she spoke to him or not. But the murder of Mark King, that could well be remembered and whether I liked it or not, that really mattered. My stomach tightened. Would John really understand if he was found guilty? In his confused madness, whatever he did, he would have believed that it had been the right thing to do, so would he be to blame?

Then I knew, it was me who really wanted to know, I needed to know that the feelings I had for my husband were based on an unspoken understanding that no matter what he did in his illness, the honest, worthy soul that was the John Wilks I knew, was real. No matter how dangerous he had become, the real John was still inside somewhere.

The cathedral clock chimed the quarter hour. It was time to call at Betty's. It was still light and the street was now busier with traffic spilling out from the school and dashing through the city. A family, mother and two children were in front of me on the path, so I kept a slow pace behind them. I was in no hurry, for I wasn't absolutely sure Betty had got home yet.

When I arrived at Betty's, the door swung open straightaway after my first tentative knock. The same warmth and friendliness exuded from the ancient walls but Betty's face was tense, her movements more nervous and hurried than usual.

'Cup of tea?' she asked.

'Can I help?'

'No,' she said as she moved swiftly towards the kitchen, her voice becoming softer as she went further into the house. 'It's been one of those days, I certainly need one myself.'

After she had brought the tray in and had poured our teas, giving me a larger slice of cake than I wanted, she paused, putting her hands down heavily on her knees, preparing to say something that was obviously going to be difficult for her.

'You know that poison pen letter you gave me?'

'Yes? Do you know who wrote it?'

'Well, yes and no.'

'What do you mean?'

'I'm not absolutely sure, so I don't know what to do. If I report the wrong person, and they're innocent, it could ruin their life. On the other hand, it can't go on, can it?'

'Besides,' I said, 'it could have something to do with Mark's murder, so if you have a strong suspicion, you must report that at least.'

Suddenly the room vibrated with the loud ringing of Betty's phone. She excused herself and picked up the receiver. The voice on the other end was agitated.

'I'm terribly sorry,' Betty panted when she'd put the phone down, 'my sister has been rushed to hospital. I must pack and go to her immediately. I'm now her only family. Do you mind?'

I stood up. 'But – who?'

'Look, I'd rather tell you when I have more time, I'd like to explain—can you come round after I come back from seeing my sister?'

'But when will that be?'

'I'm sorry I have no idea.'

'Can I do anything?'

'No, no, I'll be all right. I'll ring the school first thing in the morning.' Her hands were shaking, she rushed to the door and held it open for me.

There was nothing I could do. The cup rattled in the saucer as I hastily put it down and stumbled outside. Betty closed the door quickly behind me.

## Chapter 24

The weeks passed and still there was no sign of
Betty. Fortunately there had been no more poison
pen letters or at least I hadn't got wind of any. Like a
mesmerized zombie, I followed the routine without
any drastic mishaps. Leonard continued to be a pain
at school, Henry seemed preoccupied with keeping
the girls happy and my weekends were taken up
mowing the lawns and visiting John. I was going
later and later these days, imagining if I stalled for
long enough, something would happen to prevent me
from going, but deep inside I knew I had to leave the
cosiness of my home to face the trauma in the mental
hospital ward where John now lived.

Every moment when I was at home the shadow of
John hung over me. He was still here, the books that
he had read, his bicycle clips, the empty armchair in
the sitting room.

With a heavy heart, I finally left the house and
drove to Gravesall. When I drove into the car park,
everything appeared as normal, the rooks wheeled
and squawked like omens of death overhead.
Ignoring them, I flung open the car door, clicked the
car locked and turned towards Teveran Ward. There
was a huddle of people talking animatedly at the exit
to the car park.

'What's up?' I asked.

A tall woman with a pinched face said, 'They're
closing this ward now.'

'What? Not again? Not so soon?' I suddenly felt
very cold.

A short, stocky man said in a quivery voice, 'Yes. It's awful. I don't know what we are going to do. Mabel couldn't stand another move.'

The first speaker continued, her weathered face frowning. 'Not only that, but they say they are moving the patients to another ward that they are renaming Teveran.'

'How ridiculous!'

'I know,' she said, shrugging her shoulders, 'but what can we do?'

'Very little, I suspect,' I said, 'even if we make a fuss, they'll take no notice. They're so arrogant, they think they can get away with treating the patients like objects that can be shoved from place to place without any consideration of the consequences. They're obviously feeling guilty if they have to try to cover it all up by renaming the ward. However, whatever happens, *we'll* know what they've done. *We'll* remember and although we may not be able to do anything now, we can certainly keep trying and one day it will come out in the open!' I felt angry, very angry. I stormed to the door and banged on the intercom. There was no reply. I dashed to the curtainless window but was met with my reflection. In a fit of fury, I pressed the intercom again and again.

'Yes?' a harassed voice asked.

My voice was harsh as I said, 'It's Mrs Wilks here. Please let me in to see John.'

The door buzzed open. Looking back at the huddled group I pushed my way through the second door. There was only one staff member visible and he had rushed back from letting me in to try to appease two patients who were obviously highly distressed. One was a plump lady in a very agitated state yelling she wanted Fred, while at the other end of the room an old man was pulling a coffee table towards the centre of the room, his crinkled face set in utter determination, oblivious to anyone and anything around him. The remaining patients sat in the high-back chairs muttering to themselves, unaware of the actions of the others, or were shuffling aimlessly about the room, touching everything in their path as though it was something new to feel or something to reassure them that the world about them was real and not a place of shadows and lies. In the corner, a wizened old man was banging the back of the chairs. The lady occupying one of them cried out in protest.

Ignoring the plight of the patients, I rushed to the staff member. His tall figure loomed over a lady, trying to placate her, his muscular arms filling his thin jacket sleeves. In spite of the tension in the room he looked relaxed and friendly.

I stood close to him so that he could hear me. 'Are they really going to close this ward?'

'Yes,' he said as he moved towards the man banging the chairs. The staff member held firmly onto an old man's arm. 'Now Ted, let the people alone. We'll find you something better to do.'

'But why close this ward? It's obviously needed.'

'Goodness knows.' He shrugged. 'We've all been saying they shouldn't but who are we?'

He was right. He wasn't making the decisions. He was the one left to deal with the consequences. It was so frustrating, but I could see that there was nothing I could do or say here that would make any difference. I shrugged my shoulders and went in search of John. He was sitting in a chair at the back of the room, staring at the blank wall, his eyes fixed on something. Another of his nightmares, I thought. It took some time to get him to focus on me and even then, he didn't recognize me.

'So, I can go out with someone else?' I joked. Henry's handsome face tugged at my memory. John did not react. It was as if I wasn't there. It hurt.

He stared at the wall again. 'Spider,' he said. My blood ran cold. Was he seeing spiders or was he remembering something he'd done? Had he left a spider for Mark to find? HAD he really been the killer?

'What do you mean?' I asked. He continued to stare fixedly at the wall.

I tried to convince myself that this was just one of his realistic nightmares. He was imagining it, just as he imagined bulls, sheep, cows and flies invading his room. For now, for my own sanity's sake, I decided that he was just imagining spiders, he was not recalling something from his troubled thoughts about something he had done in the past, something that he felt guilty about.

I waited for another sign, a reaction or a word or two that would reassure me, but nothing happened. He still did not look at me or recognize me. There was nothing I could do. Next time, maybe he would know me and say some more words to reassure me. I got up and moved carefully between the meandering patients to find the member of staff to unlock the door for me. As I stepped outside, I looked for the huddle of people in the car park, but they were gone. A cloud drifted across the sun. A single rook wheeled above me.

The more I thought about the closure, the angrier I became. Something had to happen and soon. What had the police been doing with the cheque? Had Wendy been stopped from presenting the evidence by her partner? What had Gale's husband found out?

As I fumbled with the car door, I decided I would write letters. I would not expect them to achieve anything but I would certainly feel better afterwards. Maybe one of my barbed comments would make some of the culprits pause to think, and maybe even change their minds? Who could say?

When I got home, I stormed into the house. I needed a cup of tea to clear the mind. I put the kettle on, rattled the cup and saucer as I slammed it down on the counter and flung open the fridge for milk. There was none. I stared incomprehensibly at the grime on the empty shelf. Then I remembered. I was supposed to get some yesterday but had completely forgotten. I slammed the door shut. I couldn't stand tea without milk. I looked at the kitchen clock. I was much later than usual. The pub would be open. Sod it! I'd go to the pub for tea tonight, and it wouldn't be tea I'd be having, it would be something stronger.

I grabbed my coat, my handbag and the house keys and stepped outside into the early evening air. I breathed deeply in an effort to subdue the anger that was still roaring inside me. I took in another big breath. This was going to be a long haul; one incident like this was only a pinprick in the lengthy struggle I could see ahead. I would have to learn to control my feelings and think carefully and hard if I were to really help John and his situation. There must be some way to stop them closing the wards.

I looked up at the sky. The clouds gave the sky an eerie tincture. It was as though the day and night couldn't agree whose turn it was, but the very last hues of a dull sunset were disappearing behind the trees and night would soon win. A gentle breeze softened my feelings and I breathed deeply again as my shoes echoed on the pavement. The lights from the pub beckoned.

As I opened the door, I was suddenly greeted with warmth, the warmth of the atmosphere of the room and of the people gathered at the bar. It was like coming home. I glanced at the corner table where John and I used to have a drink or two at the weekends. Last time we'd come, I remembered with a wry smile, John had wandered off, got involved with someone else and invited them home to finish off the best of our whisky in spite of my protests, but that was what John used to do. I had learned to put up with it. After all, life was certainly never dull with John.

'Hello Sally.'

I turned to see Gale sitting at a table near the fireplace.

'Oh, I'd forgotten you come here on Sundays,' I said.

'Come and join us,' Gale raised her glass.

I hesitated for a moment, they looked so cosy, David and her leaning towards each other, Gale's curly hair falling gently across her pale cheek, David's dark-rimmed glasses making him look more serious and concerned than ever. They were obviously having an intimate conversation.

'Yes,' said David, suddenly getting up, 'do come and join us. I've got some information for you.' He pulled an extra chair up to the table. 'Let me get you a drink first.'

'Red wine please.' I smiled gratefully and sat down.

We watched him walk to the bar, his tall frame contrasting with the slumped forms of the tight group of regulars who commandeered the area for themselves every night. We could hear David's clear tones above the general hubbub as he ordered my wine.

'How's it going?' she asked.

'Well, you know. Just as bad. They're now threatening to close the ward John's just been moved to. Worse than that,' my voice rose but I couldn't help it, 'would you believe it, they're trying to cover up what they're doing by moving him to another ward which they're going to rename using the same name as his old ward, so that it looks as though he hasn't moved at all. Can you credit it?'

Gale snorted, 'How stupid is that? I dare say David will have something to say about it when he gets back.'

'About what?' David had moved swiftly away from the bar and put my glass of wine in front of me, the smooth skin of his hands looking tanned in the subdued light of the pub.

'Tell him, Sally.'

So I told him.

'It figures. It's the kind of daft thing they'd do. It makes our job so much easier.'

I tensed my shoulders, waiting for David to tell me what he had discovered.

'Come on David,' Gale said, 'put the poor girl out of her misery and tell her what you found out.'

'Oh, of course.' His voice softened. 'I looked—' he paused and looked around. There was no one in earshot—everyone was focused on the bar, their backs to us. 'I looked the Dightons up and as we suspected, they've been in trouble before—in Australia. It seems that Dennis Dighton was struck off as a doctor when he was there about ten years ago.'

'Really?' I gasped. 'Why?'

David waited, giving himself time to take a drink, 'It was very difficult—I couldn't find out all the details—you know these doctors are a secretive lot. However, I contacted a few mates I know Down Under and I discovered a couple of important things.'

'Yes?' Gale and I asked in chorus.

'Well,' David paused, savouring his moment. 'Apparently our do-gooder, Dennis Dighton, not only extracted extra money from his patients—'

'Really? But how—'

Pre-empting my question, David explained, 'Oh, in Australia everyone has to pay something towards their health care.'

'Of course,' I sat back. 'How could I forget?' For a moment I allowed my thoughts to return to Tasmania. Complaining bitterly, I had sat at my desk in the little office where I was working as a temp, writing yet another cheque for compulsory health insurance. With expenses like this, I'd thought, I would never be able to save enough for my world trip, the dream of my teenage years.

David cleared his throat. 'And—'

'Yes?'

'Too many of his patients died unexpectedly.'

'Really? Wow!' I sat back, taking time to absorb the information. 'Who'd have thought the mild Dennis Dighton—a thief and a murderer! And there I was thinking Tamara was the trouble.'

Gale leaned forward. 'Why didn't they do him for manslaughter? Surely he was guilty?'

David frowned. 'Not enough proof. They only had evidence about the money which gave them a good reason for getting rid of him.'

'So how come the Dightons have a lot of cash now?'

Gale added, 'And—how did they get any employment here?'

'Ah, there's an easy answer to that.' David cupped his hands round his glass. 'He knew a lot of the other doctors' secrets. That ensured their silence. My mates wouldn't tell me what Dennis had on them and I didn't press, but it gives us a good reason why the practice had to pay Dennis Dighton off handsomely to get him to leave.'

'Well I never!' I sat back, still finding it difficult to believe it all. Dennis Dighton, the mild-mannered dog walker, lackey to his domineering wife, a killer? A blackmailer? Somehow I couldn't imagine the Dennis Dighton I knew killing anybody. I could imagine confusion of medication, negligence that would account for the deaths in Australia, but a conscious decision to kill? No.

'I can't believe Dennis Dighton would ever consciously decide to kill someone can you?' I looked at David and Gale whose faces looked as puzzled as mine. 'Besides,' I mused, allowing a small smile to escape. 'Even then, the only person I can imagine him murdering would be his wife.'

'Sally!' David cried indignantly, at first allowing the corners of his mouth to twitch but within a split second, he was looking serious again.

Gale smirked, but then quickly looked as grave as her husband.

'Sorry,' I said, wondering if I should finish off my drink and offer another round. 'But then – I *can* imagine him as a blackmailer, can't you?'

Gale nodded. 'Especially if driven by his wife.'

We sat still for a moment each with our own thoughts, the muted conversations around us filling the silence.

Then Gale broke our silence. 'It's always the quiet ones, isn't it?' she said. 'He was the first on the scene when Mark died, wasn't he?'

'Yes, you're right!' I tapped my fingers on the table, unconsciously reverting to an exercise I had to do when learning the piano. 'Yes—but poison, wherever it came from—injection or spider or whatever? He had so many other, easier and less obvious ways to kill, and why kill Mark of all people?'

'Once a thief, always a thief,' David said, his features looking more impenetrable than ever in the warm glow of the pub.

'You mean, perhaps Mark caught him stealing?' David nodded.

Gale shook her head. 'But how? He's retired? Who or what could he have been stealing from?'

David looked at each of us incredulously. 'How many committees is he on? Aren't both of them school governors and she's on the health board to start with?'

I sat up quickly. 'Why of course. Tamara helps with the accounts.'

'Yes, but that's *Mrs* Dighton,' Gale protested.

David sighed. 'And *who* is Madame Dighton's lapdog?'

Gale nodded. 'Of course.'

'Now what do we do?' I asked.

David looked steadily at me. 'Nothing. Without definite proof, we can do nothing and you, especially you,' he glared at me, 'you should keep quiet. They are a powerful couple.'

'Not to mention possible murderers,' Gale said slowly, her voice cold and unwavering.

I felt slightly queasy. 'But we can't just leave things as they are, can we?'

David put his hand firmly on the table. 'Yes we can. You leave it well alone.' He looked straight at me, 'You leave it to me. I'll see what I can do.'

'You could contact someone I know on the police force, Wendy Parsons. She's a constable at our local police station. She might be able to help.'

'All right,' said David, taking out a small jotter from his top pocket and writing the name down.

Gale put her hand on David's arm. 'OK, but mind you go carefully. Don't take any unnecessary risks.'

'Me?' David smiled. 'Have you ever known me to take risks?'

'Yes!' Gale and I chorused.

'All right then.' He sighed. 'I'll go carefully and now, who's for another drink?'

Chapter 25

The next Sunday came and it was time to visit John again. As I drove into Gravesall car park my heart was heavy. The first glimpse of the dull one-storey building brought flashes of John into my thoughts, his body stooped, his angry confusion contorting his once-handsome features.

The rooks were noisy today. They were wheeling restlessly high above the trees, black witch-like creatures against dark grey clouds heavy with moisture. I reluctantly pushed the button for the intercom to his new ward. Nothing happened. On my third attempt a strained voice said, 'Yes?'

I leaned closer to the grille, 'Sally Wilks to see John.'

'Who?' The babble of voices in the ward rose in pitch, the tension obvious. Someone screamed. 'Just a minute,' the voice faded, and the intercom went dead. I suddenly missed the Sunday afternoons John and I spent walking in the fields, picnicking by the river. On one overcast day like today he refused point blank to wear his mac, his small lively frame striding towards the threatening clouds. When the rain fell, he strode on oblivious. His brown hair darkened as the water soaked in. He knew what it was to be alive and free from the shackles of the daily grind of work and sleep and work and …

The intercom buzzed, 'You can come now.'

As I stepped into the ward I screwed up my nose. The stench of urine was overwhelming. An unshaven man stepped towards me, looked up at me with his watery eyes and stared. There was no life in his face; I was just a new object to inspect in a monotonous world that he no longer understood.

'Do you know where John is?' I asked towards the melee of zombies that wandered about in the room. A voice spoke from the high-back chair next to me.

'Over there,' a plump hand pointed towards the corridor.

I walked slowly in that direction, carefully avoiding a frail woman clutching at her arm in a repetitive, meaningless action. John was sitting in a wheelchair facing the corridor, staring at the blank wall, his shoulders drooping, his clothes unironed. He smelled of urine.

I strode back to the owner of the plump hand. As I approached she looked up at me. Her dull eyes were only tinged with an element of curiosity.

'John needs changing.' I couldn't stop myself using the steel commandeering tone I had developed to cope with 4D.

She shrugged her shoulders but didn't move.

My hackles raised, I demanded her attention. 'WELL?'

Her piggy eyes defied me for a moment but then she slowly heaved her heavy frame up from the chair, grunting complaints with each movement. I remained where I was, arms folded, exuding an air of tension and incompletion just as I did when supervising a recalcitrant child.

I could feel the tears in my eyes as I watched her waddle slowly over to John, grab the handle of the wheelchair roughly and push him towards the toilet. Her final scowl in my direction made me really angry. How dare she? I stormed down the other corridor, my feet echoing loudly on the floor. I banged on the door marked 'office', did not wait for a reply and rushed in. A plump woman in uniform was poring over papers at the desk, several empty coffee mugs at her side. Her stringy brown hair needed washing.

I stood close to her. 'I've come to make a complaint,' the anger in my voice unavoidable.

She looked up, peering at me as though she had forgotten to wear glasses. 'Eh?'

I banged my hand on the desk. 'I SAID I'VE COME TO COMPLAIN!'

'Oh?' her lips curled. 'So what's new?'

My jaw dropped. 'I BEG your pardon!' I searched for her name tag but it wasn't there.

She dropped the pen she was holding and let her hands fall loosely on her lap. She swivelled her chair round to face me. 'I'm sorry.' Her tone was insincere in spite of her expression that changed into a smile, a very small, forced smile. 'What's the problem?'

'One of the carers is refusing to change the patients. I had to MAKE her attend to John.'

'That must be Ruby. She's already had a couple of warnings. It's so hard to get the staff these days. They're making so many cuts. We have to take whoever we can find.'

I stared at her incredulously.

She paused. 'I'll look into it.' Sensing my annoyance and persistence, she finally looked up at me and said, 'All right?'

I stood my ground, not convinced.

'Look, I promise you I'll look into it when I've finished this paperwork. I'll definitely speak to the girl before she goes home tonight. Will *that* do?'

I stood rigid, my hands clenched so hard that my nails dug into my palms. I wanted to say, 'No it will NOT do. You must go to her now, tell her off, sack her and fill her place and do the job properly,' but did I? No, not a word of it. It's not pleasant finding out that you are a coward, a lily-livered, no-good no-hoper. I slunk out of the room, stormed to the door so angry that when the girl finally let me out I was unable to speak. I drove home, the tears in my eyes blurring the road before me.

Every day I went to school, my thoughts constantly drifted to images of John, the smell of the ward filling my nostrils and the lazy good-for-nothing member of staff. I had to do something. I needed to see John soon.

On the Thursday, Henry was walking past the classroom between lessons.

'I say,' I called.

Henry stopped abruptly. 'Yes, Mrs Wilks?' his voice tinged with sarcasm, his eyebrow raised. He was never one for formality but within earshot of the milling crowds of pupils that filled the corridor, he had no choice.

'Can you keep your eye on my classes tomorrow morning? They all know what they should do. I should be back by the end of lunchtime—but just in case ...'

'Anything for you, Mrs Wilks.' He bowed and swept down the corridor, a gang of pupils following in his wake. As I watched him go, I realized I should have asked for the time off from Leonard and put it through the usual channels, but this was a desperate situation and I didn't want to talk about it to anyone, especially Leonard, for I knew if I did, I would surely burst into tears and he would just as surely use it as an excuse to make me leave the school sooner. On the other hand, Leonard had said I could take any time off, although an uneasy feeling nagged at my conscience as I left the school that afternoon and I couldn't be sure that if my absence was brought to his attention, Leonard might use it as an excuse to even sack me. There would be no chance of getting a transfer then. I shrugged. I had to go; I had to take the risk.

On Friday morning, I stumbled out of the house early, my thoughts clouded after a bad night's sleep. I had tossed and turned, worrying about John. Ruby's ugly face kept peering down at me accusingly. I had to see John today. I needed to be reassured that he was being looked after properly, especially after the last catastrophic visit.

I struggled to open the car door, flung my briefcase on the back seat and started the engine. Thank goodness it went without mishap this time. I pulled out of my drive, clutching the steering wheel with all my strength and I concentrated hard as I manoeuvred my way through the busy traffic shrouded in an early morning mist. A dirty juggernaut cut me up at the roundabout. I jammed on the brakes, fuming, waited for the 'bang' when I heard the scream of tyres behind me, but nothing happened. I breathed a sigh of relief.

When I finally pulled into the car park I was very tired, anxious and not looking forward to the return journey, although by then the traffic should have eased. There were only a few cars in the car park this visit. Thank goodness it was too early for the likes of Tamara Dighton and her cronies.

The air was still. All the sounds I was making were muffled by a cloak of greyness that emanated from the sky. Even my footsteps sounded different, soft and waterlogged, no longer the usual defiant steps that I took when facing John's antagonists. As if in sympathy, the rooks squawked lethargically and intermittently, as though they too had no energy to challenge the dreariness of the day.

I pressed the button on the intercom. Expecting to have to wait, I turned to take another look at the giant trees that housed the rooks, but was surprised when a breathless voice answered.

'Yes?'

'Er, Mrs.Wilks to see John.'

'Oh yes, good. I'm glad you've come.' The door buzzed. 'I wanted to speak to you.'

I opened the doors and stepped inside. A short, slim auxiliary nurse greeted me. There was still a strong smell of urine.

'There's been a problem with John.'

'Oh?' My heart froze.

'He's in his room. I'll come with you.'

I meekly followed. At least he's still alive, I thought. Or was he?

When we went into his room he was lying asleep on his bed, his back to us. I went round the bed to look at him. A long red scar stretched down his cheek.

My stomach turned. I turned abruptly to the nurse. 'What happened?'

'We were about to ring you. John had a fit in the night.'

'And?'

'Well, he wasn't discovered until the morning when I came on. He was found slumped against the radiator. He's all right now, the doctor has come to see him and the wound will heal.'

'What were the night staff doing when John had the fit? Why didn't they spot it?'

The nurse looked down at her feet.

I looked towards the sitting room. 'It wasn't Ruby on duty by any chance?'

The nurse's silence gave me my answer. I stormed out of the room and to the office again. When I burst into the room this time it was empty. The nurse who had been trailing behind me hurriedly explained, 'Ruby is being escorted from the premises. She's been sacked.'

'Oh, at last they are doing something about getting rid of lazy staff?'

'No, it wasn't that.'

I raised an eyebrow.

The nurse shifted her stance. 'She hit someone,' she said, embarrassed, as if she was forced to share some of the blame.

I stared at her, incredulous.

The nurse softened her voice. 'We will take better care of him now, I promise.'

'And when you're not on duty?'

She looked down. 'I shouldn't tell you this, but he's being moved to Suffolk very soon.'

'Suffolk?' My mouth dropped. Another move, how could they think of it! A whiff of urine announced the arrival of a woman patient who had crept up behind the nurse.

'Yes. There'll be a letter in the post for you.'

The patient, tiny, her hair adrift, grabbed the nurse's arm. 'Are you coming shopping?' The voice was urgent, clear and insistent. 'We must go now or we'll miss the bus.'

'Just a minute, Dora,' the nurse released the hand on her arm.

Suffolk! So far away? It was going to be even harder to see him. My heart hardened. Cambridge didn't want to pay, that was clear. But what if Suffolk refused to pay for John's care? Was my husband, a real person, with feelings equally as strong as mine, going to become a pawn to be tossed backwards and forwards between two authorities just to balance their account books? Who *was* going to pick up the bill?

I glanced at the clock on the wall. John was sound asleep, he didn't stir, even with the sound of my voice. I suddenly felt tired and helpless. There was nothing more I could do. Ruby had been sacked, the doctor had seen to John, and John was still asleep. At least while he was sleeping he would not feel the pain of the scar. I decided I may as well go. 'Can you let me out please?' I asked, my voice strained.

As I walked towards the car, the mist still hugging the ground, my spirits sank further. What was I going to do? Perhaps David could help. As a lawyer, he knew what should be done and what I could do. Suddenly, a figure, a large figure, loomed out of the fog. With horror, I realized it was Tamara.

'Why, hello,' she said, her artificial voice sounding even more lofty and insincere than usual, 'I wasn't expecting to see you here today.' As usual she lifted her head up slightly so that she looked down her nose at me. Whether it was intentional or not, it was both irksome and irritating. I uttered a hello back, but wished I had the courage to confront her.

She barred my way. 'It must be a worry for you.'

'What?' I stared at her.

'You know, your husband being implicated in Mark King's death.' I flinched as she put a placatory hand on my arm.

'What do you mean?'

'Haven't you heard?' she sneered. 'Why the autopsy on Mark was very revealing. He didn't die of just a heart attack at all!'

'Yes, I know.'

'They found that his hand was very swollen and thought something had been injected or it'd been a bite from something. But after the toxin scan, if he'd been bitten, it wasn't by anything native to this country. It's all very mysterious.'

'Really.'

Tamara lifted herself up to her full height. She was in her element. 'Your husband used to sell pesticides, didn't he? He would know all about poisons, wouldn't he?'

'But he'd left that job years ago. He had no access to any pesticides or poisons at all—only the ones they sell at the garden shop. Besides, you know how ill he'd become. He couldn't possibly have had anything to do with it.'

'Well,' Tamara said, 'I can tell you that the police are *very* interested in what your husband's been doing. What about all those weird insects and spiders he had in his collection? I've been told there were some very unusual specimens.'

I stood rooted to the spot. 'What collection of insects and spiders?' What rumours were being spread around now? 'Yes, he was interested in insects, spiders and the like, but so am I—there's no collection as you suggest. Anyway, how do you know all this?'

Tamara tapped the side of her bulbous nose with a finger. 'Never you mind!' Her voice softened a little without losing any of its menace. 'But you don't have anything to worry about, do you? If your husband was at fault, at least you know that he can't be charged. That must be some kind of comfort, surely?'

I glared. 'Sorry? How can knowing your husband murdered someone be a comfort?' but I was only speaking to the back of her as her ample body pushed swiftly past me and waddled towards the ward.

My eyes were blurred with tears as I struggled to put the key into the lock of the car. I sighed as I faced another long arduous journey back to school.

The bell was ringing as I entered the front door of the school. I was just in time to see Henry after the final morning lesson. As I arrived in the classroom, the pupils had all gone and he quickly gave me a rough summary of what had happened – nothing special and then said he had to dash off – he was meeting Carol in town.

'Thank you,' I called, 'I owe you.'

'You sure do. I'll be collecting later,' he pointed at me and quickly left.

I was hoping I could've had a coffee with Henry. Events at the meeting were weighing heavily on my spirits and the last encounter with Tamara needed airing. Oh how vile that woman was! Why was she so interested in blaming John for Mark's death? Why did she have to be the one making the decisions about John's care? Shunting him across to Suffolk was a stupid idea, bound to end in disaster. Why hadn't the police done anything yet?

I slumped down in my chair and leaned my weary head on my arms on the desk. I had never felt so alone, so beaten. I had to accept the changes in my life, my loneliness, and the uncertainty surrounding my husband, his care and that he, the once lively high-minded honest man I knew, could have been a killer.

'What asleep already?' I lifted my head up quickly at the sound of Henry's voice. When he saw the expression on my face, he paused and walked slowly towards me.

I raised a hand. 'Don't, don't you dare sound sympathetic or I'll burst into tears.'

'Well we can't have that,' he said, in his breezy way. 'I'm sorry I couldn't stop. After all that, Carol had to dash so I came back to grab some work. Come for a coffee? I think a couple of others are coming too.'

I smiled. 'Yes,' I said, biting back the tears. I got my bag, and left the pile of books and worksheets to be dealt with on Monday, making a mental note that afterwards, tonight, I would be burning the midnight oil marking essays. No matter how bad things were, I needed to prove that I was still able to function as an adequate teacher. The last thing I wanted was Leonard giving me the sack.

Chapter 26

When I went into the restaurant it was bustling with people. I should have remembered that most of the school met at the Old Fire Engine when they needed a break from the hassle of the daily grind at the chalkface. There was something warm and soothing about the restaurant as though its sole purpose was to lull you into a feeling of contentment. It felt as though we were being embraced by the ghosts of centuries of kindly folk sitting at the same wooden tables, having pots of strong tea and scones covered

266

in jam and cream. I slid along a seat behind a table and Henry sat opposite.

'A strong pot of tea, nothing more, I'm not hungry,' I said, making no effort to offer to get the tea myself, to ask nicely, or even consider what Henry might want. He patted the table gently and went out to order our tea. I looked around. The group nearest us was obviously a family. The parents were taking their child out, giving him the attention they'd failed to give when he was at home, but now he was a boarder, they were making a special effort. The group sat awkwardly, pretending to be happy, pretending a closeness that had been lost in the alien environment of boarding school.

'All done,' Henry slipped into his chair. He looked at my unhappy face. 'Promise I won't be too sympathetic.' He grinned. 'Can't have the music teacher blabbing in front of the parents now can we?'

I tried to smile.

'No come on, what's up? Spill the beans.'

'It's just so frustrating,' I burst out. 'The ward John's in now is dreadful. No one seems to care. He had a fit in the night and no one knew until the morning. The place stinks. Now they're suddenly moving him to Suffolk and this morning when I came out of the building I bumped into Tamara and I didn't even have the courage to face up to her and demand to know why things were so bad. On top of that she rubbed it in about John being a chief suspect in Mark King's death.'

'How on earth could they come to that conclusion?'

'Well, he used to sell pesticides, so he knew all about poisons and Mark King died from a bite or had been injected with poison, maybe from a spider not known in this country.'

'So why would that have had anything to do with John?' Henry moved his hands as if to take mine, and then realized where we were and had second thoughts. 'How on earth could he have got near enough to Mark and somehow got a spider to bite Mark and not himself. It's ludicrous!'

I put my head in my hands.

'Look! Don't forget it was Tamara who told you this, and you know the suspicions we have about her. She's obviously trying to incriminate him.' He accepted the tray of tea that arrived. 'Anyway, about the home. If his current ward is so dreadful, he may be better off in Suffolk. It'd be a different authority and they may be kinder to their dementia patients. Besides, you can't do everything and you're quite right not to tackle the Dightons. I'm not sure I'd want to face up to the likes of them. You have to tread carefully if you want anything done. What if they killed Mark? Have you ever thought if you make too much trouble you could be next?'

'No! You're kidding!'

'No? Can you be sure of that?'

'But we must do something! We can't let them get away with it can we? What can we do? We could go to the police.'

'With what proof?' Henry paused. 'Shall I be Mum?' and he poured the tea. 'You know,' he said after putting the teapot down, 'she does like to boast.

Maybe we could manoeuvre her into getting carried away and let slip some proof while she's sounding out.'

'But how? She frightens me to death.' I frowned. 'Sorry, pun not intended.'

'Carol isn't frightened of her, is she? They have another fitting this week, maybe Carol could see what she could find out.'

'Yeah. That would be great.' I could feel the tension releasing already.

'Can I join you?' Rita suddenly appeared next to me, her tall figure blotting out the light. She plumped herself down. 'I hope you don't mind. There are no other seats available,' she explained.

'Yes, please do.' I glanced at the parents and realized that any misconception about the closeness of Henry and I would be thoroughly allayed. Gosh, you had to be so careful these days.

We sat in silence for a moment, the clatter of teacups and muted chatter of the other people filling the gulf between us.

Rita cleared her throat. 'What's up? You both look a bit glum.'

Henry stared at me. 'It's just my husband,' I said in a low voice.

'Oh. I didn't realise. Would you like to share it with me? You never know, I might be able to help.'

I leaned back. Her calm assurance and uninvolved interest would make it easier for me to tell. No, I would not burst into tears this time. I didn't dare look at Henry. 'I suppose you already know hc's in thc mental hospital at Gravesall.'

Rita nodded as she sipped her tea. Her eyes scanned my face as if searching for hidden messages that she should have known but couldn't remember.

Taking her cue, I continued. 'He was sectioned there a few months ago. He became too aggressive and impossible to handle.' My eyes watered. 'But things in the ward are bad. There's no reason to treat him so badly, is there? He's still a human being.'

'You too?' Rita placed her cup carefully on the saucer.

'What do you mean?'

'My mother was in that mental hospital a few years ago.'

Henry stared. 'You never told me that.'

Rita looked at him, opened her mouth as if to say something, but stopped herself. She shook her head gently, her looped earrings swaying with the locks of her long hair. Avoiding Henry, she looked directly at me. 'My mother has schizophrenia, so when she forgets to take her medicine or when it ceases to work, she has to go into hospital.'

I watched as Henry poured out another cup of tea for me.

Rita watched too and then continued. 'At first they looked after her very well and got her medicine stablized so that she could come home. Then, after she had another episode, it was terrible.'

'Oh?'

'It was as if the staff had ceased caring. Everything seemed to fall apart; the good staff members got fed up and left. We had to get her out of there.'

'So where is she now?' At last, I thought, there would be a solution to my problem. There would be a way out, somehow. Looking at Rita it was obvious she wouldn't have a lot of extra money, so she couldn't have gone private. Maybe there was another hospital, another institution I didn't know about.

Rita shrugged. 'She's at home. Her sister came down to live with her. She sees that she takes her pills and everything is much better.'

'Oh,' I slumped back in the seat.

Henry patted my hand. 'Never mind, you know we're here to support you, although I'm not sure I'd volunteer to have John at home to entertain Carol and I after what you've told me about him.'

The image of John sorting out Henry and Carol and their home brought a smile to my face.

'A smile, at last,' said Henry.

Rita continued, 'It's like anything, you've just got to keep on going, keep on asking for more help, praise when it is due, if ever, and keep pointing out how things could be improved —like a dripping tap—some day it must improve.'

I stirred my tea thoughtfully.

Rita spoke again. 'Not all the nurses are dreadful are they?'

I shook my head.

'Well then. Get to know the good ones, tell them how pleased you are with what they're doing, and soon both you and John will become people they know well and care about. That's what you've got to do.'

Henry was listening to Rita intently, his eyes glimmering with something more than interest. She glanced at him, then looked away.

'What about the ward closures?' I asked pointedly.

'Ward closures?' Rita asked.

'Yes, they're closing ward after ward in the hospital. John has already been moved twice and they're doing it again—moving him to Suffolk.' I swallowed hard. I was not going to cry.

'The ward closures. You need to find out what's behind it all.'

I scowled. 'They say it's government cuts.'

'The government is always trying to make cuts, but the government is not closing down the wards – someone on the board is. You've got to find out who the ringleader is.'

Henry and I exchanged glances. 'What's to bet it's Tamara?' I offered. I was tempted to mention the cheque I'd stolen that was addressed to her – the one I'd given to Wendy. However, I'd promised Wendy I wouldn't say anything and her silence meant that she must be having a hard time getting her bosses to believe that the cheque was proof that Tamara was stealing. A picture of Tamara, whining obsequiously, giving a plausible reason for the cheque flashed into mind. I shivered.

Henry asked. 'Are you all right?'

'Yes, I'm fine,' I said quickly. 'Sorry, it's all getting harder by the minute. As I said, I bet it's Tamara making everything so difficult.'

Henry nodded. 'Very possibly.' He turned to Rita. 'We've just been discussing what we can do about her. Not only is she creating havoc at the hospital, she's spreading rumours that it was Sally's husband who killed Mark.'

'No! How could he have done?' Rita looked genuinely shocked.

I looked down at the newly scrubbed table. 'It might have been possible. He was always collecting weird things and even though he was generally cack-handed, every now and then he would surprise you and do something really intricate. He could've easily planted some venomous insect for Mark to find.'

Rita shook her head. 'And where would he have done this?' She paused, 'Well, I remember him creating a scene once—' she bit her lip. 'Sorry Sally—'

'No go on, it's all right.'

Rita took a short breath, 'Well, I remember someone having a long discussion with John outside the school building. I can't remember who it was but John had a shoe box and seemed determined to go inside and show it to Mark. I heard John shouting Mark's name a number of times. Things got a bit heated. John finally gave up and stormed off, so he was very, very unlikely to be able to get close to Mark at all.'

'I suppose so,' my eyes glazed over.

'There,' Henry said patting my hand again, 'Rita is perfectly right. Now will you believe us?'

'Not until I'm told the whole truth about Mark's death.'

A gloom settled over our table. Chairs scraped as the people opposite stood up, glanced over and smiled at us, gathered their bags and left noisily.

Chapter 27

Days passed and the same drudgery of school and home kept me on an even keel. If I didn't think about anything too much, I was able to carry on as if nothing untoward had happened at all. While I was busy at school, I could imagine that John was waiting for me at home, that he would put the kettle on when I came in the front door and we would share a cup of tea.

Then, on the Thursday, another brown envelope arrived. With a sick feeling in my stomach I opened the letter and under the same bold blue heading was a simple statement. John was going to be moved to a home in Suffolk next Sunday. So soon! Didn't I have a say in it?

Then I thought after such a ghastly time we'd had the last few weeks, maybe Suffolk would be the answer, maybe he would be better looked after there in a happier environment, perhaps even close to the sea. At least they were moving on a Sunday so that I could accompany him.

After another few tiring days at school, I was exhausted by Sunday but dragged myself out of bed to be at Gravesall in time to go with John in the car that was taking him to Suffolk. John sat next to me in the back seat of the car as the driver started the engine and drove steadily through the grounds of Gravesall, then turned swiftly into the main road out into the countryside.

John seemed much more docile that usual but I figured they had sedated him strongly, so that he wouldn't give any trouble. He knew me, and seemed pleased that I was with him, but this could easily have been wishful thinking, because he responded little to my talk, he just sat staring in front of him.

I tried to interest him in the different cars that sped past, in the historical buildings in the villages that we sped through, but he gave no response. I eventually gave up and sat back in the seat to admire the view, closing my eyes for a moment for some of the rest my body had been craving after the previous stressful months.

When I opened my eyes, I could see the sea stretching away from the beach at Lowestoft.

'Ah great! Could we stop a bit so that John can have a look at the sea?' I asked.

The driver pulled up, turned and smiled gently. 'Of course. I could even drive down to the beach if you like.'

'John,' I held his hand and pushed his fingers gently. 'Would you like to get out and see the sea?'

Still staring straight ahead, John said, 'No.'

'Are you sure?' I persisted. This was so unlike the John I once knew – then there would have been no stopping him, he would have stormed down to the seaside at such a pace that the driver and I would have hardly been able to catch up with him.

'No!' This time John spoke with the tone of voice that I knew would be dangerous to ignore. He definitely did not want the disturbance of getting out of the car, breathing in the fresh air before going inside. How sad! He had obviously become institutionalised already – only feeling secure when he was shut up inside.

The home was an ordinary Victorian house, with bay windows, thick brick walls and very high ceilings. When we saw his room, it was spacious, with brand new curtains and bedspread. It looked very comfortable. I joked that I could easily move in here.

The owner of the home led us to her office and as I feared, the subject of money was brought up. She told me that part of the cost would be paid for but that John would have to top up the rest. When I asked for precise details, she couldn't tell me, she was unsure, so I suggested she get the exact figures sorted out, write to me and only then could I consider releasing John's money if needed.

In my heart of hearts, I believed that as he was sectioned and as the NHS was supposed to be free at the point of need, John's care should be paid for entirely by the NHS. After all, John had worked hard all his life, paid what taxes he owed and was a very loyal and hard-working citizen. Now he deserved the care he had earned and after coming across the likes of Tamara, I was even more determined that John should have his fair share of the NHS funds available. The owner looked confused, but nodded and said she would let me know.

Then, when we went downstairs to meet the other people, I knew there would be trouble with John staying here. Seated at the table was an elderly woman, sitting very upright, very tense, her wavy white hair pulled back severely, her bird-like eyes darting around the room. She stared at John and said in an aggressive tone,

'What are you doing here?'

John stared straight back at her. There was a glint in his eye and for a moment I thought he was going to strike her. Yes, he could lash out when provoked but there was no careful planning about it. I could see it clearly now, if John wanted to hurt someone he would do it then and there, immediately. Sneaking a spider into Mark's office at school or in his own home was unthinkable, not something that John could possibly do.

He clenched his fists and leaned over the table towards her, 'I'm here for good and that's the end of it woman. It's no good whining; I've heard your whining too often to take any notice.'

The atmosphere in the room sparked and the other residents became restless.

The owner coughed, trying to cover up the increased noise level, ignoring the new enemies facing each other at the table.

'Well,' she said quickly, 'I won't keep you. It won't take John long to settle in I'm sure.' And within a few minutes the driver and I were standing outside the front door of the home, now firmly closed.

We drove home in silence, the driver concentrating on the road, while I lay back in the front seat, my eyes closed, getting some rest, while trying to blot out my bad memories of John and his new home in Suffolk.

There were two weeks left before the end of term. Leonard had stopped pestering me about asking for a transfer after we'd been told there would be a new headmaster taking over next term. The inspection had come and gone. I'd had too much else to worry about, so if I got a bad report, so be it. I made few changes to my usual teaching methods, although when warned someone would be in my classroom, I did carefully prepare that lesson at least.

The atmosphere in the staffroom had become stuffier each day as we lumbered towards the long-awaited rest in the holidays, but today was different. Today there was a buzz in the school, something was up. As I stretched my hand for the post in my pigeonhole I heard Henry call me.

He rushed up to me, waving a newspaper in his hand. 'Have you seen it? Have you seen the paper today?'

'No, why should I? I'm having enough trouble—' I stopped myself in time—

'Leonard and Tamara have been taken into custody.'

'Leonard and Tamara? Really? I could never imagine them working together. Why? How?'

'It wasn't only Leonard and Tamara involved in fraud, but Mark too. The school inspectors asked for the accounts earlier than usual, Betty handed them over before checking with Leonard, so they found out that the three of them had been cooking the books, creaming off cash for themselves.'

'Wow!' I was stunned, and then smiled to myself. Thank God I hadn't done anything about the transfer Leonard had been demanding. I could stay here. Henry was about to speak.

'And,' he grinned, 'they're scrutinising the health trust accounts as well, especially the Gravesall ones.'

I whistled. Good ol' Wendy, she must have done the trick. 'Wow, even better,' I said, and frowned, 'but Leonard?' I could hardly believe it. Leonard was such a stickler for everything being done under his control, everything in its place. I'd never ever thought of him as devious. But as I thought of Tamara and her frequent visits to the school – after all they were very pally, which seemed strange at the time, but now – now it made sense.

'Was there anything about Mark's murder, did they find out if Dennis or Tamara had anything to do with it?'

'No, no mention of Mark's death, other than just saying that he'd died.'

'Ah well,' I sighed, 'and who's running the school now then?'

Chris Masters stood in the corridor. 'There'll be a staff meeting for five minutes before classes begin. Please tell everyone. Thank you.' He turned swiftly towards the staffroom. I gathered the mail and quickly followed Henry and the other staff to the meeting.

We were among the first to arrive so while we were waiting I tore open the envelopes. The first was informing me formally of the change in headship, but no real reason given and the second was an invitation from Anthea to another of her tea parties. I groaned.

'Are you all right?' asked Henry.

'Yes, it's just another of Anthea's cream teas.'

'She is an amazing woman isn't she?'

She seemed to be dealing better with the death of her husband than I was with the loss of mine, although I had to admit she had accused almost everyone of killing her husband and was taking to the drink a bit, but we all understood, and she knew it. She must feel quite uneasy not knowing for certain what had really happened to Mark and in spite of this, she had the strength of character and will to continue on as before, holding the traditional cream tea, even when she no longer had her husband at her side.

As Chris Masters came into the room, I realized that I, too, would always feel uneasy until I knew the truth and whether John had been the instrument of Mark's death. No matter how many people assured me that it was unlikely, it didn't really matter, I knew I could not rest until I knew for certain. At least now

I knew that if John had done anything, it certainly wouldn't have been deliberate.

That afternoon after school, as I flung open the front door at home, dying for a cup of tea, there was another brown envelope in the post. I dropped my bags at my feet, grabbed it and with my heart pounding, tore it open. The horrid bold blue writing greeted me. I laughed. I could have guessed. So now, after all that fuss, the home in Suffolk was not considered suitable for John and he had been transferred back to the Cambridge hospital, back to another new ward: Yates.

Surprise, surprise, and I shoved the letter back into the envelope. I guess somewhere is better than nowhere, and with Tamara out of the picture, thank goodness, I could have some control over the way John would be looked after. Maybe things would get better now.

But this was not to be. The following week as I came home I heard the phone ringing. I dashed inside, and still panting, grabbed the phone.

'It's the manager of Yates Ward here.'

My heart froze. What had John been up to now, was he all right? Had he had another grand mal seizure or brought out the Fire Brigade again? My heart went cold. He's not dead—

'We've got John here.' She sounded quiet, timid, so unlike the bossy, I-can-do-anything tone of previous ward managers.

'Ye-es?' I asked slowly.

'I don't know what to do,' her voice croaked.

I didn't answer.

I could hear she was nearly in tears. 'They've closed the ward and he's the very last patient. He's sitting next to me in his wheelchair. I don't know what to do.'

'I'm sorry, but I don't know – contact the social services, they should know where he goes next.' I could tell by the pain in the manager's voice that this certainly wasn't what she had planned. How could they? Even without Tamara they were still heartless enough to wreck so many people's lives, passing the patients around like inconvenient parcels, treating them like unwanted animals to get rid of at the first opportunity. It crossed my mind that all these ward changes and shifting patients around might have been part of the plan all along. Maybe they hoped some of them would die in the process. It wasn't right. How could they treat human beings, vulnerable human beings, like that?

I could hear the manager breathing on the other end of the line. I had to say something. 'Look,' I said, 'I understand how difficult it is for you, but you know I can't cope with him here at home and there must be somewhere for him to go. Keep asking and do let me know where he ends up.'

There was a pause. The manager knew that was all I could say. 'All right.' The phone went dead.

Then I panicked. What if they decided to send him home? His red, contorted face screaming 'Murder!' one terrible night flashed into my thoughts. Would it all happen again?

When I came home the next afternoon there was an answerphone message. With trembling fingers, I pressed the button.

An officious voice intoned: 'Your husband has been admitted to Luke Ward, in Callwell Hospital – the acute mental health assessment ward for people who have John's condition.'

God, was he never going to be settled?

The next Sunday I hurried to see him. John sat in a wheelchair, unhappy and disinterested in his surroundings. After a long time, a nurse suddenly appeared.

'Are you John's wife?' she asked.

She came closer and whispered very quietly. 'I've been fighting for him to go to Ivory Home.'

'What's the problem? Why didn't they send him there in the first place?'

'The trouble is, it's a private home, but I keep telling them, they haven't got any NHS places available, they've closed them all down.'

'I know, tell me about it! Surely they wouldn't think of sending him home, would they?'

'No, I shouldn't think so, although the way things are going, who knows?' The nurse quickly wheeled another patient towards the toilet.

Every day after this visit, I turned the corner into my road with trepidation. What would I do if there was an ambulance outside? What if I found my husband being wheeled to my front door? I gripped the steering wheel hard, very hard. If that happened, I decided I'd have to turn around and leave, go anywhere, where they couldn't find me. I couldn't possibly cope with him again. Visions of his face, his features twisted with unfettered anger, his eyes wild, fists clenched, flashed into mind.

There was no ambulance outside, thank God. Inside, I found yet another brown envelope had been delivered. I tore it open and grinned as I read. At last, he was to go to Ivory Home! The nurse hadn't been told, obviously. Surely this would be the last and permanent place for him to stay, and hopefully, it would be right for him, if the nurse's comments were anything to go by. I would see for myself.

The home was still some distance from my house, but the following Sunday I drove down the long driveway with trepidation. It's all very well for a home to have a good reputation, but you only need one or two bad nurses. I parked the car awkwardly, but didn't care. I needed to see John, to see that he was all right. I stormed through the front door and asked the first person I came across where John was. They showed me to a room at the back of the building. He had a room to himself! He lay in his bed, quiet, and his face was much smoother, more relaxed than it was before. Yes, at last, he was in safe hands, there would be no more trouble. So, it was with a lighter heart that I prepared to go to Anthea's cream tea party later that day.

Chapter 28

When I arrived at Anthea's home, grey clouds had
gathered to fill the sky. The house looked colder and
darker than ever before and even though I could see
the silhouettes of people through the latticed window
the place seemed lost and lonely. Somehow Mark's
absence had clouded the building with extra
starkness and depression, as though reflecting the
heartache Anthea must be feeling. Straight after I
rattled the brass knocker, the door was swung open.

'Hi.' Henry's serious face greeted me.

I smiled, said 'Hi,' and he opened the door wider.

'Come in, I don't know where Anthea is, I seem
to have assumed the role of doorman.'

'Thank you,' I said, 'and what a good doorman
you make too.'

I stepped across the threshold.

'They're all through there,' he said, pointing
towards the sitting room. I went towards the noise.

The voices were subdued. No one felt like trying
to socialise. It was the end of term, and we all just
wanted to go home and have a rest. Even Anthea was
not her sparkling best. Her perfect smile was blurred,
as though she'd had a few too many, fortifying
herself to cope with this influx of people. The black
circles under her eyes were more marked than usual.
She tried to hide her unease as she walked slowly
among the guests handing out cups of tea.

Betty was the only cheerful voice, chatting to the
small group of quiet figures in the corner. I decided
to join them. Henry and Rita were like automatons,

standing side by side, their eyes glazed. I scanned the room.

Nearly everyone was here. Bill Greenland was gazing towards the window with his teacup balanced on his rotund tummy. Chris Masters was next to Leonard Hall's wife Dorothy and they were standing stiffly next to Teresa, their silence spelling out the huge gap that the absence of both Mark, and, now Leonard created.

Teresa stood close to her husband George as if he could shelter her from the almost untenable situation. Vicky Lowe stood awkwardly at the side of the group, her face grim and uncommunicative.

'It will be the first cruise I have ever taken,' Betty enthused. I was only half listening. I willed her to continue for none of us really had the energy to make polite conversation.

No matter how hard we tried to ignore it, we could still feel the insidious atmosphere of tension that had crept into the school and into this room. It would not be resolved until Mark's death had been fully explained. I glanced around our group. It could have been any of us, yet when I focused on each face, I could not believe that any single individual would be capable of planning someone's death like that. It must have been accidental.

My stomach tightened as I faced yet again the prospect that John had been the culprit. But how had he done it? It didn't make sense.

Anthea arrived with a tray of tea cups.

Betty took hers carefully. 'You know,' she said to Anthea, 'it would do you good to get away sometime. Maybe next year, of course, after you've had time ....' The unspoken words hung in the air. Anthea waited silently while we fumbled to get our cups and moved on to the next group.

Betty said to us, 'She's taken it hard, you know. She puts on this facade that makes everyone think she has recovered well from losing her husband, but I know better.'

'Oh?' I took my first sip of tea.

'Yes,' Betty continued, 'it was only yesterday that she came into the reception area just before I closed up. She sat on my chair and poured her heart out, poor dear.'

'And there I was thinking she was one of the most self-sufficient people I knew, only slightly affected with drinking a bit much these days, but – don't we all?' I said.

Suddenly there was a loud crash. Anthea had dropped the tray to the floor, scattering broken china at our feet, spilling tea onto the pristine carpet.

'Bugger!' she shouted. The room froze.

Vicky said nervously, 'She bumped into me. It was an accident.' She quickly knelt down and started to gather the broken china pieces.

'Leave it!' Anthea screamed. Vicky knelt back on her heels and stared wide-eyed up at Anthea.

'It's no good looking at me with those cow's eyes of yours. You've done enough damage already.'

Vicky looked stunned. 'Pardon?'

'You couldn't leave Mark alone, could you?'

Anthea glared around the room of astonished faces. 'Huh! You have no idea, have you?'

Chris was the first to break the silence, his voice edged with steel. 'No idea about what, Anthea?'

Anthea bowed her head and mumbled, 'Never you mind.'

Chris stepped forward, his voice assuming his manager's there-there tone that always made me cringe. 'We know you have had a very difficult time Anthea, and we are very grateful that you have gone to all this trouble in your time of grieving. We know that you supported your husband admirably. Perhaps it's time for you to have a rest, have a break, go on holiday. We really appreciate what you do for us, but at some stage you must look after yourself, and your own feelings.'

A teaspoon clattered to the floor.

'Oh yeah?' Anthea glared at Chris, her voice edged with a sarcasm I had never heard in her before.

Chris moved forward again, his hand ready to placate the distraught Anthea.

'Now don't get like that, Anthea. Come, let's go and sit down for a moment and calm down. Vicky will help clear up the tray, won't you, Vicky?'

Vicky nodded and started gathering up the broken cups again.

'Now, Anthea,' and Chris held out his smooth hand.

'No, listen.' Anthea thrust Chris's hand aside and glared at him and then at Vicky.

'You had no idea, had you Vicky?'

Vicky's lips were closed, her eyes moist with tears, waiting for Anthea to continue.

'Asking me to water your plants while you were away was not the best idea you had.'

Everyone was listening now.

Anthea sneered. 'Such a loving couple you made. Mark's dressing gown hung behind your bedroom door. You thought I wouldn't recognize it didn't you, you naive prissy whore?'

There was an audible intake of breath in the room. Nobody moved.

She turned to me, 'And you, you idiot, you had no idea what your husband got up to did you?'

Anthea pointed her finger at me. 'You didn't know your loving husband kept bringing a lot of those ghastly spiders to school. I was the one who stopped them getting past the front door. I saved you both from so much humiliation and what thanks do I get?'

I opened my mouth to speak but stopped when I saw Anthea take a deep breath to continue.

'Well, you're done for now. John was the one who had the redback spider. He was the one to blame. God knows where he got it from – no doubt from your connections Down Under or perhaps you'd got hold of it and planned to make your husband have an untimely death yourself. After all, he was being difficult, wasn't he? Is that what you had in mind?'

I stepped back, my mouth agape. 'No, how could you think of it! I didn't know anything about this, honestly.' Tears began to fall down my cheeks.

'Enough, Anthea,' Rita stepped between us, her hands still holding her teacup.

'Oh, enough, you say,' Anthea snarled at Rita. 'Who are you to presume to interfere? You, who are nothing more than another of Mark's little trollops. You didn't think I would find out about you either, did you?'

Chris cleared his throat. 'Now Anthea, be careful, don't say anything more before we get a lawyer.'

'*We* get a lawyer!' Anthea shrieked. '*We*—look, I'll do this on my own thank you very much. I'll say what I like when I like. It's worth it to see the look on your faces you pathetic people. You never did listen.'

By now Betty had moved forward. 'Listen? So it *was* you who wrote those horrible letters?'

'You don't know that.' Anthea crumpled, her tall frame now hunched, her features tortured.

'Oh yes I do, Anthea. I recognized your writing.'

'No you didn't—you couldn't. I'd disguised—'

'Exactly,' said Betty, 'in the same way you changed your writing for my Get Well card when I was in hospital. That's how I recognized it. Why on earth did you write those ghastly letters?

'Why shouldn't I? You all needed it, you have no idea how to behave; someone had to do something!'

Vicky faced her. 'You mean with your husband too?'

'I don't know what you're talking about!'

Vicky's face lit up with revelation. 'It was you who left the spider for Mark!'

Anthea didn't reply.

Vicky pointed at Anthea. 'It had to be you. All that detail about my bedroom – you'd cut your own key and had been snooping hadn't you? You knew that Mark would come to my house instead of going to work. You'd told him to collect the keys from the box in my hall cupboard.'

'So?'

'So *I* know he was the last one to touch that box. When we checked for the keys, you rushed in and shook the box. You knew there could be a redback in there still. You were the only person who knew for certain that John had a redback spider and with your spare keys, you'd come into my house and planted it. You didn't care whether it was Mark or I who touched that box, you wanted to hurt one of us and you did.'

No one moved. Anthea folded her arms and glared.

Then Chris took the initiative, walked purposefully over to the phone and dialled.

About the author

The author is Australian-born teacher and writer Dr Rosemary Westwell who lives in Cambridgeshire, England. She moved to the UK in 1971 and settled with her British husband in the county, teaching in a number of different schools. After the birth of the second child, her husband began to show signs of an illness that degenerated into dementia and he is now permanently in a care home. Her experiences inspired her to write her first novel: 'John, Dementia and Me'.

She has five university degrees (in music, the arts and education) and completed her PhD ('The Development of Language Acquisition in a Mature Learner') in 2007. She has two daughters and six grandchildren who live in the UK.

The author gives light-hearted talks about her book, her experiences as an Australian-born citizen establishing a new life in the UK and about her difficulties of learning Spanish after acquiring a flat in Spain. contact: rjwestwell@hotmail.com

publications:

Her PhD thesis is available free on:
http://eprints.ioe.ac.uk/48/

Other publications (available on Amazon):

- 'John, Dementia and Me' a novel based on the author's experiences when her husband developed dementia
- Out of a Learner's Mouth', a humorous account of her language learning experiences in Spain.
- 'Teaching Language Learners', a book of suggestions and ideas for teaching languages, especially English.
- 'Twenty Tips for Teaching IGCSE ESL', a book of ideas and suggestions for teaching English as a Foreign or Second Language.
- 'The Spelling Game', a book of ideas for teaching spelling.
- 'A Close Look at Unseen Poetry' a book which supports students studying poetry.
- 'Spontaneous Survival Lessons in English' and 'Activities to Engage with The Woman in White and The Lady in the Lake' are available on http://zigzageducation.co.uk

51932176R00165

Made in the USA
Charleston, SC
07 February 2016